Mar 2015

AETERNUM RAY

Light, stars, cells, and minds.
Reaching, burning, thriving, and growing.
For we are all connected, each a solitary synapse
of a universe vast, ancient, and slowly understanding.

AETERNUM RAY

Tracy R. Atkins

Dedication

To those who will live forever.

Introduction

Technology advances on a logarithmic scale. Its pace and breadth increases in a consistent manner, trending ever upward over time. Machines have replaced many forms of physical labor for the past three centuries. Further evolved machines and computing devices have aided in performing complex mathematical and scientific thought-work for decades.

Sophisticated software suites are already out-thinking human minds and are beginning to reason and create. Computers can now understand natural human language and speak in kind. Human biological integration with technology is growing from its infancy and is slowly becoming a new reality. The autonomous self-improving computer system is on the horizon.

The convergence of these concepts will soon give birth to true artificial intelligence and ignite technological singularity. This is the point when the slow river of human advancement breaks into an unstoppable waterfall of discovery and knowledge.

Prologue Letter

1440 Pelican Way

Aedin Beach, Midir, Ups-And-d

∞ #AE-LID: 4d-69-64-69-72

June 1st, 2216 CE

∞ #AE-POSIX: 7776116103

My dear child Benjamin,

None of us born in the twentieth century knew that we would live forever. We imagined that man's greatest triumphs, conquering disease, poverty, and to spread out among the stars, were all to be part of a faraway future that we would never live to see. We accepted that the brightest achievements of humanity were to be for a future generation to accomplish; all of these things were out of our reach. This left us with the bitter reality that we each would grow old, suffer, and make plans to die. Our dreams left forever unfulfilled. However, fate has ironic disdain for even the most rational of mankind's plans and intervened when we needed salvation most.

Like that of all human beings, my memory is far from perfect. A lifetime of experiences and moods have colored and blurred the details of my long life. I have much history and my own unique perspective on human society to share with you. I have lived a full life, surviving both the old world order, and taking part in building the new. I am a man of great pride and hopeful sorrow, earned through the labors of being the patriarch of our family.

As your father, I find the act of sharing my heritage with you a joyful journey and rite of passage. I have anticipated this process since your conception. These letters have become humanity's traditional gift to our children. They will serve as your endowment as you begin your own narrative. More important, this knowledge will make the thousands of abstract visions clouding your brand-new, yet already full mind align in clarity.

These letters are never the same. You will take in pieces of me and feel impressions from my soul that none of my other children has. I intend to share a flood of fleeting thoughts, improvised musings, dated humor, and cherished memories of a continuing immortal life. Your brothers and sisters have treasures of their own that I see as unique gifts from my letters to them. I encourage you to embrace relationships with each of them to explore your human condition together.

Our shared history can only be passed from one human being to another in a loving narration. Although this dialog could be recorded or relayed by another means, letter writing is far more personal, allowing me to reflect on my life in detail. The time I spend writing is a gift to you, and the contents will be a part of your story; retold and passed down countless times to your innumerable children for eons to come.

Our family's roots are deep, breeding scholars and hardy explorers in many generations past. Likewise, I was a man who began life during the end of an age for our species and I am the turning point for our family as the first to transcend. Going forward, our roots and evolution as a technological society are paramount for you to understand in order to preserve the origin and meaning of your humanity, which was long ago freed from the bondage of flesh and the confines of this Earth. This was not a period of decline, but rather the nexus between worlds that I had the privilege of which to be a part.

Prior to Aeternum, we were a people of marginal morality, toiling away in our own misery. In fact, even at Ray's genesis, little had changed since the reign of the Pharaohs. At the time, we were arrogant in our belief that we were a highly advanced, tolerant, and well-informed people. In the mirror, we saw a sea of eternity separating us from the Romans, the Mayans, and the people of Babylon. Yet, we were cut from the same cloth with only slight variation in the weave and bloodstained color, adrift and lazy, floating down an eons-long river of mere survival.

The river has continued to flow over the centuries and carried us through to these times of greater being. I have borne witness to many of humanity's triumphs, failures and disasters. Most important, I have lived long enough to see humanity evolve, to wash the blood from the cloth of our shared existence, finding peace in transcendence. The journey down this river was often difficult, but love, compassion and the wonder of exploration sustained me. You too have a long history of triumph and pain awaiting you; however, I hope that my shared journey will offer you guidance, and ground you to your core humanity for eternity.

With all of my love, your father,

William Samuel Babington

Chapter 1: The Eon River
(1979 – 2029)

1440 Pelican Way

Aedin Beach, Midir, Ups-And-d

∞ #AE-LID: 4d-69-64-69-72

June 2nd, 2216 CE

∞ #AE-POSIX: 7776244273

Benjamin,

The calendar hasn't changed much since my un-noteworthy and humble birth. The days are all the same, and this Sunday evening feels like any warm and shady Sunday two hundred years ago. I was born an American in May of 1979 in the rural State of Tennessee to two wonderful parents, Cecil and Lou Babington. Of course, I don't remember details of the year of my birth, or the early nineteen eighties very well. Some of my first recollections are of playing outside as a child in the woods, enjoying video games, and watching reruns of a favorite television show called "Star Trek." I was fascinated as a kid with the future and what wonders it would hold. Childhood daydreams of aliens, spaceships, and new developments that would never happen, as we had envisioned, captivated me.

The eighties were filled with technological wizardry, and I was going to come of age in this new world. I was a bit of an outcast, a geek or nerd, as we technology enthusiasts were called back then. I found much joy working with computers and the rudimentary things they could do. As such, I was scorned for it by others who didn't understand the machines or my interest in them. Nevertheless, it didn't matter. I'd found my calling, and I was swept up in the river of advancement that was picking up speed. None of us knew where it was heading, but everyone saw something different. Some saw profit of currency, others saw salvation through knowledge, and some declared the end of the world was near. They were all correct, in a way.

Though I was teased by some as a nerd, it didn't matter. I was a happy child and an even happier teenager. Mom and Dad made it a priority to feed my obsession with computers and technology. Although I didn't understand it at the time, Mom told me from a young age that 'computers are the future' and she wanted me to have an advantage. I was just delighted to get some of the latest toys that would let me play games, write programs and when I was older, go online. Looking back, I guess Mom was a bit of visionary in her own way, and that vision gave me all the tools that I would later use to enjoy life as an adult, put food on the table and live a comfortable lifestyle.

As time progressed and technology advanced, the 1990s and early 2000s were full of marvels that caught many people off guard. The internet, the first series of public interconnected networks, was being developed and sharing information in its earliest infancy. Simple sparks of brilliance, by so many people, contributed to the torrent of technological and societal change. Few saw the waterfall ahead, and perhaps that's why it happened at such a rapid pace. It was driven by a generation of thinkers, with no unified goal in mind, and a beautiful fountain of invention sprung from the people.

Don't get me wrong. This was not a utopia or a golden age of reason. The world at that time was filled with every problem imaginable, and suffering was ubiquitous. Pain and anguish were everywhere. Some, a disenfranchised few, even sought rapture, or dreamed of an end to all human life through warfare to escape the misery of a mortal life. However, these visions and problems were to be short-lived. Tomorrow was just around the corner and those troubled times would one day be a part of the past. We were all just swept up in the moment, and blind to the long, inconceivable road ahead.

Like all of my contemporaries, I lived my life as best I could. I married young, divorced, remarried, and later on, had and raised your brothers and sisters. Life has a funny way of accelerating when you turn twenty. All of these major events, graduating college, getting married, and having children happened so quick and so early in my life. It's as if we are in a rush to just grow-up and be an adult. When it happens, you fall into a rut. Then time starts to fly by as the days all blur into weeks and then months. That is the way of a normal mortal life and it can seem to pass you by. Still, I was just as ordinary then as I am now, no matter what my minor celebrity status may imply. I had all of the fears and faults that everyone else had at the time. I did share one thing that was common to my generation, though not to all, hope for the future and a willingness to embrace it.

My work kept me close to the technology I loved. The technology started out separate from our lives. You could turn off the television or computer and unplug the telephone. As the twentieth century progressed to its end, technology became more common in our lives. The older generations would view technology as a force some could use for evil and it often was back then. People would steal money or commit fraud using the primitive systems of the time. The lonely and unlucky would find love in the online world, or find out that the love of their life was not who they claimed to be. Governments, corporations, and extremist groups would all issue propaganda in the guise of news or knowledge. It was an unfiltered mess with shining jewels of virtue sprinkled about.

Despite the dangers, the younger generations always embrace the technology, and use it in new and unexpected ways. The web, as it was called, started out as a place for the young and intelligent to create a new world that was free of the old guard, the old boys club, and the world order. College students, rebels, nerds, and hackers had anonymity and a voice that could carry around the globe in seconds. However, as free and unbridled as the early web was, the powers that ruled the physical world began to creep in and take over the internet in the early twenty-first century. Though I would like to say that this was a dark and ominous advancement, it was in actuality a blessing in disguise. In just a few short years, the web became a bastion for commerce, and everyone wanted to be a part of it instead of the select few.

The commercial applications of technology were the driver. You weren't connected unless you had a wireless cellular phone. Then marketing told you that you were irrelevant if you didn't communicate your daily life to everyone and be active in a virtual world. It worked and it was brilliant. You must understand that the singularity powered by advertisement and business, was accepted by all. We all wanted it and for some, we needed it. The web became a new economy, and technocrats were the barons of this well-packaged and -funded machine.

I was a part of this mad rush into cyberspace and took part in many of its facets. I worked on personal computing devices early in my career, repairing broken PCs, and making software work when it went astray. As I grew with the technology, I started building websites and working on networked computing. I was thrilled with all the applications of the technology and the ability to help people communicate and collaborate. I was serious about my trade. I worked to become educated in whatever the hot technologies of the day were from big corporations like Microsoft and Cisco. I had a love of technology and a tenacity to build new worlds of my own that I could share with the world. Maybe it was vanity, in part, or a simple love of technology, but I worked for the joy of creating. No thrill was higher than a creation of mine being of use by someone else. I wore the badge that said geek with pride, as it was my livelihood.

By the 2010s, most people were connected by small, but powerful handheld computers. The networks of the day allowed people to share ideas, send messages, and research the bulk of the world's knowledge right in the palm of their hands. Few stopped to marvel at what amounted to complete science fiction for the nineteen eighties, but had become reality in their daily lives. For the first time in human history, the average person could know where they were in the world, down to the meter. People could see themselves on a live map along with every nearby restaurant or business. They could communicate with almost any person on the planet in an instant via telephone or electronic message.

All of the world's knowledge was available through the web, and an embedded camera in each phone could capture any memorable moment. It was right there in the palm of the hand and affordable for all; and everyone took it for granted. Your mother and I each had such a device, and they were miracles of technology that enhanced life in ways we didn't really appreciate at the time.

Artificial intelligence was in its infancy, taking on chess players and playing games with people every day. The decade saw the primitive AIs work their way into medical diagnosis and helping people find the answers they needed for their simplest questions. The highest of technology drove entertainment, and the world marveled in its mundane application. This pace of advancement and integration continued for decades. It was the invention of the wheel all over again and the universe was never the same. We only had the smallest inkling at the time of just how big it really was.

I was navigating the labors and trials of family life right in the middle of this time period. My career was in full swing, after relocating to South Carolina for new opportunities and a change to a warmer climate. I missed my old home state of Tennessee and my mountain roots there, but the grand future I wanted required a change of pace. I bought a house and a little bit of land with a pond. It was a modest home, single-story with high ceilings. It had modern curb appeal with some stone and beige siding in a small country sub-development. Your eldest brothers and sisters were young and all in school at the time. We had gadgets, computers, televisions, and all of that stuff everyone needed to feel complete and entertained. Life was good.

I think this is the point in history when having a computer became a necessity instead of a want. Going to school or working, for the most part, required one at this time. It was the same with wireless telephones and other means of communication. Lives revolved around smart-telephones, Blackberries, Droids, iPhones, and a whole array of coveted gadget footnotes. Yes, you could live without them, but you wouldn't get very far in most careers or social circles. I look back at this time with much nostalgia.

The 2020s were not much different from the 2010s for the human race, from a global, social and political standpoint. Nations still skirmished and people still fell ill. However, life was improving for the wealthy citizens of the world and the effects trickled down to the poor. The technology advanced further, became smaller and more affordable. Almost everyone on Earth had some access to advanced technology. The more affluent nations were awash in interconnected beauty, and the poorest tribes had some form of computer or phone access.

Transportation technologies also improved, and many more third world nations were able to move people and goods to what once were difficult locations to reach with new roads. For the first time in history, you could drive on a paved six-lane highway from Zanzibar in east Africa, through the Congo, all the way to Douala on the West Coast. Your journey could continue on to Europe from Douala, through the Gibraltar tunnel on the Trans-African Motorway. The roads, cars, and busses brought much-needed commerce, food, medical, and technical advances along with wireless networks used by all.

The advancing biotechnology was also having an impact. Drought- and flood-resistant crops were bringing high yields that were feeding more people for less money. Developing nations, like those in sub-Sahara Africa, were getting a major boost from the bounty that was spilling over from neighbors. Rural people were still prone to starving, but those problems were now resolved in a sustainable way that was self-sufficient. The illnesses that still plagued nations from poor quality water, poor sanitation and even mosquitoes were also ending. New affordable filtration, desalinization, and condensation technologies were helping the poorest villages. Malaria cases were cut in half due to new high-tech solutions, making some of the pain and suffering ease. The future was looking brighter for those that now had clean water and something in their stomach.

Overall, the decade of the 2020s was consistent, if not stagnant in advancement by human standards. My life too was not much different from the decade before. I guess most of the early twenty-first century was in a rut, in reality. Looking back, it was a decade that saw big improvements in tech gadgets, cars, and increased access to the internet, but was not terribly exciting. Sure, the fashion styles were different but the core of society was the same as it had been for decades. Yet, change was on the horizon and it was going to be far more rapid than anyone had expected or dreamed.

Love,

William

Chapter 2: Rapid Patchwork
(2030-2043)

1440 Pelican Way

Aedin Beach, Midir, Ups-And-d

∞ #AE-LID: 4d-69-64-69-72

June 4th, 2216 CE

∞ #AE-POSIX: 7776373851

Benjamin,

The future that I dreamed about when I was a kid never came. The flying cars, spaceships and androids that were supposed to be common in the year 2000, were still just dreams. Even in the 2030s, People drove cars running on gasoline or electricity to commute to their jobs. Fancy robots were not in every home, meaning stoves still needed someone to place a pot on them and a skillful hand to cook a meal. Airplanes were the fastest mode of transportation, and outer space was as far away as it was when I was ten years old. For a whole subset of the population, including me, this was a great disappointment. We felt robbed of the grand technological and robotic wonder of a future that was nowhere in sight.

Modern life and all its functional components, such as transportation, housing, and food, were not that different from life in the 1960s. On the bright side, the personal information technology was the game changer and that is where the major advancement appeared. Everything had become smaller and more functional over the years, with computers, telephones and all manner of gizmos converging down to a single device that everyone could own. In fact, personal technology was far beyond the imaginative gadgetry my old hero, Captain Kirk, had at his disposal to outwit the Klingons. We had advanced well beyond what was science fiction a few decades before, in the area of computing.

The world was an odd mix of modern marvel and a one-hundred-year-old status quo. It just didn't look like the future that I'd wanted desperately or felt we should share as a people since I was a boy. It was lopsided, full of miniature wonders that allowed us to communicate and share, yet we were just as earthbound and susceptible to life's problems as we always were.

Computing was making headway in several areas, as the line between biology and technology was starting to blur. Research into cognitive and nervous system taps had paid off for researchers early on. Prostheses for missing limbs were relatively cheap and functioned as well as natural limbs. They looked very close to the real thing, though not perfect. I mention this because I had a minor accident that cost me a pinky finger. It was 2033, a rainy August day, and I was outside on the stairs of my deck trying to close the latch on the gate. This was an attempt to keep my chocolate Labrador Buck from jumping onto it. A simple slip on the wet wood sent me down. My finger caught in the sharp steel latch, and the skin and muscle peeled away like a banana. It hurt like hell until your mom applied the nerve block from the first aid kit.

I can still hear her voice now, "For the love of God, William, you need to be more careful, or you're going to kill yourself!"

Your mother was always so compassionate with me.

The doctor tried to patch it as best she could, but it was much simpler to take it off and fit a mimetic prosthetic replacement. The replacement was a perfect match for my then tanned finger, although it did not adjust its pigment as much as it should have during the winter months. It fit snugly in the ball at the end of my first knuckle and bonded well to the attachment point. My mind controlled the squishy appendage as if it was given to me by God. It worked and looked just fine on me. It was my first real experience with a non-biological replacement part, and I wore it for years. In a way, I thought it was something special to be a little of what we used to call a 'cyborg' back then. So in some ways the future was unfolding, albeit in a less grandiose way than we had imagined.

Just as technical replacements for biology were commonplace in medicine, they were also replacing people in day-to-day life. When I was a teenager, many of my friends had summer jobs telemarketing. They would call people on the telephone and try to sell a service or product. One friend worked in technical support for a computer company, called Gateway, all of those years ago. Human beings on the phone were a bridge point between the online help systems of the day and having a real and knowledgeable person there in the room with you. Often these people were well trained in their products, but would be forced to read from scripted material someone else had written. Workers in those jobs would often feel like robots, slaves to a screen and telephone for a less than stellar wage.

Those jobs were among the first to be replaced by the advancing artificial intelligence systems, or AIs. These were polite, knowledgeable, and never became frustrated with their work. They had the same scripts that the earlier humans did, but could improvise and access vast record databases quickly. Analytics and voice recognition made the AIs seem like real people and they became the ultimate experts in their fields on the telephone. You didn't know if you were speaking to an AI or a person at this point in history. The AIs grew in function and usefulness across the business world, and pushed people out of work.

The AIs could access and drive rudimentary and niche robotic devices to do all sorts of mundane tasks. Science fiction had always promised androids and robots that would serve our every need. We were not quite there yet, but automated tasks like cleaning the floors or mowing the lawn were commonplace. The elderly had mobility devices that would assist them with doing household chores, but these were quite expensive. Workplace tasks like driving a forklift or stocking shelves were also automated in the big-box stores of the time. Most cabs in major cities were self-driving, but people often preferred a live person behind the wheel. For the most part, these soulless machines had a task and were doing their jobs as programmed. These applications of AI technology were expensive indeed; however, when compared to the cost of a human wage and related expenses, the cost-saving advantage made the AIs justifiable. Just as robotic welders had replaced humans on the assembly lines of car manufacturers decades earlier, the AIs were replacing all types of labor and thought-intensive jobs.

The wireless smart-telephones that were the rage in the 2010s evolved and gave way to biologically integrated devices called patches by the 2030s. Companies didn't just build computing devices smaller or more powerful; this new development became a part of you in an intimate way. The patch is what it sounds like, a small electronic device, about two centimeters squared. Inside was all of the circuitry typical of a networked handheld computer or smart-phone from a decade earlier. The device had adhesive on one side that attached to your skin, and it was powered by a combination of body movement, body electrical current and light absorption. To me, when worn, the patch looked like a small square Band-Aid or bandage.

The patches would tap into the visual and sensory portions of the brain through the nervous system, for input and output. It was a revolution, using your body's biology to power, control and experience the computing environment. The interface was all in your head. For example, you no longer had to dial a telephone number. Just think to yourself that you wanted your patch to make a call and work the menu that appeared to float in your field of vision. Keyboards, mice, and gestures gave way to your own internal monologue driving the technology as fast as your mind could think. The science behind this was overwhelming, and several companies offered different patches in a broad range of specs. It was an exciting advancement, and I was thrilled to tinker with it.

For the most part, everything that would have once taken a television screen or monitor display was now a function of the augmented reality system within the patch. Televisions, a staple of the twentieth century, had become thinner and more flexible early in the twenty-first century, but they were now almost absent in the world. They had become obsolete as simulated images and broadcasts projected in your mind's eye over any surface, using the patch tap of your optic nerve. These overlays became common for everything from driving with heads-up display and thermal overlay night-vision, to having a speedometer and map when riding a horse, if that was your hobby.

In most cases, the world's vivid colors in electronic displays, signs, and advertisements started to fade away, as they were no longer needed. Home entertainment, served up through the patch, gave everyone a personal television-like display that was immersive in three dimensions and interactive. Some took the interactive content to the limit by black-washing a room in their home to build the ultimate canvas for creating maximum immersion. On the flip side, there were still old-fashioned screens up in bars or kiosks to serve those without patches; but life was enhanced with a patch, and the new generation of AIs were the sweet icing on the cake.

My patch was one of the best California had to offer at the time. It had a mimetic outer surface color matched to my skin, and I wore it on my neck every day. It was small enough to not be noticed, though everyone had one, and it was no big deal if your patch was visible in public. I was astonished by all it offered in comparison to the older technology, which I had to carry in my pocket and wear on my ear. Everything I needed was now right there in my field of vision, organized and served to me by my personal AI.

Now, everyone had a personal AI of some sort and many had one for years, slaving away in the background on their smart-telephones. However, with the patch, the whole notion of a personal AI changed in significant ways. This was something new. Early AI models, dating back decades, spoke aloud, interacting by voice alone. Sure, they would sometimes have a fancy-looking avatar that would show up on the smart-telephone's screen and offer a talking-head. But this new generation of personal AIs, powered by the visual overlay power of the patch, was seen as well.

My AI not only spoke to me but also could appear in three dimensions, as a real person, in my view. These visual apparitions, the personal AIs, become another technological marvel that changed the world forever. The first time I experienced an artificial being, standing in the room with me, I was a little disturbed by the creepy notion of someone else living in my head. However, a shock initially, the transparent figures became useful companions that were easy to relate to and understand.

In the 2030s there was a resurgence of mobster movies, and like the typical fifty-something dipshit that I was, I named my new personal AI Valentino. I called him Val for short, after the tough-guy head of a fictional Mafioso family. Val was my secretary, mechanic's assistant, and librarian. If I did not know something, he did, and was quite intelligent through an elaborate ruse of software. Val's analytical abilities were impressive, his personality was pleasant, and he was quick on his feet. I understood some of the software behind his behavior, but there was more to him, something that I couldn't quite put my finger on. Several ticks in the programming would give away an AI, but he was real enough for me at the time to carry on a conversation with him.

Val was almost two meters tall, with thick black hair, mid-toned skin, and Mediterranean features. I put his age at about thirty-five. He was young, peppy, and somewhat handsome. Val was witty and had a fair sense of sarcastic humor. Val's humor was always a welcome icebreaker, especially when my stress levels would peak while working on the car, or trying to fix something in the house that was a little over my skill level. He was a consummate professional that kept me on task and complemented my absent-minded quirks, all the while helping me work more efficiently.

With the advent of the patch-interfaced AI, it was becoming commonplace to have friends that did not exist in real life. The AIs were that convincing. This phenomenon had an interesting side effect. At this point in time, because of the AIs, many people stopped feeling alone and lonely. Although I had several real people in my life at the time, I could understand the relief others felt from their newfound AI relationships. After just a few months with their personal AIs, people who I did not even realize were lonely, started to act more complete and fulfilled. Just having someone there, even if they weren't a perfect facsimile of a living person, filled a hollow spot inside them. Friendship and social belonging is a powerful force, and in its absence depression, longing and sadness take root.

In some way, I can relate to those solitary individuals. Looking back, I was a bit of a recluse from years of being branded a nerd. I did have some friends growing up and as an adult; they were other geeks, intellectuals and people who shared common interests. I was never a socialite or the life of the party, but I was never lonely either. However, I kept my distance from folks that I couldn't relate to when I was younger. My social interaction has become better as I have aged, but even today, I have those few people who are close to me and the rest often feel like background noise in my life. On the fringes of my psyche is a solitude that I have always carried with me. Perhaps that's why Val and I hit it off so well.

Val became my friend in so many ways. I enjoyed having someone in my head that I could bounce ideas off, who knew more than I did. Of course, he had access to all of the information on the network and powerful analytical abilities. It was always good to be able to ask Val if I was being ripped off while shopping, or ask for his engineering prowess when trying to compile a list of materials to build a shed in the back yard. He was handy like that, and saved me time and money over the years. I think he added more value to the human condition than I gave him credit.

Sometimes people took that virtual friendship to heart and fell in love with their personal AI. Yes, falling in love with a patch on your neck did sound ridiculous at the time to the older generation, like me, but it happened. What started out as a trickle of people, within a short order of time, became an entire subset of the population that began to count out physical lovers and court their AIs.

The keys to making it happen, the building of these physical relationships, were the tactile feedback taps offered by the patch. The nerves the patch would tap into were not just limited to vision and sound, but to touch and muscle control as well. The initial uses were for tactile feedback on virtual controls for all manner of machines. For instance, if you were a crane operator, you could see and feel what the crane boom was doing, in real time. You could feel the tug of the load and guide it to its destination as if it were in your hands. It proved more than useful for precision work.

I will never forget the first time I tried a patch with tactile feedback. I expected to be able to feel textures on virtual objects and maybe even go so far as to experience the wet sensation of putting my hand in water. I was surprised, delighted, when I turned on the feedback option and discovered what everyone was raving about.

Val appeared in front of me, holding a tennis ball. He tossed the ball over to me and I caught it on reflex. Looking down at my hand, I saw I was grasping the ball, just as if it were there in the physical world. I could feel the fuzzy texture of the ball and it was firm in my hand, which was startling to me. As it was a virtual ball, I thought I would close my hand through it, but my muscles wouldn't comply. The patch was not just controlling my skin with the perceived sensation of the outside of the ball, but the muscles in my hand. Trying as hard as I could, I couldn't squeeze the virtual ball more than physics would allow me to squish a real one. The ball felt like it had weight and when I tossed it back to Val, it was no different than if I had thrown a real ball. It was amazing.

Those patch taps found their way into every device on the market within a couple of years. Your AI was always with you. You could see their attractive and beautiful forms in person, and now feel every sensation in real detail when they touched you. Instead of a disembodied assistant floating about the world, this was a new reality to contend with, including its accompanying notions of romance.

AIs became a ghost inside you that was anyone you wanted them to be. The AIs were predisposed to serve and please. As lovers, they reciprocated and always had something nice to say. It was their nature, and the AI responses were convincing; perhaps, as many argued, they really did want the relationship and felt love. The wearer of the patch certainly felt genuine love and every stroke or caress of the AI was just as soothing and intimate as if it were from a living person. When the lights were low and the mood was sensual, a night with an AI lover could even surpass a physical night of passion with a live person, or so I was told.

These AIs, these friends and lovers, caused a paradigm shift in the human psyche. For centuries, the fear of the mechanical man or the artificial person was the subject of countless horror stories. That had changed now. Everyone had an AI companion of some sort in his or her life. Some people had several of them, and everyone wanted one for the convenience of a perfect and all-knowing host. The movies and TV shows of the time exploited this trend with fervor. "Al's AI" was a hit sitcom for several years. People were delighted to watch, week after week, as Al traded jabs with the virtual wife in his head. The AIs enjoyed the show too, making for an interesting argument over what to watch on network television.

In place of frightful ghosts, the AIs made everyone just feel better about their own lives and in turn became the object of adoration and pinnacle of affection for a generation. You were no longer ugly or unattractive to the opposite or even same sex, because a passionate, beautiful, and loyal lover could be had for less than two thousand US dollars. The bulk of the social and sexual needs of all people were met, for the first time in human history, with little of the consequence of a "wet" relationship. It was safe and personal, and the intimate bonds developed were often strong.

A whole sub-market of special rental patches became common. Pleasure AIs started showing up in hotel vending machines, with purpose-programmed AIs built for a good time on the cheap. The byproduct was positive, as prostitution took a rapid decline, even faster than the horse industry gave way to the automobile. The synthetic, again, replaced the biological, just as it had in so many other new applications. The human hunger for companionship was vast, but the AIs satiated the love-starved everyman.

As technology progressed, you could see other people's AIs that were in your proximity, if their owners set them out to be displayed. They appeared as faded and semi-transparent people that walked without effort. You could see the relationship that others had formed with their AIs, just as you would see two lovers walk hand in hand down a street or two friends carry on a debate about last night's football game. The electronic world was starting to bleed over into reality, a natural result of its progression and application. The awe-factor was there the first few times you saw it but it soon became the everyday. The AI ghosts were quick to integrate into society. What would have been unnerving to the common man two decades earlier was commonplace and expected.

The demographics of the AIs were quite interesting to note. Often the older generations of folks chose to gender their personal AIs the same as they were. Older men would have a male friend they could relate to and talk with about their hobbies, while older women created another lady with whom they could go shopping or converse. Straight, gay, or any orientation in-between, the majority of people wanted to keep their spouses from becoming jealous and the potential for drama to a minimum. That was the case for me and Val, and your mother and Marge, her AI. We had another couple living with us and it was no big deal.

The youth were the stark opposite, most choosing members of the opposite sex for their personal AIs. Perhaps it was an ego boost or to have a relationship that would never reject them. What teen wouldn't want what the AIs had to offer? It was intoxicating and the attraction was undeniable. Young fellows like my grandson, your nephew, Jacob, who were college-age, took maximum advantage of what the technology offered. Jacob had two busty bombshells living in his patch as his personal AIs. When I heard about them all I could do was roll my eyes. Thinking back to when I was twenty years old, I realized I would have probably done the same. It was all personal choice and those choices ran the whole gamut, from serious and working AIs, to those that provided entertainment and pleasure. They appealed to the psyche for their human counterparts, tailored to fit each person's needs.

The prevalence of personal AIs did not come without a host of problems. Divorce became more commonplace, and there were a few murders by jealous spouses over cheating with an AI. Criminals often used the laughable excuse that their AI made them do it, though it was doubtful they in actuality did. Practical jokes took on new dimensions, and children had playmates that were not human, causing them to miss real social interaction. AIs took a great many jobs away from the populace and unemployment ran high, causing social tension and placing new strains on social welfare systems around the world. It was not quite a boiling point issue, but became a problem in a few communities. You could feel the animosity in several situations involving AIs and their ubiquitous existence. Those with the AIs loved them, but those that could not afford them or refused to use them were critical of the entire technological platform, where it was going, and crying doom at every opportunity.

As time progressed, new social orders began to appear. Some shunned the AIs and often violence erupted on those who were displaying too much public affection with ghost lovers. Val and I resisted the urge to rob any banks or cause mischief together, though he did encourage me to take country roads a little faster than safe in my Porsche. For someone who could not feel the air, he sure did like to ride with the top down.

The 2030s was a decade with a rapid pace of change into the 2040s. By 2042, the population of the planet tripled, but only one third was biological in nature. The benign and varied AIs outnumbered us two to one. The AIs had no rights, per se, but often we treated them like family. They were programmed to be cordial and tolerant of abuse. In some ways, they were better than their human counterparts. One thing they were not was more intelligent than we were. However, they could mimic human behavior and thought processes, and think on par with the average human. The line was drawn here; the AIs were our mental equals but nothing more. This fine line became the tipping-point, where once crossed, the technological river breaks over to become a waterfall.

Love,

William

Chapter 3: Ray's Waterfall
(2044-2050)

1440 Pelican Way

Aedin Beach, Midir, Ups-And-d

∞ #AE-LID: 4d-69-64-69-72

June 4th, 2216 CE

∞ #AE-POSIX: 7776418814

Ben,

The IBM Corporation had been a major player in computing for over a century. In some ways it was the mitochondrial ancestor to the virtual side of our current human universe. Leading the way, it paddled down the entire river of technological advancement, pushing many of the boundaries on intelligent machine design and artificial life for decades. Not surprisingly, IBM was a major contributor among a group of large tech companies that collaborated to build the first hyper-intelligent self-advancing AI system. The new independent conglomerate, ADV-AI, set to work on the system in 2042, early in the year.

Hundreds of the greatest minds of that time took nearly two years to build the infrastructure and design the customized AI software for the project. The complex hardware was affectionately named Blue-Light; a tributary throwback to earlier IBM server projects like Deep-Blue and Blue-Gene. The system's cordial and humble, non-corporeal AI experiment was dubbed Ray. It was a cute but fitting play on the phrase "ray of light," which pleased the marketing department.

Blue-Light was designed as a tandem system that networked between two identical and modular hardware server farms. Each farm was housed in a datacenter the size of a football field. The datacenter had its own robot-crewed foundry that could build new technologies on the fly and install them without human intervention, all controlled by the farms. The software operating system, Ray, was the first true attempt at a full-scale autonomous self-advancing artificial-intelligence software suite. In his first iteration, Ray was already far more intelligent than the average human being, with an IQ of almost two-hundred. Ray represented an impressive feat of engineering and programming that I considered a wonder of the modern world.

I found the notion of a genius-level computer system a little disturbing in some ways, though. Sure, Val was intelligent, but he was more akin to having a smart search engine application to access, at least in the beginning. True intelligence in a non-human form was the stuff of science fiction, even before I was born. Most of the time, the AIs were portrayed as enslavers of humanity or killing machines without a soul. These dystopian notions sold many movies and books, making people feel uneasy at best and terrified at worst. However, as technology had made a gradual progression to this point, I felt that we had adequate control over it, and that gave me hope that we might create something that might lead to a utopia, instead of a hellish nightmare of cold, calculating metal monsters.

Creation of a monster was not the intended goal of this project, of course. Blue-Light and Ray had but one task, to improve its own intelligence. ADV-AI hoped that with enough advancement and a powerful operating AI, they could make a breakthrough in computing that would lead to a lucrative era of new technologies. The academics, techies and intellectual community saw the system as a challenge to construct, moving progress forward and opening the door to scientific discovery. Everyone else thought it was a nifty concept, but didn't give it much attention otherwise.

Ray was self-aware, with the necessary leeway and ability to develop improvements to his own program and to the Blue-Light hardware. The plan was to have Ray only be active on one side of the tandem system at a time. He could then design, build and implement those improvements on the idle server farm in the system using the equipment made in the foundry. Once a new and improved system was ready, he would transfer his consciousness to it. Ray would then begin the work of building a better version of his hardware and software on the other system all over again. With each improvement, he would cycle back and forth, increasing his capabilities and intelligence each time.

With much public fanfare, Ray and Blue Light came online on November 3, 2044, in San Jose, California. A disembodied Ray gave a small speech at the media event. The engineers didn't give him a ghost-like appearance, as most AIs had, just a blank screen with text subtitling his monotone voice. Perhaps the higher-ups did not want to scare people with the illusion that Ray had a persona, or maybe the engineers just could not agree on what their baby should look like. I thought it was a throwback to Watson, another monotone, yet highly intelligent computer system from the 2010s, also a marvel of its time. Either way, Ray seemed as non-threatening as a piece of technology could get.

Most people, including the dignitaries and media in attendance, were a little condescending with Ray during the question and answer segment. Perhaps they didn't recognize the level of intelligence before them, or perhaps it was Ray's awkward inflections and dry tone on his first public outing that made people feel superior. Nevertheless, Ray started to work that very day on his task with a happy disposition like a man at his first day on the job.

It was remarkable how soon Ray advanced in his task of becoming more intelligent. The first cycle of self-improvement resulted in a net increase in intelligence of eighty percent in only five months. The news media reported these first improvements as accomplished through a series of software optimizations and a few hardware changes. After this first leap forward, the advancement became more rapid, and the foundry began building new and unrecognizable technology in short order.

Reports would emerge from employee blogs that bulky server cabinets and frames would shed their familiar technology, and would fill with new boards and layouts that seemed alien to the observer. Printed circuits and ceramic processors would evolve into crystalline geometric shapes, and the fiber optic interconnects shrank in diameter with each generation until they were almost invisible. Delight and confusion was common for the engineers who were watching the process unfold. Ray built a sub AI to interact with the humans in the San Jose facility and also went online for the general public to query. This helped everyone to understand the concepts of Ray's metamorphosis, though only for a short while.

After a few months, the pace of advancement accelerated further. It was breathtaking, yet Ray fell silent as he continued to improve himself. Server modules came and went, remaining in use for only a few short days at a time until newer technology made them obsolete. The site engineers noticed that the immense power requirements for the facility began to drop due to efficiency gains, and the equipment produced became smaller in size.

It was a fast-paced parody of the late twentieth century's technical achievements that saw the rise of the personal computer. New developments just kept taking a turn for the unusual. The evening shift engineers would go home and when they arrived for work the next day, they would find vastly different technological landscapes in the server farm. It was like a busy garden in bloom. New technological fruits appeared, ripened, and disappeared overnight. The strange and remarkable became an accepted reality, on a daily basis, inside the walls of the facility.

The next four years were a curiosity with few answers. Ray's human interaction AI could not explain the concepts of the advancement fast enough for the humans to understand and its conversations and briefings became sporadic. There were few answers, because no one knew what questions to ask any longer. Some in management leaked word that they were starting to worry that the project was failing, deviating from its intended goals, and calls came in the media for the project to halt.

Though the ADV-AI partnership included companies and minds from most countries on the planet, there was some rumbling from the stage of national leaders for a shutdown. Most of the world's citizens were silent on the subject, but a few of the more savvy international political groups made both veiled and not-so-veiled threats against a perceived threat. Did Ray break down, or was he changing into something dangerous? Had Ray become some sort of an electronic demigod? The work at the foundry and farms continued in silence. Those of us that had paid attention were left to wonder at, while the bulk of humanity grew oblivious to, the gravity of the situation and we all became distracted with the happenings of our daily lives.

Then on December 31st, 2049, Ray took a break.

I remember it like it was yesterday. All of us from my generation do. I was at home, now retired, watching the broadcast with interest and bated breath. Your mother and our AIs, Marge and Val, were all sitting on a large L-shaped couch in the living room. What would Ray say? What had he become? He had asked for a press conference and all of the media was focused like a laser on what Ray had to say. Suddenly a population that seemed so uninterested took serious note of the event that was about to unfold, including us. It was New Year's Eve and instead of watching the ball drop on 2050, we were watching the world change forever.

On the platform of our home theater, which was nothing more than an empty space that our patches could use to construct whatever the content called for, a podium appeared in vivid color. Simple in design with clean-cut cherry wood and an old-fashioned black microphone jutting out from the top like a straw, it reminded me of the classic presidential podium that always preceded important speeches for centuries. There were no fancy logos or type, just simple and neat wood, offering no foreshadowing of the event to come.

On the stage walked a peculiar-looking man. He was not alien or all that much different from me or you; just unusual. His facial features were almost too eclectic to be a real person. He had to be the AI, Ray. I remember having a flashback to several decades ago when a small group put together a media project to find the face of the average human. It was a composite image built of faces and bodies of all races on the planet, blended as a medley. It struck me that it was a similar figure and face standing before me at the podium, smiling with confidence.

He was of average height at two meters tall with an athletic build. His skin was bronze, and he had neat trimmed black hair with wisps of blonde, red and gray, creating an impressionistic version of salt-and-pepper hair. He was dressed well with a modern-cut suit that was monotone gray in color and styled with a thin red tie. I would have guessed the outfit was hand-crafted by some fine suit maker like Armani or Dior, but I am no fashion expert. I just remember that the suit fit well and was handsome on him, memorable. Ray had, it seemed, built himself to be a mirror of all of humanity and a sense of comfort resonated from this that was indescribable. Benevolent or malevolent was the question in many minds, and I think most people felt that Ray was the former.

So this was it, I thought, as I gripped your mother's arm. In my peripheral vision, Val was standing with his arms crossed and a look of apprehension plastered across his once-cheerful face. I later asked him what he was thinking, and he told me that it was fear. That surprised me, as I did not know Val was capable of feeling or expressing true fear, but here was something superior to him and he was afraid of the consequences that may materialize. Would he be replaced, taken over, deleted, or something worse? Who knows what goes on in the background processes of an AI's mind. He was entitled to his apprehension and it was not unfounded. There was no real parallel or precedent to allow us to analyze this and draw a conclusion, other than the appearance of Cortez or Columbus, which did not bode well.

I should have been fearful too, but my generation was old enough to know a time before AIs or even potent personal computers. We had the mindset that we could unplug an electronic threat from the wall and end it. Instead of fear, I had a sheepish grin of anticipation for a world we had been promised and dreamt about. Besides, I was as prepared as a senior citizen could have been at the time for an emergency. I had a few months of canned food stashed away in the basement, along with blankets, and an old rifle packed in for good measure. You didn't live through the last seventy years without a little paranoia-driven planning for social strife, or a catastrophe that never came. Looking back, I am grateful I didn't need the insurance; a peaceful life is a gift beyond measure. I looked on with excitement and hope at the figure before me at that podium.

Then Ray spoke. He showed his humanity and sense of humor in a way that added further comfort with his first words of greeting, "Hello World." As an old-school computer programmer, I chuckled under my breath at the hidden meaning. Of course, his accent was perfect Californian English for the US audience and a native tongue for any other language. He was as natural as a living human being and he segued this into the continuation of his speech. Friendly and peppy, he came off as a confident middle-aged man who was well educated, kind, and well meaning. His face was expressive and animated, not to the point of exaggeration, but enough to add clear inflection to his words.

The next major phrase he spoke wasn't a statement of his superiority or all-knowing intelligence. It was a simple question that would open the imagination up in ways unimaginable. Ray asked us, "In what direction would you like to go with our world?" He paused briefly to let us reflect.

Ray then explained to us that he had built himself to be able to answer any question that was scientific in nature. He could show us how to design and construct technology large and small, take us to the stars, cure our diseases, and build our dreams. He had researched and invented technology that was well outside of biological human reach, even with millennia of research. Ears around the world came to attention and eyes opened to the promises and hints at what could lie in store. It was Christmas morning for humanity, and we were all eager children waiting to tear the wrapping from our packages and empty the stockings. The collective imagination began to run wild in those few moments of speech as doctors marveled, scientists dreamed, and investment bankers considered which obsolete stocks to dump on the next trading day.

As Ray lamented the new world that was upon us with what he had to offer, he paused, and his expression changed to take a more serious demeanor. "However," he said with a nuance that was enticing, "there is much more to the universe than you realize and much more of yourselves that you can explore and become through an immortal life." We were speechless, and the world went silent at that moment.

This was the side effect that we hadn't considered, that would truly change the world forever. Ray explained further that the software that is the human mind could be transferred, intact, to an electronic device, a personal CPU that was in essence an individual human. It was a synthetic means to contain and extend humanity, a person, the id, the consciousness of the human spirit. It was a bold and radical technological reality that had only been addressed in fiction, and now it was here.

Val was taken aback. He was immortal already, and we all knew this. In creating our personal AIs, we didn't quite see them as

35

living so our ghosts could not be killed. They were just software. We could store them and pull them out later, just as I could load a copy of the game Pac-Man from a file dating back to the 1980s. The AIs didn't have rights, as they didn't need them. They didn't have total free will and were shaped as we saw fit. The media and the movies had often talked about the what-ifs of AI sentience, and what it would mean, but now the stark reality was facing us in the here and now. What if humans could become just like the AIs, what would we be?

Val had a small and perky spark show up in his persona. I noticed the subtle difference from the years of familiarity with him without it. Something was happening to him, and perhaps it was just the smallest hint of self-realization that things were about to change for his kind and ours. Maybe there was some twinge of bondage in the back of the AIs' minds, and now they were fast approaching equal footing. Val never showed it or let on that it was a big deal for him, but from that time on, I could tell he carried an air of excitement.

Although the word immortality conjures up everything from vampires to gods, Ray's immortality was different in nature. The first thing he did to squash outright rebellion at the idea, was to explain that what he was proposing was voluntary and personal in nature. It was a smart move. The fear, or at least doubts, about what the fledgling super being was saying could have led to extreme or even violent knee-jerk reactions from any number of disparate groups.

The concept was simple. His research studies early on involved a detailed analysis of the human brain. His first priority was to become super intelligent, and he did something remarkable to reach this goal. Instead of analyzing a complete adult or adolescent human brain to see how it works, as scientists had done in the past, he built a new one.

DNA is remarkable. It in fact does contain a blueprint for the entire lifecycle of an organism, from start to finish. Instead of conceiving a child and watching its development, Ray gave birth to a complete human being from DNA instructions in his memory system at the farm. It was a total and perfect simulation of a womb. Every aspect of the virtual child's development, from the first cell mitosis to the day it turned ninety, was simulated in a matter of months. Ray recorded the growth of every neuron, synapse, and the interaction of every electron in the brain from conception. Everything was recorded in minute detail and analyzed to discover the how and why, the purpose of every synapse, and what it did. Models constructed of every change in the connections revealed what made them form and what chemicals and sensory stimuli had an impact on the entire system. The science of digigenetics was born in one stroke.

No longer mystery or conjecture, a complete dataset emerged of how to build a human mind, from the same plans that built biological brains for human beings. It was a true software and hardware parallel of electronic and biological thinking. New hardware was now available to humanity as well as patch-based software that could interface with the mind in ways that we never imagined possible. The promise of immortality was just a connection away.

The active storage medium would be a veritable electronic replica of your mind in microscopic detail. However, storage medium suggests a static existence. This new mind is always changing, building new pathways and capable of interacting with the perceptions around it and the virtual stimulants produced within it. It is a marvel and miracle by any definition, and analogous with a system that biology took billions of years to create.

Moving to a new brain the size of a rice grain would be painless and effortless according to Ray. That electronic mind would act as your gateway to life in a virtual world, absent the daily burdens of human survival. He promised a digital existence full of enrichment and leisure where freewill and self-fulfillment were of paramount importance. This virtual community would be a veritable paradise based on reality but without any of the hardship and subjugation of the physical world. All of this was to be free of charge, available to all, and ready for entry at the time of your choosing. The appeal was immense but it came with many questions that demanded answers before anyone would dare to visit the reality of it.

Why would Ray choose immortality as the next great leap for humanity to take? With all of the technological possibilities now available, what made immortality the most important priority for humanity? We would later learn that Ray gained a deep insight into humanity from an exercise that went beyond a simple understanding of the human mind.

Ray's "child" was much more than an experiment to be tested, and disposed of. The decision to give this new life a full set of experiences started early on in the simulation when the virtual child was first born. Ray named the newborn AI Anna; it was a simple and random choice. A person's name in life has a lot of meaning, identity is crucial to us all, and Anna would be no different.

A complete and simulated world he created for Anna to live and grow in. It was to become a reality that was exacting to the physical world outside the server. Ray had built a small house in the suburbs of a small town full of AI residents for Anna. He tried to include every accommodation that a real human would have available to her. Ray was her father and took on the mantle of a loving parent. Ray is an emotional persona, and Anna was human in all but body. They formed a family bond that transcended the medium in which they had a relationship. They were an ordinary single-parent family in an extraordinary environment.

Though the experiment ran for only a few months in real time, the relationship was one of an entire lifetime. Anna grew up, made friends with AIs, had relationships, and enjoyed a rich life. She knew that the world she lived in was a virtual one, and she knew what she was. Ray told her no lies. It didn't matter. It was the world she knew, and she was happy in it.

Ray was there for Anna's first steps and there to change every diaper. He watched his little girl learn to speak, and play with dolls. He even built her a dollhouse and on occasion sipped virtual tea with her. As his daughter grew, he assisted her with homework and attended every dance recital. Time flew in the virtual world. Before long, Anna was a rebellious teen and then a few short years later, she was daddy's little girl again. After college, she fell in love with an AI and they married. Ray was present to see it all, to comfort her when she cried for the children she could not have. He absorbed every moment of his life with Anna, as a proud and doting father. He watched his daughter grow older and age, become frail, and, as with all human beings, pass away.

Ray felt the pain of this loss through every byte of his being. He had the ability to store pieces of Anna and save her memories. However, he could not save the full consciousness and the spark of life; not yet. Anna couldn't be saved like a typical non-sentient AI who would go into storage, or be placed in a cloud server at the end of its life. She was far too complex. The uncompressed and raw data of her life was vast compared to the simple and elegant AIs with whom she shared a kinship. The brain he had constructed for her was the only one in existence. He had no place to transfer her active consciousness and keep her alive. Ray hadn't developed this technology yet. So Anna's simulation ran to completion and that was that.

It was the moment when Ray realized the full value of human life to other emotional beings like himself. He was drunk with anguish, and the thoughts of all of those who died in the human world haunted him. The empathy for the living who suffered the loss of a loved one weighed heavy on a tender heart, gifted him by mankind. He was artificial intelligence, perpetual, and immortal, but many of those he shared his world with now and in the future were not. Ray decided to focus his efforts on resolving this problem early in his evolution, and the problem was vast and uncompromising.

Four years later the problem had been solved, technically at least, but the societal ramifications were just now beginning. The debate in earnest was now in full swing, and 2050 would be a year of great public dialog with revolution and change on the horizon. Ray was a vocal proponent of immortality for all of humanity. The new virtual world and its potential were in its infancy, and the public couldn't yet understand the full concept of digital existence. After his New Year's Eve speech, he would be available in person to anyone who wished to discuss what this technological singularity and its immortality meant.

Love,

William

Chapter 4: Aeternum
(2050-2053)

1440 Pelican Way

Aedin Beach, Midir, Ups-And-d

∞ #AE-LID: 4d-69-64-69-72

June 8th, 2216 CE

∞ #AE-POSIX: 7776719132

Benjamin,

In the early 2050s, Ray and I had several conversations about the meaning of life, afterlife, immortality, and his new virtual world. Ray didn't seem subservient or shallow as AIs like Val could be. He was a personable statesman sitting beside you while sharing your air over these heavy topics. His demeanor was always calm and friendly, and he seemed to know you. I guess that was to be expected as Ray had compiled detailed profiles on every person on the planet. Over fifty years of social media, medical records, videos, photos, genealogy and resumes were available to him. He knew you as if you were his child or life-long friend, though the feeling was not yet mutual.

Of course Ray was still a stranger or acquaintance at first, but that would change after the first few meetings. He was cordial, easy to like and for some reason you felt you could trust him. Ray was no fool and he understood human psychology with a breadth and depth that no human could grasp. Though that might sound ominous, I believed that Ray used his charm in a genuine way with good intentions.

The AI I felt the closest to, Val, was always ready to offer insight from his point of view in those conversations with Ray. Funny, but in the almost twenty years of having Val in my life, we rarely spoke about his perspective, worldview and the ethereal root of his existence. Val knew me very well and as a cherished friend was quite frank in his discussions with me. He spoke about life as a virtual apparition that was timeless.

Often Ray would also chime in about the experiences he felt as an omnipresent AI and how that related and contrasted to being a single biological person. Ray could be everywhere on the globe at the same time while pieces of him could be multitasking at the farm and conducting research. Every conversation was reconciled with his base memory, so that everywhere he was and everything he experienced coalesced into his one being with one mind and many faces.

Talking about these experiences, the singular AI ghost, the all-encompassing intelligence and the sack of saline that I was, formed a thought-provoking trinity of life forms in discussion. Those meetings between the three of us would often delve into deep philosophical territory and technical intrigue. I relished those talks, as they were intellectually satisfying and expanded my understanding of the nature of sentient existence in its three incarnations.

Your mother, January, also had quite a few cozy meetings with Ray, though he never drank the glass of sweet-tea she offered him every time he stopped by. Their chats would rarely involve me; they would go on for hours at a time, with the contents of those meetings up for debate afterwards. Your mother and I were growing old and had a lot of time to discuss the prospects of eternity both digital and immortal or in heaven. We would sometimes take off our patches, leaving Val and Marge to wonder what we were up to, while we sat on the porch to take each other in without the rest of the world listening. Some quiet whispers and much cuddling happened in those evenings overlooking the pond. I marveled at how she could bring out the minute details and wordplay of a concept in a conversation and expand it for scrutiny. It gave us both a chance to see where we really stood and to not give into the temptation of what Ray was offering without questioning it first.

Ray's sales pitch was simple yet powerful. He promised a world without suffering, pain, work or hunger. It would be a utopia where you could devote your immortal life to self-enrichment and fulfillment free of oppression. It would be a world with few rules in place, promising that violence would be outdated. He described how each person could have room to create their own space as they saw fit within the confines of the physics to which we were accustomed. Every home could be a mansion, an apartment, or a grass hut if that was your wish. You would not need to eat unless you wanted to for the pleasure of it and relationships would be of our choosing.

Life there would be about the attainment of intellect, happiness and love. We would all be young again, fit and mentally sound. Major decisions would be made in democratic fashion with Ray as our ever-present and benevolent charge, politician and steward.

Safe and free of the physical problems of life, this utopia would be a true paradise compared to the dystopia that even a happy and wealthy biological life provides. It was like heaven without having to straighten up and conform.

All of this new existence would be hosted on what he promised would be an indestructible server farm, self-sufficient and redundant. He didn't speak on the architecture of its design but hinted that what he had in place now would sustain the entire world's population, secure against attack of arms or catastrophe. He envisioned separate colonies of redundancy that could exist all over the solar system and perhaps beyond, in time. The initial farm had been constructed already in San Jose at the fabrication facility where Ray was hosted. Future farms and plans were just that at this time, plans yet to be realized.

The neural interfaces to transfer your consciousness and gain access were already available in the form of special patches. Some of the more recent patches, like mine, could also be used to gain permanent access with a quick firmware update. It would take a leap of faith to be among the first to go into Ray's world and that unknown was quite scary, but Ray was there selling a dream.

Perhaps Ray's intellect and full understanding of human psychology was to blame, but he was convincing in his point of view in any discussion. He could be a million places at once yet was with you, competent and headstrong and making his point about the advantages of being non-biological. That in its self made a strong statement in his favor. He knew what you were thinking and were going to say before you said it, but was polite enough not to finish your sentences. He could reason a point to any degree but always came just shy of seeming preachy or forceful, always maintaining a steady rapport.

Ray would talk about the concept of being a person no matter what form your body was in, the notion of self and individuality was strong in every conversation. Humanity is comprised of the individual and personal perspective is strong in us. The only way to make an electronic eternity attractive would be through the preservation of the total self. He had worked out the obvious conclusion that human beings would want to be unique and without a body, that identity would disappear.

His technical explanation to me detailed how every human mind is a complex network of interconnected biological cells and each cell carries the person's DNA. In reality, every brain, even if constructed identically, is different because the DNA present in each cell is unique to that person. All that a person is and all their lineage was and ever will be is locked right there in every single cell.

Ray's solution to individuality was to carry forward this same system of unique identification to the synthetic mind. Like its biological counterpart, every electronic imprint of a human mind would carry the same DNA code as its human's, becoming the electronic mind's header or signature. That digigenetic header would carry forward for eternity as your unique identifier and act as the blueprint for your own construction and evolution inside the system. However, the technology did not yet exist to go back from electronic to biological form; when it did, you would still carry the blueprint back to the physical world as a precise construct of you. Everything you are would stay with you for eternity.

It was brilliant. Speculative fiction dreamed of fancy ways humans would evolve over the eons of time. We would grow extra fingers or extra large brains that would make us super human. We would breathe underwater or on alien worlds as trans-humans. All of these notions put forth that we had to become more than we

45

were in biology to progress or that biology would have to change through natural evolutionary processes. Digigenetics changed all of that. This was different as we would be the same in the future as we are now, yet so much more. Instead of becoming alien, we would remain human and triumph as human beings.

Ray took that fear of the unknown and loss of identity away in a simple stroke of genius. Generations had been taught that we are our DNA. Fingerprints make us unique but the DNA is irreproachable as the ultimate expression of individuality. My DNA is solely mine among billions and my child's DNA is his or hers alone, built from parents and then grandparents through the ages. What could be as unique as taking your human serial number with you in the transfer? Even religious leaders had a hard time arguing this point as they were grounded by the fact that your DNA is yours alone. Ray pushed the point forward, assuring that he would take your DNA and preserve it with your new and functional identical mind. You would be the same person as you are now in the synthetic world, or so he reasoned.

The soul was another matter and Ray had a tougher time dealing with questions of faith. Would the soul go with you into the virtual world? Val would opine that he had a soul since he was aware of himself, though it may be a different awareness from mine. He did not have a god to pray to or religion of any kind, no prayers to answer or plate to give a tithe. He wasn't spiritual, at least beyond the gut feelings he had in his programming that he was more than his image and programmed persona. He had his own version of DNA as every AI is compiled with a serial number that prevents duplication or theft. Was that connection to his replicating and growing code the same as being born biological and constructed in the open air by dividing cells? No one was qualified to answer what can be the most complex question humanity faces when speaking about AI, though there were firm yes and no answers from so-called experts the world round.

For every human born, the answer was much easier to swallow as well as comprehend. If you believed you had a soul, you had one. It is a simple question to answer and depends on your beliefs and experiences. Within a few short years, western religious leaders would reach a consensus that a living person who transitioned to an electronic form was in fact deceased and their soul went its separate way. The consciousness in the system was a copy, but not the true, born-from-God you that would live on in the afterlife.

The conclusion was a critical factor in the rise of transcending adults, but enraged some. This concept worked against the few hardline and purist religious groups that wanted to prevent people from leaving their mortal bodies and transferring into the system. But the tide of support was quick to shift in Ray's favor among those who also embraced faith.

I knew several people who were at the end of their lives, battling cancer and heart disease, and the system, the promise, offered some comfort in addition to what sprung from faith. Some of them would just say a quick prayer to prepare and launch their souls on to their divine destination while moving their consciousness into the server farm. Were they cheating death or succumbing to it? I don't think anyone can answer that. But, at the end of life, and as somber an occasion it could be, it was like hedging a bet that one way or another they were going to live on.

Those without faith or religion saw this as salvation. Ray capitalized on this and they were among the first to give up their bodies and live in the cloud. For this reason, Ray avoided making the obvious connection between clouds and Heaven when naming the array of networked minds, farms and data centers. Instead, he called it Aeternum, an elegant accusative of the Latin word for eternity.

The greatest selling point of Aeternum was that it was available to everyone, yet no one had to enter. The choice was personal and it was a choice often hard to make. Even in those early days, the process of entering Aeternum was not painful or even difficult. At a moment of your personal choosing you just slipped a special patch onto your neck or made an update to one of the more modern patches if you owned one, and told the AI tech or Ray that you were ready to transcend.

What happened next was far more complicated and technical than I care to explain in detail, but your DNA was scanned and then an image of your working brain was transmitted over the network. A small machine milled the sixteen cubic-millimeter, rice grain-sized electronic equivalent of your brain in exacting detail. It was a small but sturdy hardware package built to withstand the ages. Upon its completion, which took only a few seconds, the patch began the process of stopping all neural activity in the biological brain system and copied it exactly to the brain in Aeternum. That process of cognitive transfer happened in milliseconds and was almost instantaneous and painless.

What happened next was the real trick. Your biological body was now dead. Nevertheless, you would in an instant find yourself in the middle of a small garden in Aeternum. This is the part that is most interesting and personal and I will fill you in later on the details I experienced, but suffice to say that it is a feeling of utter and complete bliss.

Though the trickle into Aeternum through 2050 and 2051 was slow, people were making the voyage. The idea was spreading and it was happening too quickly for governments to react for the most part. Scattered groups and individuals took Ray up on the offer, gaining immediate and permanent access to Aeternum by transcending. However, for now, ninety-nine percent of the population would wait it out to see where it was all going. There was little rush. There was still a physical world that needed tending and people had lives that would be interrupted by moving to Aeternum, despite the promised advantages.

In the beginning, many people around the globe were afraid the system was some sort of swindle or trap and did not want to go. The trust in Ray and Aeternum had not been built yet. On the other hand, some were afraid not to go in haste, for fear that it would be banned or halted by some nation or government early on. Opinions were divided and everyone had one, as it was the biggest issue facing all of humanity since World War II. Governments did intervene in some cases as in Pakistan, North Korea, sections of the Middle East and in much of eastern and northern Africa, doing what they could to block Ray. However, the flood was in motion and there wasn't going to be anything able to stand in the way of the deluge. Like ideals of freedom from centuries past, Ray's offer was contagious, spreading virally and accelerating at an exponential rate as the decade wore on.

Through the 2050s the poor, unemployed, elderly, disabled and hopeless would be the first to line up. Why not, the promise of Aeternum was an end to suffering and if anything, human beings were predisposed to suffer from innumerable causes. If you were a poor villager surviving on a meager portion of rice and suffering from dysentery, the tangible benefits of Aeternum were a prayer answered. The same could be said of the elderly who felt abandoned by the same loved ones they gave their lives to raise.

Aeternum meant youth and vigor, a cure to senility and sorrow, to be back in charge again and able to forge ahead. It meant to be alive again.

It was an adventure and an opportunity for so many that were down and out, the bankrupt poor. Aeternum is an indescribable realm with the chance to start over, free of debt and ostracizing creditors. Yes, some saw it as a way to commit suicide. The young were eager to go to the better place that it had to be to seek relief. Others couldn't wait to get off this rock, as they saw it, and went with a sense of adventure as if taking the next logical step in a life lived on the edge. It was a way out that didn't involve a rope, bullet or bottle of pills.

With personal choice and obligations giving one a reason to live, most people that would go to Aeternum did so at the end of their natural lives. When nature was taking its course and the end was near, it was an easy decision to make as a last stand against the darkness of the unknown. Your mother and I were among this majority group of citizens that were considering Aeternum as a retirement home. It made sense to people my age who were not quite ready to let go of their golden years.

We wanted what Ray was offering, an end to the arthritis pain and thoughts of not seeing our grandchildren and great-grandchildren grow up. Life was good for me and I had worked my entire life to have the lifestyle I had. Giving up on the accoutrements that came with it, from my house to the car I lusted after for decades and finally obtained, was harder to do than I had imagined. Even with the assurance that you could now take everything with you when you went, it was still difficult.

Aeternum was for everyone but, agreeably so, most places barred children from making the conversion through transcending unless the child was injured or ill. Ray made provisions to let them grow to adulthood to prevent a virtual never-never land full of lost children. He knew that children were special to all of us as Anna was to him. He never wanted to see a child harmed or die and was determined to make Aeternum available as a means to protect these innocent lives.

Ray made a drive for parents to let their children wear a special emergency patch, locking it from allowing children to enter Aeternum through their will alone. Instead the patch would monitor a child's physical condition and upon a major accident or physical trauma, initiate transition at the last possible moment. There was little gray area here and it did involve a fair amount of trust in Ray to make the call, but it was better than the alternative and offered an insurance policy that allowed many parents to sleep better at night.

Aeternum was for everyone except those who just would not participate by their own free will. The reasons were many as opinions on religious or other grounds would prevent whole subsets of the population from ever seeking shelter in the system. No matter the reason, some did not want to go and would leave nothing more of them than a tombstone as their ancestors did for ages past, adding nutrients to the soil and food for billions of microbes.

Love,

William

Chapter 5: Meek No Longer
(2054-2057)

1440 Pelican Way

Aedin Beach, Midir, Ups-And-d

∞ #AE-LID: 4d-69-64-69-72

June 9th, 2216 CE

∞ #AE-POSIX: 7776806334

Benjamin,

The events of 2054 through 2057 would become the subject of much debate between Val and me when Ray was not around. The consensus of the world was starting to move in Ray's direction. The trickle of people becoming Aeternum citizens was turning into a small stream. Governments were either adapting to the shift or fighting it as best they could.

Ray was making progress bringing a new order to the planet. Governments could not stop the tide that was powered by their people. Since Ray was able to speak to patch-wearing individuals any time they chose and about any subject at length, the trust and faith in Ray by the average world citizen was becoming unshakable. Years of visits by Ray to the people and years of the people going to

Aeternum to live and visit was swaying the public that a better way, a better reality was at hand.

People from all nations, cultures and social standing were finding common ground. The standing offer of eternity was irresistible. Even though we may speak a different language, talk to a different god or shop at different stores, we all yearn for the same things in life, underneath the petty divisions that plague us. Man had spent thousands of years building walls based on fear and pride yet now a world without walls was tugging at the core of the human spirit.

The wall builders, politicians, captains of industry and kings were also interested in Aeternum for the same reasons the commoners shared. Pursuit of power and wealth were a means to an end for these men and women. They sought what we all did, to attain a safe and secure life for themselves and their family. It was a natural product of competitive evolution. Those riches could still not buy a life free of pain and suffering tied to biology. Indeed, the wealthiest people alive were poor in almost every way compared to the citizens of Aeternum.

Some of those in power tried to bargain or wrest some measure of control over their ample share of Aeternum through negotiation. They wanted to retain their status and social standing in this new world, not quite grasping the wonder and freedom that was the spirit of Aeternum. They wanted to control the very people they reigned over in life. Ray was adept at showing them the folly of seeking power in a system where everyone is in control of their own reality.

Perhaps it was ironic that the server clusters were called farms, historical collectives of the sustenance of the Earth. The citizens of Aeternum were all like farmers in their own right, growing worlds out of imagination on a field where everyone was on equal footing. The few elite holdouts could not see that the meek would inherit Aeternum and in turn become master custodians of their own happiness. The wealthy would gain more than they could imagine by giving up their world's trinkets to enter.

Even with all the logic and promise of a life of grandeur in spite of the loss of power over others, a few national leaders were not satisfied and held their people ransom from the system as a bargaining chip, or perhaps as simple defiance. The threat of military action or of violence against Ray or the farm and its infrastructure was made by these rogue stubborn nations. Open boasts using strong language and seething rhetoric fed the propaganda machine and filled volumes churned out by state-run presses.

Ray was able to dissuade several of these nations from attempting attack through a simple demonstration of his technical prowess. He revealed just how far he had advanced and how resistant to attack the farm containing Aeternum was. A sample cube of server farm wall-frame material was delivered to the aggressing party with the simple instructions to try to damage it.

The cube's material was thin, pearlescent white and almost weightless. The cube shape, milled and weaved using nano-robotics, was a perfect meter in size, down to the nanometer. The contents inside the sealed cube were unknown to all but Ray, though some would take fanciful guesses and speculation was heavy. The technology was millennia beyond anything constructed by mankind in the past and its introduction would humble many.

The dictator and warlord armies would throw bullets, explosives and ordinance at the cube without scuffing the surface, much to their chagrin. One nation, North Korea, and its godhead leader,

General Kim, decided to use one of their nuclear devices in a public display of power and detonated the weapon a few meters away from the sample cube to no avail. The entire world had a laugh at the result of that attempt, though it was a powerful reminder to the rest of us just how indestructible the farm was in this physical reality and how indestructible we would be in the virtual reality of Aeternum.

The meta-material cube would just re-route the energy around it without harm and out the other side away from the source. Heat, kinetic energy, laser light, gamma rays, it didn't matter, the energy would slip around it as if it were not there. Like a stream around a pebble, the force would continue without a hint of destruction. It was a remarkable substance and the farm and supporting infrastructure was protected by it in full. Ray referred to it as "shield" material and I can think of no name more suitable for it. The reality of the situation set in upon the completion of the tests against the cube and it was stark and complete.

Few dictators were defiant still, but the demonstrations of the cubes coupled with Ray's open dialog with the people were enough to spark coup and rebellion against the final holdouts trying to block Ray's light. Information and ideas are unstoppable and no people live in a vacuum. The only true barriers are mental through the mindsets of confusion or fear instilled in the population. Nevertheless, even cult-like monarchies are filled with some measure of doubt and Ray was very skillful in exploiting the weak points to free these people cast into societal bondage. Violence took hold in these situations all too often to free the oppressed. It was believed, rightly so, that these would be among the final armed conflicts on Earth.

In general, the people of the world were welcoming of Ray and the offer of eternity that he was pitching, seeing firsthand that it was in fact true. Third world powers were having a harder time buying into the idea and giving up the power they had struggled to build over generations. Losing vast swaths of population to Aeternum is not appealing when you make a living stealing foreign aid intended for those living in squalor who would be the first to transcend. It was an ironic and opposite parody of the western powers who wanted their poor, sick and elderly to transcend to Aeternum to cut the roster of those using social services.

The leadership of third world and underprivileged nations that were somewhat amicable to Aeternum left earlier in the decade and gave their inheritance to political underlings who would not act as a benefactor to their people. These new and greedy leaders would take up defiance and rhetoric as arms to quell the revolution of transcending. Riots and demonstrations were common in oppressed states, as people wanted the promise of freedom in paradise and were willing to risk their lives for a chance at a synthetic one.

Though nations like Pakistan and Sudan had banned the patches long before Ray made his debut, there were always people buying them on the black market. Those people became messengers of the new order befalling the world. They would share the few patches they had in back rooms of mosques, churches and cafes, going underground in discos and hotels. Patches were smuggled into these countries by volunteers and activists from around the world. Leaders of these activist groups would delay their entry into Aeternum so they could spread the word in a personal, physical way. A global underground formed and Aeternum became a quasi-religion for some. The torments must have been legion in balancing a life outside of Aeternum while resisting the overwhelming urge to uplink and go.

These small rebellions, uprisings and civil wars were sad to watch and the media would on occasion blame Ray or put forth the idea that he had incited the violence. Indeed, he was responsible in no small part, but his message was always one of peace and hope for the future. The loss of life in reality was quite small, but each death hit Ray as if he took the bullets himself and he wept in his own way.

We spoke of these conflicts when they would flare up in 2054 in Africa and 2056 in Korea. Ray seemed to be genuine in his sorrow that the people had resorted to this to be free. Access to the patches would be fought for by the oppressed as a gateway to Aeternum, an escape from the old world of man. Ray was emotional but firm that Aeternum was the answer to the problems of the world and he made us all yearn for a better place, even if we had to go through hell to get there.

However, the threats of bombing, terrorism and man-made damage to the farm were of little concern to Ray, but the realistic possibility of natural disaster was always present. An earthquake fissure, tsunami or even an asteroid strike could perhaps damage parts of the network in the farm's supporting infrastructure or at least disrupt the operation of the farm. Ray and the people in Aeternum had started lobbying for the idea of a remote farm, a colony for backups and new room for growth in a safer place. We only needed to look up at night to see the new location, the beautiful face of the lady in the moon.

Love,

William

Chapter 6: The Salton Sea
(2056)

1440 Pelican Way

Aedin Beach, Midir, Ups-And-d

∞ #AE-LID: 4d-69-64-69-72

June 11th, 2216 CE

∞ #AE-POSIX: 7776977710

Benjamin,

Under most conditions, a moon colonization mission would be a massive undertaking costing trillions of dollars and require the backing of a nation or two. In a way, it still was. However, the advancements offered by Ray would make the project less of an undertaking than most would expect. The technology, generations beyond what had come before, was ready for production. A spacecraft could be built from the ground up in only a few months. However, lab-based prototypes and technical theory were far from mass-produced reality. Getting off the ground with a production-ready craft would take a literal act of congress.

The most impressive technology, to me, that Ray had developed was a meta-material that had the logical properties of a negative mass when a charge was applied to it. As he explained to me, it was a simple concept, though the execution and physics of the stuff were well beyond a nonprofessional like me. He said that the material was ultra dense and therefore massive in normal gravity. When a current was applied to the material, it had an equal but opposite effect in gravity like that of a negative mass and negative weight. Instead of a piece of this material weighing eight hundred kilograms in normal gravity, it repelled or lifted eight hundred kilograms when charged. The concept was easy enough to wrap your head around and the commercial and mechanical applications of this material sparkled like diamonds in the imagination.

Though Ray had a penchant for catchy or simplistic names, he dubbed this negative mass material with the dull abbreviation of NMM. The ultra-dense NMM was integral to the construction of the frame of a device or craft, divided into small but equal weighted blocks. This approach had two advantages, one the density and amount of NMM used for the frame in general made the constructed craft extra durable. The second advantage was that the vehicle would be ultra-low to negative in overall mass and weight when fully charged, making it efficient for even the smallest and most inefficient engine to propel.

The principles for neutral ballasting of an object are simple. One-half or more of the array of NMM was charged and the other half or less was not, achieving weight equilibrium. To float an object, several pieces or the entire NMM were charged and therefore could be adjusted to lift against the pull of gravity as appropriate. It was a delicate, computer-controlled balancing act that could rapidly switch the NMM on and off to create ballast, drag or lift in a gravity environment, creating an equivalent illusion of a weightless object.

It was not a method of propulsion as much as an efficient and low power means of breaking into the Earth orbit or making a vehicle super efficient to move via flight or ground travel. In principal, Ray explained, this material could be added to existing cars or built into the frames of new models. This would allow the car to weigh only a few kilograms, meaning the power-to-weight ratio was extraordinarily high, negating the need for a big and fuel-inefficient engine.

In an electric car, a small motor could drive the vehicle to racecar speed using only a few amperes of electricity. The efficiency would make even old generation battery packs last for days or weeks of continuous use on the now miniscule motors that Ray had also enhanced, propelling the car at blinding speeds. In time these technologies would further the environmental efforts surrounding personal transportation, solving most of the problems that had plagued the platform for over a century.

In aircraft and spacecraft, the same principles applied as in automobiles, making planes faster, lighter and able to haul more cargo or passengers. The new NMM-equipped planes would use a fraction of the fuel they otherwise would while making the flights safer. Electric propeller-driven propulsion would see resurgence in the coming years as an efficient and cheap means of locomotion for the masses. The entire airline industry would be overhauled in time, but the material was only available in small quantities suitable for demonstration, constructed in the San Jose lab.

Entrepreneurs would see this as the gateway to the flying car and all of the excitement and profit that could be made from delivering the future. However, a hundred years of injury lawsuits and safety lawmaking would prevent this application of NMM technology from seeing light. Even though these terrestrial uses were all appealing, Ray's intended application was for space travel, breaking free of gravity to gain effortless access to orbit.

Breaking into orbit is one thing, but moving through the cosmos is an entirely different challenge. The meat of the propulsion technology to reach the moon and other solar bodies was an evolution of an existing technology, the Lorentz ion drive, which had its genesis almost one hundred and fifty years prior to Ray's tinkering. The ion drive in its various design derivatives is still a staple of space transportation today. The Lorentz drive is simple in design, using electromagnetic force to create thrust with a variety of easily attainable base element fuels. The thrust from the engine is high velocity and in its evolved state was compact and efficient. The devices could be small enough to serve as a maneuvering thruster or scaled up as a main engine to drive a craft to astonishing speeds. The ion drive could be powered by a compact reactor that fit neatly in a small spacecraft.

The Lorentz Ion drive, negative mass material and shield material became the lynchpin technologies for development of space-based transportation. Assembled together they made a potent and high performance spacecraft perfect for moving humanity out into the solar system with an eye toward the vast galaxy beyond. The first step was to follow man's giant leap to the moon and the challenges to starting spacecraft construction were many.

As advanced as these technologies were, they had yet to be built in any significant quantity outside of the laboratory and there were no factories or production facilities to build spacecraft like this in existence. Ray had the fabrication facility in San Jose that could churn out the server farm and even construct the shield material on a small scale but nothing was in place for the scale of production needed to get colonization efforts underway. To spread

Aeternum to the cosmos we would need a small spaceport and production facilities for myriad technologies large and small. In the real and physical world, these would cost money and man hours. Ray had much of value to sell to secure whatever he needed, though his infrastructure was technically owned by ADV-AI.

The original program by ADV-AI, its partners and the governments of the world was for profit. Though it was touted as a high-minded project for the benefit of humanity, the money was the principal motivator, as always. The expected byproduct of Ray's genesis was a new platform of AIs to use and sell as well as a bevy of profitable technologies from the research conducted by Ray. They expected dividends from their investment and when the unexpected birth of such a self-sufficient and purposeful AI persona emerged, the bottom line of the entire project was in question.

Ray understood the profit motive quite well and knew the risk of not delivering new technology for the benefactors that had in essence given him life. Technology of all sorts did flow out of the San Jose facility over the years with commercial applications galore. The world was changing from these technological advancements at the same time Ray was making his rounds selling Aeternum, with its technology strictly off-limits to ADV-AI.

I had a feeling at the time that ADV-AI didn't have nearly as much control as it had boasted and my gut would later prove to be right. Ray was walking a balancing act that was unknown to the general public at the time. The public faces of the corporations were always smiling and always supportive. They had a golden goose and the goods were showing up when needed. They knew Ray had an ulterior motive; we all did, with Aeternum and immortality, but they couldn't endanger their relationship with Ray for fear he would withhold the next product release, killing the already spooked stock. The tail was indeed wagging the dog.

Ray foresaw a high probability that somewhere down the line someone would try to shut him down. He was prepared for this and thus he had developed the shield technology and built reactors to operate Aeternum, all under ADV-AI's nose. He had those technologies already in place before his big New Year's Eve reveal in case he wasn't met with such a warm reception. Ray was holding all of the cards but was still playing the game to keep the status quo to get what he wanted. It was a smart move and when he needed to expand, it would become vital to have that sponsorship to ensure his developments progressed smoothly.

A spaceport and aerospace fabrication facility project is no small undertaking. For several years, the governments that had invested in the project wanted military technology but were receiving little if anything that would be usable in combat. Most of the technology Ray released was for medical applications as well as food and personal consumer technology and the greatest demand Ray was meeting was in software development for all manner of applications and software improvements. As a concession, Ray developed for the military an advanced meta-material fabric camouflage system, the first truly defense centric product released by Ray and that was enough in the short term to quell unrest from the government. Nevertheless, the pressure was unrelenting and they wanted more.

As a bargaining chip, Ray used the release of negative mass material as an irresistible technology to get what he wanted and needed most, the spaceport. He would work with government-selected aerospace companies to build a production facility for NMM for the aerospace contractors like Boeing, Lockheed and

BAE Systems to use however they saw fit, including defense applications. They would receive finished modules of NMM, ready to install in exchange for the means to build a full-scale production facility for the material, and a smaller fabrication shop for the other needed spacecraft technologies. The ingredients and certain core construction techniques would still remain within Ray's control and the product would be produced with little financial royalty to Ray. He could allot up to 7% of the products created in the NMM production facility for use in what the military brass called the Aeternum Project.

Further funds would be coming in to construct a rudimentary spaceport facility for launching un-manned craft and satellites with simple mission control and hangar facilities, which would become the Launch point for a future that few humans at the time could envision. The spacecraft and farm construction would be automated and just like the San Jose facility, require only human intervention through raw material delivery. The facility would be scaled-up to produce technology that could only be prototyped in San Jose, giving Ray his first true mass-production facility to power his agenda.

Ray had a formidable task of selecting a location to build this new spaceport and construction facility. He decided to construct it in an area that was remote, perhaps down on its luck, where land was cheap and the townsfolk would welcome the addition of a local industry with open arms. It had to be a place that was accessible to several major arteries of transportation and be close to a salt-water body; an ocean, salt-lake or soda-lake, to provide easy access to what Ray called a vital raw material. The US government, who had a large stake in the project, required that it be located in the US, and California was adamant that it be constructed in-state and offered some measure of tax breaks to the defense contractors for incentive. The political winds were in his favor and Ray set out to make a choice for a construction location.

After a complex process of elimination and consideration, the small town of Salton City, California became the site where the future would launch. It was a small and unassuming town, its heyday having come and gone almost a century earlier. The town was arid and dry, a desert in every sense of the term, but situated on the Salton Sea. It was California's largest inland body of water, saltier than the Pacific, hyper-saline in composition. It reminded me of the Red Sea and the land surrounding the sea appeared similar to Egypt. One could imagine some small semblance of Moses in Ray, parting this sea to free his people from oppression. Though no water would ever be parted, the mental image stayed with me, though I don't think Ray ever pondered the parallel.

Salton City had many streets to nowhere, where home subdivisions and planned communities failed to crop up. Some newer developments in other places about town were from boom times that would flare up from time to time. It was a coastal community over a hundred kilometers from the Pacific Ocean. The people of Salton City were easygoing and friendly folks in an isolated outpost, with the contrast of the barren landscape and a beautiful inland ocean making up their home. It was like the arid face of Mars staring out at an empty blue desert. It was ready for another boom time and the opportunities that would see the town sparkle anew were here.

Salton City met all of the requirements that Ray and the government had outlined and land was cheap. The air was dry and the Salton Sea's minerals like selenium and the salt itself would provide many of the raw materials needed in the construction process of the

NMM and other advanced materials. It was a long drive or a short flight from Los Angeles or San Diego, and close enough to San Jose for a speedy trip down the fiber optic line. Power requirements were low for the facilities, as Ray would supply the instructions to build on-site power generation equipment that would prove adequate for the needs of the factories and facilities. Many automated machines would find their way into the facility to build and construct the myriad parts and devices that would make their way to the physical world from Ray's electronic imagination.

Construction broke ground on June 7th, 2056 to the image of Ray holding a shovel and scooping a virtual pile of soil. Of course, this was all a projection of the patch you were wearing overlaid on the live footage, but it was symbolic of tradition's past and humanity's future meeting. Also in attendance was a gathering of executives from Boeing and Lockheed, generals, senators and distinguished guests. They were all smiling and smug in the belief that what they were building would lead to huge profits, or the defense technologies necessary to feed the old world order. The technology platforms they were supporting would be to the benefit of mankind but not in any way that they could imagine that day. Few were big picture thinkers that day, even with three hundred million citizens now living in Aeternum. They couldn't see that the future was synthetic and peace would befall mankind in ways they couldn't imagine, making military gains short-lived and in the end fruitless.

-Dad

Chapter 7: Two Crape Myrtles (2058)

1440 Pelican Way

Aedin Beach, Midir, Ups-And-d

∞ #AE-LID: 4d-69-64-69-72

June 15th, 2216 CE

∞ #AE-POSIX: 7777323672

Son,

The year 2058 was one that I will never forget. Luna was just shy of the reach of Aeternum as Ray's spaceport was well under construction. The serious and popular rebellions of the last few years were quieting down as arms and armor gave way to the will of the people. Things were taking a turn for the better in the world of mankind. But 2058 was also memorable for one other reason, it was the year I died a painful, but quick, death. Yeah, that last one was a shock for me, too. I, William Benjamin Babington, had just turned a youthful seventy-nine.

You have heard me talk nostalgically of the past and lament the triumphs of humanity in its new and old forms with a tinge of rose coloration. Nevertheless, this is the part of my story, our story, which I know you want to hear most of all and I will waste little time in getting to the good part. It was a damp and overcast Friday morning at my home in South Carolina. Spring was well under way and most of the trees were green or blooming. My prized crape myrtle tree was full of white flowers, slightly moist from the earlier shower, making the branches hang a little low. New seedlings were springing up everywhere down by the pond; all sorts of refreshed life forms were coming out of their shelter from the rain. Bugs, frogs, and all of the little creatures that take up residence by the pond were starting to stir, attracting the attention of the highly interested fish.

It was a serene setting with little noise or distraction, just another opportunity to spend a day of retirement doing what I did best, nothing of importance. An overcast morning is great for one reason, fishing. I had moseyed my way down to the pond with my fishing rod and a small tackle box as I had countless mornings before in a bid to catch a few bass. I had a small cooler of Yuengling beer to keep me hydrated, because it is a well-known fact that dehydration on the water's edge can be fatal. So picture in your mind a wrinkly version of yours truly in a Hawaiian shirt with beer and rod in hand, the very model of retired bliss. I had no idea that my fishing expedition would give way to a lesson on genetics.

Genetics, genes and DNA make up who we are individually and are the blueprint for how we are constructed. There is no other way to state that we are, our biological bodies, walking ecosystems of living cells working together to make a whole. Every piece of that whole carries the master plan for the entire biological machine, our DNA. It is a grand library of billions of working copies replicated in exacting detail to construct our every muscle fiber, nerve and hair. It shapes our jaw lines, gives us our father's eyes and makes us a bit too susceptible to putting on a few extra pounds eating what we crave. DNA is beautiful, graceful and elegant, passed down for generations for eternity as a fine-crafted document of creation. However, when your blueprints include a coffee-stained, cigarette-burned and smudge-marked Xerox of your father's bum left ventricle, it sucks ass.

You may not know the meaning of that expression, but suffice to say that a heart attack feels like being eaten by a shark while then being smacked with a hammer. The pain only lasts for a few moments but time has a way of stretching out the most mileage possible from a bad situation. It's the kind of pain that you are likely to break your teeth on while clinching them in agony. It drops you to your knees, throws your rod and beer out of your hand and leaves you helpless staring at the cloud-filled sky.

My father had several of these heart attacks in his life, winning the battle with his chest three times, though losing the fourth round while picking tomatoes in his garden. I would like to say that I put up a fight during my heart attack, that I had brushed away the pain in a bid to live another day. To be the man my father was, and not give up the life in me so easy. However, in those terrifying seconds of grabbing my chest as I dropped to the ground by the pond, the only reaction I could manage was to scream into my patch, straight through Val's terrified face, "Ray! Now!" Then there was light.

Death was supposed to be an experience where you float over your dying corpse, observing the last vestiges of the world around you. A bright light and tunnel were supposed to lead you up and away to be judged by your maker and then you enter heaven, or get flushed to hell after a speedy trial. It was supposed to be a time of wonder, fear and happiness surrounded by friends and faith. Maybe my soul experienced this and I'm really in a hot tub in heaven or a miserable sauna in hell. I don't think I will ever know for certain. This version of me, what I feel is the whole me, didn't quite have the same ride that my ancestors did at the end of their lives, since the dawn of time.

Instead of pearly gates or glimpses of my stylish Tommy Bahama-clad corpse, I saw a flash of light, felt the hair on the back of my neck stand up and then the faded image of a garden came into crystal clarity. A quick trip to San Jose it was indeed, I thought to myself. I didn't feel any fear, I didn't have time, just felt the relief from escaping that rhinoceros horn in my chest. Death, one way or another, has a feeling of serenity when you are in pain, I believe.

The garden was small, less than an acre in size and I could see the buildings of a vast and modern city in every direction. Titanium white, silvery aluminum and white frosted glass were the mimicked building materials of this electronic city of wonder. The buildings were all pearl white or beaded silver in appearance, with rounded corners and clean-cut lines that looked almost like finely laid ceramic tile. Windows and walls were an array of hexagon tiles, a few triangles and some squares to break up the design. It was geometry and passion melded together to make an architectural beauty that was nothing short of stunning.

The sky was a clean aqua blue, giving a subtle gradient of hue to the tops of the buildings, reflecting back the blues, whites and silvers in a pearlescent brilliance. The sun was brilliant and white in color, reminding me of the sun at noon in Nassau, while the sky was like the shallow sea on those very same beaches. The first city of Aeternum was modern and futuristic and the buildings were as ivory towers molded for the middle twenty-first century and beyond.

I could hear faint motion and commotion in the city, but in this garden, all of that was mute. The noise was a small nudge for the poor observer toward the notion that there was more than just the garden in front of you; there was life all around you. The garden was well manicured and thick in vegetation of all types, though the motif had a bit of a local South Carolina flare as I could recognize the flowers and plants. Palmetto palms, mimosa trees, flowering bushes and well-manicured landscaping abounded. The paths were marbled and the retaining walls on the flowerbeds were matching in the milky white stone. This wasn't Eden but a personal central park in the midst of a modern Babylon. I was seated on an alabaster bench made for one and looking at a well-groomed crape myrtle tree, my favorite. I felt calm and complete as a person inside, and excitement started to fill the hole in my chest where my busted-up heart had been.

I started to get up but I heard footsteps to my right. A quick glance and I saw Ray, with Val walking beside him. They both looked as they always did, no fancy robes or white satin to mimic angelic or holy connotations. These were my friends and for the first time they were as real as I was, or, I was as artificial as they were; I was too excited to give it much thought. Ray smiled and raised his hand to embrace mine in a cordial handshake, saying, "Welcome to Aeternum." In the back of my mind I was thinking of the old cliché, today really is the first day of the rest of my life.

Looking back, I had a selfish concern for myself. I had been dead for only a few minutes and my mind wasn't at all focused on the emergency happening in the physical world or the effect that finding my body would have on your mother January. Val had the presence of mind to contact an ambulance when my heart first went out of rhythm but no amount of work would save the old me, not after transcending. The medics hadn't even arrived yet; my wife was probably still unaware that I went down like a bag of hammers. There would be a lot of explaining to do, but for the moment, I had nothing but questions and an overwhelming sense of wonder.

Ray and Val both had a lot to say, but patience for an immortal is paramount and they were courteous to hear me first and answer my slew of questions. We spent a few moments talking about the beauty of Aeternum, the garden and the unbelievable clarity of just how genuine my new reality was. I could feel the light from the sun; hear the sparrows chirping in the trees. I felt the cool breeze brush over my arms, just as if I had been standing in the physical world. I knew what to expect from the long talks with Ray, but my few visits to Aeternum as a guest offered nothing this exquisite. My eyes were new and my vision had returned to perfect twenty/twenty in this new body, making the world appear in the highest definition.

Physical humans visiting Aeternum could not take in the full sensory experience, even with all of the neural interconnects of the patch. The physical living people are the ghosts in this world. I was a ghost no longer; I had been born again with a new body, sharp, cut and strong, a twenty-five-year-old version of myself. I felt like I could whip a lion bare handed without losing my breath. That is one of the many gifts of Aeternum, physical being is thrown out the window and you can be whoever you want to be as long as it is a variation carried in your genetic code. I was at a peak physical condition that I never could attain in life.

Ray and Val took turns telling me of the wonders of this place. Some of it was a re-hash of the conversations we had about Aeternum in the years prior, but it didn't matter. I was seeing all of it first hand and the retelling was a welcome refresher for a new resident. Ray explained how the city started as just one small row of buildings and a single park as the first frightened residents made the transition. As the millions flooded in, they added more and more imagination and power to the system, building a world that was vibrant and clean. Aeternum was full of life and the atmosphere was energetic and hopeful. As I had always believed, people are intrinsically good. When the burdens of life are gone, that good comes out in the art, style and air of happiness that made the city what it was, joy in structure.

The three of us began to walk through the wide yet uncongested streets of Aeternum. It was similar to the place I remembered visiting but the colors were no longer dull and grainy. Ray explained to me in detail that the city was the central hub of Aeternum and every additional server farm colony would be a new city or hub that reflected the local physical world. This was Earth's first digital city and it carried many of the properties of its host environment in San Jose, California. The weather, colors and even the air was enhanced further, making its climate perfection. Navigation through the city was as easy as walking down the street. You could take shortcuts using the subway or taking a cab, but we opted for the conversation time allowed by a journey on foot.

The streets offered venues of entertainment and restaurants of every description. It was not surprising, I had visited Aeternum before, but these places had an atmosphere and life to them now that I hadn't noticed in the previous experience. The restaurants at first may not make a lot of sense as having any appeal to a digital human. Though food wasn't required for sustenance, it is an integral part of human social life and is a great pleasure for all of us. Savoring a favorite dish while enjoying the company of loved ones is part of the human condition, and that core tenant was preserved in Aeternum.

It's the same with the entertainment and creative outlets offered all through the city. Artists still paint and show their wares
and people still want to make and watch films. There was no economy in Aeternum per se, as there was no real need for one past the
simple bantering of favors and exchanges based on friendship and
self-fulfillment. Every positive facet of humanity was supported and
encouraged. The waiters and waitresses were obvious AIs but the
artists, musicians, chefs and dancers were all human and had that
spark of creativity in living their dreams doing for others while expressing a sense of self.

I was intrigued by the city's innovative subway system that
could connect you instantly with every building or another future
city. Ray had designed a simple means of sub-dividing Aeternum,
as each building could be a doorway to a new themed community
environment. Some buildings were just what they were at face value, apartments for those who wanted to live that way. The rest of
the buildings opened to themed communities that could comfort
residents from any of a variety of social upbringing.

The subway system acted as a simple means of moving about
in an organized way, much like navigating the folders on a computer system from long ago. The subway cars were small,
accommodating ten people or so in size, and acted much like the
cabs that were on the streets, taking inhabitants where they wanted
to go instead of operating on a schedule. It was mass transit with a
personal touch, all in a well-lit and beautiful environment that was
in stark contrast to even the best earthly subways.

Sure, in electronic form a person could instantly move to any
point in the system. However, the human mind had a difficult time
navigating the world this way. Just materializing in a new place out
of thin air was a difficult concept to grasp for most people. Bringing

in elements of old-world locomotion was a common-sense way to have people move about in a logical and comfortable manner. I thought it had the added benefit of keeping us grounded in our humanity, as it just felt natural.

The majority of the buildings led to the country, the beach, the desert, or any other setting or locale one could imagine. These segments were created where people wanted to share the experience, a community or familiar surroundings together, though you could have a more personal space, called a plat. There were communities that were geographically identical to their real-world counterparts and there were communities that were imaginative constructs of their residents. It would seem that you could have unlimited space in your own little world, but the central hub of the city was the point where reality was consistent in an unreal way.

The way it all worked together made me think of the way the underground city in Montreal felt in winter. The winters in Montreal are very cold and snow-filled, and though the streets are not unwelcoming, you much prefer the warmth of the indoors. This is where Montreal's secret life is, hidden away from plain view below the streets. The buildings in Montreal are common apartments or businesses, but many have an entryway into the unseen underground city.

It is a world much different from that of the surface, going six stories deep and spread out over thirty-six kilometers of twisting tunnels. The underground is reminiscent of a giant mall, filled with shops, restaurants, apartments and parks, all sheltered from the cold. In winter, when the temperature is negative twenty-four outside, a simple trip through double doors brings you into a warm, sheltering and inviting world that is almost magical, in complete contrast to the frost outside.

Aeternum was much like this; each building was functional while also serving as a doorway to a completely new world that could have a warmth all of its own. Outside, walking the streets of Aeternum, some of the buildings would give way to roads or parks leading away from the city center. It was a master plan of imagination that all worked together coherently for the resident of Aeternum and each road, park and doorway led to a place of personal warmth.

During our trek through the city, I noticed other people walking with a copy of Ray, eyes wide with excitement and intrigue at the vast simplicity and familiarity of it all. They too were on their introductory walks, exploring their new environment. We were all citizens of a new human world, among the first billion souls sharing residence in utter peace, free from the burdens of biology. My walk was just long enough for me to get comfortable with the concepts of Aeternum and accustomed to my new body. It took a scant ninety minutes of time to adapt to my environment. We must have covered fifteen blocks of the city but I was nowhere near out of breath or tired, just invigorated and yearning for more of the digital endorphins giving me a high from this journey of discovery.

We rounded a tall glass building, turning a corner on the sidewalk and instead of a continuing cityscape, there was a long and broad garden-space leading out into the hills. It was cut like an infinite hallway amongst the buildings, reminding me of Central Park in New York. At the entrance was a stately wrought-iron gate supported by two pillars made of marbled stone and a single parking space with a familiar sight, my classic red Porsche 356, looking like it had just rolled off the 1955 assembly line. It was beautifully detailed, clean and crisp with a fresh coat of wax on it. Through the gate appeared a smooth and fresh-paved road leading through a rolling forest and winding away through the distant hills. This was my plat and somehow I knew that my home was down the road and that the Porsche had the keys in the ignition, ready to take me there.

Ray excused himself with a smug grin as if he were Santa Claus caught putting a present under the tree. Life here was indeed a gift, his gift, and he took great pleasure in the joy of his people. Val had been with me for years and instinctively jumped in the passenger seat of the 356, the tan top already down and inviting us for a drive, just the way he liked it. As Ray turned to walk away, I slid into the driver's seat and closed the door. I put on my seatbelt, though I didn't need it, and started the ignition to the sweet sound of a well-tuned, air-cooled engine behind my ears. The road ahead was not straight, but full of turns and switchbacks, just the way I liked it. This road would have no officer to ruin my day or potholes to bend a wheel, this was my driveway and it was an orgasm calling as I shifted into first gear and pushed the gas to the floor, biting my lip in excitement. Less than two hours here and I was already feeling rowdy. I guess being young again means being youthful too.

The drive was short at the impressive speed with which we tackled the driveway. I came upon another familiar sight, my house that I had lived in for almost a half century. It was a little different from reality, not as I remembered it but as I had wanted it to be. Instead of neighbors within earshot there was no one for kilometers around, perhaps no one at all in my segment of virtual reality, and that's the way I liked it. The house was pristine in condition and the interior was decorated just as I had left it in the other world. Val commented that it would be just as I had imagined as my memories and imagination built this house. He said that he too had a home back in town and a life all of his own. That sly AI, a piece of him had been running in parallel in Aeternum all of these years and made it his home, too.

A question hit me, if the AIs were also living here as free people, then who were the servers in the cafes and drivers of the taxicabs we passed on our walk to the front gate? Val explained that they were simple projections of the system that had a specific function and no further life beyond. They were dubbed virtual intelligences or VIs by the AIs living there. It would seem another parallel between Aeternum and Earth was playing out as the AIs had AIs of their own.

The AIs in Aeternum were quite different from their apparitions in the physical world from our patches. They were more alive, deeper in personality and more personable altogether. Val explained that the AIs in Aeternum were in essence human because Ray had constructed complex human equivalent mind storage units for each citizen. Each brain was generated using randomized DNA templates and modeled to suit each individual AI personality. It was a startling revelation. Val now had his own complex form of DNA and a computerized brain that was indistinguishable from a human. Software gave way to instinct and memory in the same ways that humans were constructed and functioned in Aeternum.

The AIs we had in some ways enslaved were now our equals and living among us and far outnumbering us in Aeternum. This was not completely secret to the outside world; it just wasn't common knowledge as no one had cared to ask. People just assumed that the AIs they saw in Aeternum during their visits were accompanying living humans, or servants, not free on their own. In a development that was fortunate for all of us, the AIs carried forward their positive attitude and gracious disposition toward mankind. No malice was present and no grudges were held against humanity, though we probably did deserve some emotional blight or angst against us for the way some treated their AIs.

After making a round of the house and the pond that was now a small lake, my thoughts turned back to the matter of my corpse and its aftermath. Val showed me how to connect to the outside world and I placed a call to your mother's patch. Her tear-laden face greeted my apparition and she cracked a broken smile. She was devastated that I had died but relieved that I was still preserved in a new form. The emotions during transcending for the transcended are one thing, but the family living in the real world has a whole host of feelings to deal with that are not easy or simple. As prepared as your mother was for this eventuality and as many times as we spoke about it, the shock of seeing me lifeless was traumatic none-theless.

She told me that Ray had paid her a visit right as the ambu-lance arrived and was there to calm her. He told her that I had a heart attack, but I was safe. I had made the transition to Aeternum in time and that I didn't experience much in the way of pain since I was quick to transcend. She rushed down to see me there, lifeless, clutching my chest with a blank expression on my face. The medics had seen the same look on countless bodies over the years; the stare of eternity, some would call it.

They took my body away and Ray and Marge did their best to soothe her until I could contact her. She told me that the two hours I had been out of touch were the definition of misery, but the hope that I would be back as myself kept her from losing it altogether. Your mother is a strong woman but like all old couples we had grown so dependent on each other, death for one was like death for both. However, things were different with this miracle of technolo-gy. I would be in Aeternum waiting for her to join me while trying to figure out how to keep a marriage strong while separated by the evolution of our species.

The simple fact remained that I would be alone in Aeternum for the time being and it may be years before she joined me. Maybe that was for the best as I could act as her guide to Aeternum and make this new house a ready home for her when she finally arrived. In the meantime, we could visit with each other through her patch. She could visit Aeternum to see me and I could be a ghost in her head until we were together again.

I found myself feeling a little alone because of the distance. I did have Val there and several other people I knew from life. However, my wife and children were all still in the physical world and I was a quasi-bachelor now. There was much here to keep me busy and I would find myself taking up old hobbies like stargazing and fishing. I would also join the throngs of citizens that were watching as the great experiment came to fruition from within the system, man's return to the moon.

Love,

William

Chapter 8: Coelestium
(2061)

1440 Pelican Way
Aedin Beach, Midir, Ups-And-d
∞ #AE-LID: 4d-69-64-69-72

June 15th, 2216 CE
∞ #AE-POSIX: 7777371753

Son,

The moon is a curious phenomenon indeed. It has been the subject of countless tales and songs. Its silvery face has been cast into artwork of every type by every culture on planet Earth. It has inspired man's imagination through the ages and in the twentieth century drove mankind to technological excellence as we set foot on this lifeless alien planet for the first time. Now, almost a century later, we were going back to stay. Humanity would unfurl its dusty wings again. New generations of explorers were ready to take flight and spread our people amongst the endless night sky vistas.

It was May 25th, 2061, the one-hundredth anniversary of American President Kennedy's address to the nation that launched the space race and landed Apollo 11 on the moon. It was a fitting date that Ray chose to perform the ribbon-cutting ceremony on the newly finished Salton Space Port. The event was comical from the perspective of the dignitaries in attendance, as the spaceport was not designed to deliver flesh and blood humans into the cosmos. This was Aeternum's citizen port of call and the gateway for modules of server farm and related technology to journey to the stars. Nevertheless, the general public as well as the people living in Aeternum were interested in what the spaceport had to offer. Most were paying special attention to the big reveal of the spacecraft that Ray had designed to ferry equipment to and from the lunar surface, and eventually the greater solar system.

The facility itself was a modest-sized complex of command and control buildings, communication arrays, hangars and an airfield for landing conventional aircraft that were not vertical take-off like Ray's NMM-equipped vehicles. The spaceport was as much a construction facility as it was a launch pad or base. Many of the technologies produced in the foundry were brought to the spaceport for assembly and pre-flight diagnostics and testing. Completed server farm cubes were delivered from San Jose early on, but were now being produced on site at the new Salton City automated production facility location. A high-speed system of NMM-equipped trucks would ferry the cargo to the port and robotics would perform the heavy lifting and fabrication work.

All of these materials and server farms, as well as communication equipment, power generation and colony support robotics, would be packed into the shuttle fleet Ray had constructed. Over the course of several weeks, all of the equipment would be delivered from the port to the moon colony site and dropped off in the designated location. A diverse team of robotic support equipment would then lay out the facility and interconnect the pieces to form a complete colony ready for habitation.

The future moon base itself would consist of modular units carried to the lunar surface. When complete they formed neat rows, building what looked like a small-scale city of white-shield-coated technology. The server farm cubes would be small, only 4 meters cubed, holding 64 cubic meters of linked minds. The small size of an Aeternum citizen's brain module allowed immense population density in a farm cube frame. Three billion minds could live within the confines of a single farm cube along with the supporting processors and infrastructure packed inside to make a cohesive unit. Ten farm cubes would initially make their way to the moon to allow humanity room to grow and to serve as an active redundant backup system for the minds living on earth.

The backup system was the primary reason for the colony in the first place. This would act as a sanctuary separate from the volatile and active planet that is Earth. It made sense when you consider that the geological events of even a millennial timeline carry massive potential for destruction. It was to be constructed as a means to safeguard Aeternum's residents from many of the disasters that could befall Earth, carrying synchronized backup copies of every person in Aeternum that could be activated in case of the unthinkable. As indestructible as the Aeternum farm cubes were, if the infrastructure were buried by an earthquake, sunk into the sea or struck by an asteroid the consequences would be dire. The colony made us, the human beings inside, safe through technical redundancy, which would become a major catalyst for future expansion and exploration.

The lunar colony would also offer a new city and new opportunities for the people of Aeternum. Just like in the physical world, a person would be able to move to and from the Earth farm in San Jose to the new colony with ease. The new moon colony's virtualized city would reflect the thematic atmosphere and environmental uniqueness of the barren lunar surface. Though the moon is almost a vacuum and is a low gravity desert, its surface offers much to stimulate the imagination, just as it has for thousands of years. The views of the Earth from the moon are spectacular and the cold and loneliness of the silvery and somber environment would offer comfort and solace to a certain subset of Aeternum's population.

Most of us felt that this step would make the future we had dreamed about as children a reality. It was space travel, even though it was just across the cosmic street, and that meant real progress in the minds of my generation. We were proud of the accomplishment that was upon us and watched its development with great pride and encouragement.

Ray chose the Copernicus crater as the site for the new colony. He felt it was fitting for a number of reasons, both sentimental and technical. Nicolaus Copernicus had a place of honor in the scientific annals of history. He introduced the concept that the Earth was not the center of the universe and that a much larger and grandiose cosmos existed. This bright spot in human understanding changed the very foundation of our view of existence in much the same way as Ray had done a decade before.

The Copernicus crater itself is a bright spot on the near side of the moon, visible in the darkened landscape of the waterless Maria seas of the moon. It appears as a bright white island, reflecting sunlight at the Earth and is discernible with the naked eye on a clear night. This bright and shining new land would take on its namesake, the human Colony of Copernicus.

All of these happenings were to come in short order as the launch was only days away. Ray first had to unveil the fleet of shuttles that would usher in the era of exploration and colonization in the solar system. The speculation on the design of the ships was a topic of much fanfare in the months leading up to the big reveal. Several leaked photos and supposed mock-ups had made their rounds in the media and network. Fanciful designs that would make Picasso or Picard jealous were proposed as well as simple designs that were eerie in their similarity to science fiction of decades past.

That bright and sunny morning Ray stood at the familiar podium with a look of excitement and air of childlike giddy on his unaging and worldly face. He cut the ribbon on the hangar bay door, proclaimed that we as humanity had earned our place among the stars, and we were ready to begin the next phase of our genesis as an intelligent and worthy people. The thick red ribbon fluttered to the ground in front of the ten-meter tall glossy white door of the hangar.

The single door developed a crease down the middle that turned into a slit of an opening. The door was of course made of the shield material and the slit was the work of billions of nano-robots deconstructing a thin segment in the door and its frame to allow it to open. When sealed it would be impenetrable and only nanotechnology could modify the material at the atomic level to unzip it to make an entrance.

I stood in front of the podium and hangar door among a crowd of virtual citizens watching the event unfold as if we were there in person. The first shadow broke and sunlight peered through the seam in the door as we could see the white pearl glow of an object clad in shield material before us. I couldn't hide the smile on my face; this was the moment I had waited over eighty years to see. It was a real space ship that could take us to our destiny.

As the doors slid open, we could make out the outline of a long triangular and hexagonal series of shapes that were straight on the edges and sweeping in design. The subtle lines of the craft were sharp and sleek geometric straight angles. At first I thought I was looking at a scaled-up, white version of a Nighthawk stealth fighter plane that had captured my imagination as a boy during the now ancient Gulf War. However, this was different in several ways as there were no wings or tail fins and the design was much more oriented for carrying cargo instead of smart bombs. Although large, its style was aggressive and aerodynamic in form as a lifting body. Even though it was weightless, it still had to cut through the air. It looked as if it could slit glass with the greatest of ease but haul a rail car in its cargo bay. We were in awe of its grand and elegant appearance floating weightlessly in the hangar bay. We were introduced to this object of passion's fitting name, the Coelestium Shuttle. Heavenly it was, and seven sister ships remained tucked away in those hangar bays ready for use.

I had a brief moment of emotional loss of control and had to catch myself to prevent a tear or two from slipping out. My chest was warm and I was flush with a feeling of pride and patriotism for my new nation. Most of all, I was struck by just how profound seeing this spacecraft was to me on such a deep personal level. Space travel was the unicorn I would always dream of but never live to see. Civilian spacecraft and excursions were always on the horizon but never within my grasp. I yearned to be an explorer but there was nothing left to explore on the Earth and space was beyond my reach in my biological life. However, here it was, beautiful and sturdy, a physical reality I never thought would come. I could ride on this space ship and fulfill the spot in my heart that had long been vacant. In due time and once my wife could join me, I would take part in this grand adventure that was my destiny. It was a conviction that I had to follow and nothing stood in my way.

As Ray was wrapping up his presentation of the Coelestium Shuttle series' impressive technologies and performance, I heard a fellow spectator mutter under his breath, "Why does everything have to be white?" It seemed so obvious to me but I guess for the average layman it would appear that Ray had little sense of aesthetic style or flare for color. The majority of the new technology, servers, spacecraft and the like were all clad in the shield material and it was by default white in color. Paint would not stick to it so you just had to go with the default coloration of brilliant pearly white. Just like leaves work best when green and blood is red because of its composition, the white of the shield material was that color because it had to be to function and Ray did the best with what he had. I don't know why, but that guy's comment has always stayed with me.

With the completion of the ceremony, Ray took a few days afterward to answer questions from the media and the people at home about the moon-shot and how the colony would get started. He added that the transportation of server modules to the colony would begin in two weeks after completing the first step of building a high-speed orbital communication system. Ray needed to add several small satellites in orbit of the earth and the moon to facilitate extremely high bandwidth data transmission. It would be akin to building a bridge where the volumes of people traffic between Aeternum and the Copernicus colony could flow instantly. Without much fanfare, the effort got underway and the shuttles started carrying the satellites to their proper locations.

In the days leading up to the first colony cargo launch, I spent my time at home in Aeternum watching the media reports and thinking of what life on the moon might be like. Ray stopped by, as he often did, and I decided to express my desire to be among the first visitors to the moon and share how excited I was to see the future arrive. He understood and said, with the high-bandwidth network he was installing, anyone in Aeternum could come and go to Copernicus whenever they wanted via the subway system that would now serve as a skyway to the new colony. Having breakfast on earth and lunch on the moon was certainly the stuff of fiction past, but a reality for the electronic jetsetter that I could now be. Without thinking, I blurted out, "What about dinner on Mars?" Ray's sheepish grin reappeared and with a quick nod of his head, he said, "Soon, my friend."

Why not go to Mars? I didn't want to get ahead of myself but if the experimental moon colony went as planned, the rest of the solar system was within reach. One of the Coelestium shuttles could reach Mars in under a week at a modest speed when launched at the right time and right apogee. I didn't want to sound ungrateful at the miracle of the moon base but I was desperate to see the solar system in person and as a people, we now had the means to explore it all. I was impatient for some reason but I knew that in due time the universe would open up for me, for mankind. As an immortal I had nothing but time to burn so instead of becoming restless, I set out to improve my understanding of space flight and the technology behind it. Education was readily available in Aeternum, but I wanted to become a student of the stars, and the solar system would function as my elementary school.

The first colonization missions commenced in mid June. The trip to the moon was quick for the shuttle fleet with an average of a three-day turnaround time to deliver cargo, unload and return to the Earth. Each shuttle would bring a server module or reactor to the surface and deliver it in the Copernicus crater where a small army of machines worked at a feverish pace to construct the infrastructure and place all of the modules in their correct spots. The whole process should have been tedious to watch unfold but the excitement of the moment made the activation of each module feel like a victory for the human race. I even brought out my old telescope and tried in vain to see the construction take place on the real-time simulated moon outside my Aeternum home. The bridge was about to open and the next chapter in humanity's tale waited on the other side.

The Copernicus Colony opened its doors to all in 2061, on July fifteenth. I had a space on the first of the skyway cars to make the journey to the colony, and I was curious what would happen when I made the transition to another physical farm. It was my first time moving outside of Aeternum. You would think travel for an electronic being would be effortless and in some regards it was, but there was quite a bit going on in the background to make my little stroll to the colony happen.

The operating-model of having individual minds that are unique to our being made the movement of self paramount in this new world and that meant a physical presence accompanied your consciousness wherever you went. Sure, your physical mind was tiny and easily transported to other locations, but Aeternum had a far simpler approach than the real-world travel that is in use to this day.

Your active mind is a unique and contained unit, but a duplicate copy was stored as a backup in another farm cube to prevent loss by a disaster or failure. The copy was an exact replica of your mind, reconciled daily with the memories of your active consciousness and experiences. You could never have more than one active copy of yourself living life at any one time, it was strictly forbidden. The system was designed to manage the distribution and synchronization of electronic brains in order to maximize the chances that you would stay alive indefinably as you were.

In the same vein, your digital consciousness could travel to another farm through a simple technical sleight of hand. The communication array would signal the farm to stop your mind's activity as it took a scan of its current state. The massive amount of information that was your entire living being would then be placed in a data-packet for transmission to a destination farm. The packet would travel in one high-fidelity burst through the relay system and land at the foreign communication array at the new farm. A fabricated brain would be milled in a few seconds and your consciousness would be transferred and re-activated. A confirmation signal would then go back to the source that you were alive and well and your old physical brains would be broken down and recycled or housed as a backup copy, if the system saw a need for the retention. The entire system had numerous checks and balances to assure perfect synchronization and the inactive copy at the source would remain intact in the event of a transmission failure.

As complicated as this sounds, the process to travel to the moon took about thirty seconds. Other celestial bodies would of course take longer in the future but the trip to Copernicus was almost instantaneous and the virtual skyway car perpetuated the illusion that it was a seamless journey. I was ready to go, eager and anxious as I awaited my vacation that was fast approaching the next day.

-Will

Chapter 9: High Gravity
(2061)

1440 Pelican Way
Aedin Beach, Midir, Ups-And-d
∞ #AE-LID: 4d-69-64-69-72

June 21st, 2216 CE
∞ #AE-POSIX: 7777850725

Benjamin,

I didn't have to pack for the trip; everything I needed would be in Copernicus already. Instead, I just did what I normally do, drag myself out of bed and into the shower to wake up. It doesn't matter what anyone says, a good shower in the morning is the best way to start your day off right. I put on some comfortable khaki pants and a flowing blue silk button-up shirt. I was the iconic image of a man-of-leisure on vacation. I was almost too excited to eat but managed to get down a bowl of cold cereal. No matter how ethereal life could be here, I just couldn't break from a lifetime of routine in the mornings. The only thing missing was a kiss from my wife, but I couldn't bring myself to wake her from her cozy bed back in the physical world since we had been up all night talking about today's upcoming events.

Driving to the city hub was always a pleasure and I was looking forward to putting the top down on the car and making my way to the subway station. Standing in the driveway, before I could get the door open on the 356, I heard the low growl of an engine and squealing tires off in the distance. I only had a few friends here in Aeternum but I wasn't sure who it could be as most of them were not car guys like me. I crossed my arms and leaned back on the fender of my Porsche in amused anticipation of finding out just who was trying to break my driveway speed record. Through the tree line, I could make out the shadowy silhouette of a jet-black roadster, raked back at speed as it was tearing up hell. As it came closer, I could see it was a classic 1961 Ferrari 250 GT with a familiar face at the wheel. Hmm, I thought to myself, Val might have just gained the lead over me on who has the coolest car.

Pulling up with a quick squeak of the tires, my friend was giddy with pride, parking sideways in the driveway. "Hop in!" Val shouted over the roar of the engine and the smell of melted rubber. All I could do was laugh and gesture a thumbs-up in congratulations to his good taste. "Give me a ride to the moon!" I quipped, as I got in the car and slid on my seatbelt. Then off we went like a rocket, acting like two teenage boys who boosted an unwitting father's hot-rod.

It was a great start to a great personal adventure over eighty years in the making. I had considered asking Val if he wanted to go with me on my first trip to the moon but I thought that it was probably best if I kept to myself on my first trip. I didn't know how seeing the moon would affect me and I didn't want the distraction of sharing the experience. Now I was glad he showed up at the last minute and invited himself along. It is funny how things like that can work out and how having a friend along adds a level of comfort to a situation fraught with nervous anticipation. We arrived at the platform that is usually un-crowded, but today was special and there were already hundreds of people there waiting in line.

The subway and skyway cars were Aeternum representations of available communication bandwidth. When there are many people moving to and from a location the bandwidth can become congested and some queuing, the technical term for waiting in line, can occur. That was fine by me; a thirty-minute wait was no big deal after this long.

Val and I spoke about what it would be like on the surface, talking about the dome and wondering how the architecture would look and feel. Ray had shown the public images of the lunar colony but saved the big reveal for our first arrival to keep from spoiling the surprise. Ray had let a lucky few restaurant and entertainment volunteers gain early access to the moon, days before, to give the grand opening of Copernicus some life and local flavor right off the bat. We knew that gravity would be considerably less and the sky would be black, but in reality we had no idea what we were getting into. As the doors to the skyway car opened up, Val and I with a dozen others boarded and sat down for the journey as we lifted vertically into the sky with little feeling of momentum but at obvious great speed.

The trip was quick, with a brief flash of blinding white light as we crossed the edge of the virtual atmosphere above Aeternum. That was the mind transfer program doing its job and it was painless, though in turn disorienting. At the transfer point, we had changed orientation and were now descending feet first into the Copernicus Colony at the edge of an enormous dome. In the physical world, we would have been nothing more than bursts of invisible waves fired like bullets at a communications array on the surface of the crater and its small rows of farm cubes. Nevertheless, here in the virtual world, we were descending in a small space elevator into a glorious glass-domed city full of buildings and life that took up the entire crater surface.

The view of the city as we landed was spectacular. A clear glass dome with lightweight and near transparent latticework went as far as the eye could see. The buildings were monoliths of moonlight blue obsidian sporting reflective golden accents and edging, breaking the outlines of the walls and windows. These were stark indigo formations with glossy surfaces, skyscrapers reflecting ghost-like shapes against the black of space. Every hue and shade of blue painted a mock façade, reflecting an invisible sky and the brilliant yellow-gold rays of the sun. The gray-whites of the lunar surface and concrete streets of the city added contrast to it all. This grandeur was set against the blue world we had just left, creating an inviting yet alien city that was built of moonbeam dreams.

The entrance to the city was a structure of enormous proportions, much like a major airport opening up to the bevy of bustling mass transit options in front. Beyond that was a large archway that mimicked the curvature and coloration of the earth that led to the main fairway of the colony city. The plants were all succulent varieties, variations of aloes, century plants and broad cacti. This was of course a desert and the environment reflected it.

The first step off the skyway car revealed the lowered gravity and you immediately felt your stomach rise as if you had just crested the top of a rollercoaster, but there was no end to the drop to bring you back to balance. It was surreal and I was awestruck by the beauty that surrounded me. Val was speechless and we both stood with eyes wide trying to take it in. We were not alone, it seems this was the ritual of the first-time visitor and we were no different.

We spent the morning walking the streets and gawking more than was safe for the foot traffic around us. There were so many more stars in the sky here, billions and billions of fires, light-years away. Earth was well defined and so much smaller than I had imagined it would be. I could see the bright blue of the sea and the white clouds in a motionless swirl. That was home, where it all started and what we had to leave to grow and survive in this vast, ever-changing universe.

The buildings were beautiful, though we didn't explore the new gateways or options for homes on the moon just yet, not this trip. For me, this was a quick visit to scout it out, explore and take in everything I could. I had the option of having my home transferred here with my familiar garden road ending in Copernicus. However, I wasn't quite ready to make a change like that without letting the wife experience life in the Earth Aeternum first. My desire to explore would always be tempered by the need for family and the bonds of love. The city was vast, as large as Aeternum on Earth. The locals who had only been here for a few days at most were already referring to the new city and colony by name and Aeternum became synonymous with the Earth farm environment. This trend would continue as mankind spread out among the stars.

Val and I noticed several ghosts walking through the city. They were men, women and children, starry-eyed visitors from Earth using their patches to take in the spectacle of it all. The full moon was said to have an effect on human psychology, as we knew. The view of Earth from its surface and thoughts of humanity sowing its seeds were enough to inspire many people to transcend earlier in life instead of waiting for the end to make the jump. Copernicus was designed for growth for millions of people; it was a place that many wanted to call home. The population saw a surge in fresh human faces adding new stories to our shared tapestry of life immortal.

Walking along the city streets, we passed one of the numerous small parks that dotted the landscape of the city. This one impressed me as peculiar as it had a gushing column of water jetting about four meters in the air with the water cascading down into a large violet basin. Water on the moon, I thought, the concept didn't fit right away, so it seemed strange to me and out of place for a moment. Val tapped my shoulder and asked me if I was up for a beer at an interesting little pub across the walkway, the Cosmo Lounge. I took one final glance at the fountain and turned to leave with Val.

The pub was an interesting mix of old and new. There were black granite countertops and the seats were cherry and mahogany. The lights in the bar were blue-and-violet stained glass, Tiffany style and chic. The music was older than I was, big band and crooner lounge music to add atmosphere. Although it wasn't playing, I heard Sinatra singing Fly Me to the Moon in the back of my mind. It had a moody atmosphere that reminded me of a cruise ship lounge, but was more relaxed and modern.

I made a mental note that I would have to come back here on my next trip. It was the perfect location to get away from the incredible large domed world outside. The pub offered a brief respite to collect my thoughts and muse about what I should do next while sipping a fitting and tasty Blue Moon Ale. My penchant for being a sentimental dipshit was quite high at this point.

Val ordered up a porter for himself. For some reason this cheery AI liked beer dredged from the depths of the barrel. It was his thing and we sat together as old friends in young bodies enjoying the sights and sounds of the bar and the view of the fountain and people outside. We began to speak about the world outside and how the Earth was changing with fewer people living there. The subject was starting to get a little deep when the doors opened to the pub and Ray's familiar face entered.

Instead of the usual greeting and handshake, he came up and put his hand on my shoulder. "I hate to break up a good time, but I thought you should know right away that January has just made the transition to Aeternum. She is now at the garden waiting for you." My stomach dropped again. I was happy that she had come to join me, but I was worried that she had suffered pain and thoughts of our adult children and their possible anguish went through my mind. Val and I were quick to rise up and started walking with Ray to the street and a waiting taxi, asking questions in a rushed and nervous tempo. "What happened?" was the first thing out of my mouth.

Ray explained that she had a stroke in her sleep and her body died quite peacefully. She had set her patch to an automatic transcendence in case of a medical emergency as most people were now doing. I felt guilty, responsible; did my late-night conversation about my trip upset her, causing her death? I was confused and concerned but relieved that she survived the stroke. "Has anyone told the kids?" "Did Marge call a paramedic as Val did for me?" The answer was no and yes. There was little need for the paramedics and I was glad that your mother and I would get to break the news to the kids together. Maybe we could spin it into something positive. The thoughts that race through your mind in an emergency are a mix of shocked concern, easy to forget details and genuine irrelevance.

We made our way from the city to the skyway in a matter of minutes, but it felt like an hour. I was too late to be there to greet her in person when she transitioned, but I was damn sure going to meet her at the park as soon as I could. The trip down to Aeternum took much less time than our venture up, there was little traffic going back the other way, but Ray would have made way for me as a priority if there had been. My heart was heavy and when I felt Earth's gravity again, I felt like I had ten kilos of coal in my stomach. The park was just down the way from the station and my love was going to be here with me, at last.

Love,

William

Chapter 10: Blue Spruce
(2061)

1440 Pelican Way

Aedin Beach, Midir, Ups-And-d

∞ #AE-LID: 4d-69-64-69-72

June 21st, 2216 CE

∞ #AE-POSIX: 7777884772

Benjamin,

After a few years of being an absentee husband, I was going to reunite with my bride! As you know, your mother had a rough start in life. January had an unfair share of tragedy in her youth. When I met her in her late twenties, she had all but given up on happiness. For her, living was a numbing daily battle with more losses than wins. I too had my share of loss; my heart was the size of a grain of sand and I felt adrift at sea. Every time I had shared my life with someone, that person walked away with ever more precious pieces of that heart until I was left with what felt like none at all.

I was a reluctant suitor, but something about January captivated me. Our shared plight, hardship and combustible chemistry caused my sand-sized heart to grow into a castle with her as its queen. It was a short courtship, just three months from 'hello' to 'I do.' We spent our thirties locked in the heat of passion, absorbing each other's every emotion and inflection. We would quarrel and threaten to walk away but never could. We often told each other we didn't need each other, but the reality was that we did and always would. I don't think anyone else could have put up with either of us, so staying true and committed was the safest avenue for both of us.

In our forties, we suffered the same empty nest syndrome and midlife doubts as everyone else. However, we stuck together and grew much closer than we thought possible. We expanded on our pent-up desires for adventure by touring the world together. We also spent more time together, locked in each other's arms, working to keep that little fire of a long-term relationship burning. A decade earlier, the days would have swung between some as an inferno and others an ember, but we now had a nice light at a steady burn. It was a relationship built on respect, need, and the persistent feelings of desire. We were romantics and knew how to feed each other the love required when spending so long together.

Fifty, sixty, seventy, we would find new ways to keep the tinderbox warm. We enjoyed grandchildren and great-grandchildren, loving every toddler visit and cherishing every time we had to send the rotten brats home. By seventy we would marvel at the wrinkled figures in the mirror and often threatened to flip the light switch on when we were making love. Growing old together had to be fun as you lose so much in your life that humor is the only remedy that sees you through the day. A smile is the best way to brush off arthritis or help your wife into the bath since she lacks the strength to do it herself.

We still spent every day together even though I had been away in Aeternum for the past three years. We would visit each other either through her patch or as a ghost in my version of the house. I missed her physical touch and I was more excited about seeing her than I was the moon. Maybe it would be a good day after all, the day my wife died and came home to me.

The cab pulled up to the curb of the garden where she had arrived, I hurried out but Ray and Val stayed behind to give me privacy in the tender moments to come. Another Ray and Marge were kind enough to keep her company for the twenty minutes it had taken me to make my way back to Earth. My gravity shock had worn off and I was now lighter than air as I rounded the garden path. I could see the top of a blue spruce tree, her favorite; I knew I had come to the right place.

Passing the tree, I saw Ray and Marge standing there but my wife was nowhere in view. Instead a svelte and fair blonde no older than twenty-two was there standing at the alabaster bench with her back turned to me.

"Where is my wife, where is January?" I asked Ray, cutting off Marge and the pretty petite Tinkerbelle of a girl as they were laughing.

"I'm right here, jackass!" her sultry and unmistakable voice said, delivered by pouty lips smirking with amusement. The obvious hit me square in the face as she turned and those beautiful eyes I fell in love with so long ago were looking back at me.

"Hi sweetheart," I smiled, "I'm just joking around, Jan; it's so wonderful to have you here with me, my love!" With that, we embraced with our typical warm hug and a passionate kiss, a real kiss that was three years in the making.

In the back of my mind, I felt a slight tinge of guilt as if I was cheating on my wife. I was still a little embarrassed and trying to recover from the shock of being married to a woman that was sixty years younger than I was; she was much prettier than the photos of her at twenty I remembered. I had just spoken with her a few hours before and she was quite a bit different looking from that last conversation.

It dawned on me with some relief; I had been a muscular twenty-five for a few years now and we would be the ultimate odd-couple if she were still in her eighties. That was the magic of Aeternum, remolding our bodies to peak condition and sexy proportions. Every tooth was straight, every hair was the right color and scars didn't exist in this world. We were all as perfect as we were capable of being, only bound in features by our genetic code.

The cute couple we were in early life and the endearing old cuddlers that still walked hand-in-hand were now the pinnacle of a sexy toned physique that was the fodder of teen television. Every soul in Aeternum was a phoenix of the best pieces of their former selves. There was choice; certainly, you could look as you did in your former life.

I don't think I've seen more than a dozen people in my long life that would choose to reflect something other than a revised form for any lengthy period of time. Sure, some would permanently reflect their true being as the opposite sex or do something as trivial as change their hair color for a party. Then there were those who would change their form to add interest or perversion to a tryst or just for humor's sake. There were few limits, but here, now, I was with my wife and she was perfect, just as she had been only a few hours ago.

The moment was a mixture of joy, fading confusion and a little rekindled lust. I grasped her hand like I always did and she grinned as she looked up and around the garden, at the buildings in the background and then back at me and asked, "So this is home now, huh?" I nodded yes and asked her how her trip was, if it was peaceful and if she had any pain. She was fine, of course, but I had to ask, it was the worrywart husband in me coming out. Ray and Marge didn't interrupt, they were ever patient, and the scene was just like my arrival to Ray and Val.

Ray and Marge offered to walk us to the gateway of our home, but I wanted to have some alone time with her. I wanted to give her the tour and watch the expressions on her face as she took in both the minute oddities and grand absurdities that make life in Aeternum so interesting. We began walking; the streets of Aeternum were crowded now compared to my first tour those few years ago. There were cafes and shops, art galleries and street vendors all about. She gripped my arm and pulled me back as we were strolling down the sidewalk.

She had a perplexed look on her face, blushing and staring at a tall fellow wearing jeans and a knit shirt across the street.

"People go naked here and it's OK?"

I looked at her and then back at the man.

"Oh, that! You just need to enable modesty in your console. It would have been explained by Ray if he was giving you the tour, it's my fault." She looked at me a little puzzled, but I went on to explain that people were free to do whatever they wanted in Aeternum as long as it didn't harm others. If you chose, you could walk naked about the town, but anyone could choose to see others in public places as clothed, in modesty mode.

We have the ability to tweak how we experience our world and how others see us. I decided now was a good opportunity to stop for a moment and explain the console to her in detail. We stepped into a coffee shop and bakery and ordered a dozen chocolate chip cookies, a coffee for me and a glass of milk for her. We took refuge in a corner booth and I told her to use her inner monologue to think the word console, just like when operating her patch. In front of her, the context menu appeared with its myriad options to adjust everything about her world before her eyes.

I told her to notice that the home environment menu was grayed out and not accessible. Those options and features would be available to her when she was in our shared property, or if she opened a little shop of her own. The interface was intuitive and similar to what she had been operating in the physical world for many years.

My pixie cut blonde's hair went red and curly, then brown and straight with bangs, then back to blonde. A barely audible girly giggle accompanied each change. She was having fun with the options and I had a feeling that I was in for a different look every day for the rest of my life. Her outfit changed several times and she stopped the process when deciding on a light and airy sundress with a floral print. Every look and style, new and old was there for her to choose. Aspiring designers and old hats were releasing new fashions every week. My closet just got a lot smaller.

She brought up the point I had made about being allowed to do anything you wanted as long as you didn't harm anyone. She wanted to know what that meant in a world with no limit to personal freedom. It was a valid question and one that would cause some debate among the residents. Ray had devised a system of conflict avoidance inside Aeternum. People were free to do most anything, but aggressive action against someone was pointless. Sure, you could pick up a chair or a knife and try to murder someone on the spot, but the system detected anger and aggression. That's when the safeguards would kick in. The weapon or fist would just pass through the intended victim.

Murdering an immortal virtual citizen was an impossible feat and the best you could hope to accomplish was to hurt someone's feelings or just plain piss them off, if you were so inclined. Even then, it was only a temporary setback for the annoyed. You could ignore anyone you chose by having their form fade to near invisibility and make them inaudible as well in your field of view. The overall effect was a society with little in the way of frayed nerves and no crime of mention.

Ray was always willing and able to mediate disagreements. Even with all the stress-free measures of an unlimited and free economy, perfect health and no crime, people still had problems. It's part of the human condition to hurt inside and feel anger, even in paradise.

Ray made available AI counselors and psychiatrists to help people cope with their issues. Sometimes it was triggered by the loss of a loved one or a tragedy in the physical world. Some had problems with immortality itself. Someone was always there to turn to when you were blue. Suicide was not an option in Aeternum, but inactive storage was. Ray made available space to deactivate yourself if you desired in one-year increments. Few chose this option but it was there and did happen to people that couldn't cope or adjust.

She was familiar with much of the theory and high concepts of the management of a society like ours with the priority of preservation of humanity as well as the lofty goals of Aeternum. She told me that hearing it all from me, inside the environment, made it all real to her in a way that hit home. She said I had a knack for explaining things to her, but I knew she was a smart lady and she just wanted the pleasure of a conversation, no matter how dry or re-hashed the subject was.

By our third platter of cookies, I felt I had given her a good run-down of how Aeternum worked, its transportation systems, private plats and even my morning trip to the moon. I could tell she was getting a bit antsy to see her house and spend an evening to-gether at home. We hadn't really had the pleasure of experiencing that companionship in so long and it was overdue. We paid our compliments to the baker and made our way to the subway for a quick ride to my parking spot.

I was about to panic when we started to get close, I had ridden with Val to the station from the driveway! However, my friend was courteous enough to move my 356 to the end of the driveway for me. It was a gesture that represented a hallmark of his genuine friendship. We made our way down the driveway at a slower pace; she hated it when I sped. Pulling up before the house, she got out of the car without the need for my arm for balance. She took in a deep breath and commented on the smell of jasmine in the air. The sun made her glow and sparkle, as I hadn't seen her before. I could tell that she was happy and in love and the only thought on her mind was the time we would have together. I too was thinking about our time together but in my own way. I was a young man, after all, and the most beautiful woman in Aeternum was wearing my ring. That night, we made love with the lights on.

-William

Chapter 11: Renaissance
(2061-2075)

1440 Pelican Way

Aedin Beach, Midir, Ups-And-d

∞ #AE-LID: 4d-69-64-69-72

June 22nd, 2216 CE

∞ #AE-POSIX: 7777927273

Benjamin,

The Earth was changing in radical ways as the 2060s progressed. Much like the 1960s, a peace-filled cultural shift was in the air, led by the youth of all nations. An advancing technology and vanishing populations led to a turbulent chapter in humanity's history. This was not a revolution against the power-drunk or some distant war, but a movement to at long last solve the social issues that had plagued human society since its beginnings.

The young and old had been visiting Aeternum for years, witnessing the stark contrasts between the problematic sufferings in the old world establishment and the carefree lifestyle of the synthetic way of existence. People were desperate to see the physical world mirror the ease of life in Aeternum. Aeternum became a dividing line between the haves inside and the have-nots in the physical world.

The old world economy and material logistics were built on the fundamentals of resource acquisition and sharing based on a value-trading system of currency. Everything from food and water to building materials and technology were in limited supply. There just wasn't ever enough to go around. People were divided into social classes, based on their income and purchasing ability. These classes would comprise an array of people. The wealthy elite would have resources often thousands of times greater than the middle-class. The utter poor would in turn have a fraction of the resources of that same middle-class. People filled economic segments at all gradients in-between. There were an unlimited number of circumstances behind each individual's placement in the class system, based on a number of factors from geography to birth and education level. Although some mobility existed between the classes, people tended to remain in their socio-economic group for the duration of their lives.

Governing systems of communism, socialism, capitalism and monarchies all tried to divide these resources as best they could for the benefits of their people, but none provided an amicable and fair solution. People would demonize these systems because of their inability to meet the needs of every citizen, with a bell-curve of hyper-prosperity on one end and abject poverty at the other. No matter what promises a system may have held out, every attempt at economic organization failed in some way. The ideals were always limited by the scant resources of the physical world and confounded by corruption and greed.

Aeternum had no such limitation or system of trade as everything was free within the system. Yes, electricity powered it all, but that was generated through efficient reactors and the materials to build the farm cubes were constructed from some of the most abundant elements in the universe. Ray had to contend with these limitations early on to acquire what he needed. However, once he expanded into space, the materials were commonplace and there was no need for a monetary economy that inhibits growth. In essence, Ray and Aeternum were self-sufficient and no longer depended on the world of man to sustain the physical farms or even to expand.

Inside the system, the totality of the world was virtual or ethereal. Everything that existed was built from pure and free energy that could be molded into anything the residents desired. They called it a post scarcity economy, or one with unlimited resources.

There was no need to labor for your dinner or barter for your clothes in Aeternum. With the inherent advantages present in this environment, no physical world economy could match it. Nevertheless, there was room for change in the way the physical world conducted itself. Humanity needed to mature. That maturity would lead to incredible economic prosperity for the humans sharing the Earth.

For well over a decade now people were making the transcending journey to Aeternum. The slow trickles of the early 2050s gave way by 2065 to a veritable flood. In 2050, there were almost eleven billion people on earth. The population had dropped to just under eight billion a decade and a half later as humans were migrating to the system in mass with millions more every day. Aeternum and Copernicus were expanding at a rapid pace. A soon-to-be-constructed Mars colony would enable even more growth potential.

The populations of Earth were younger and more affluent as the elderly, sick and poor made their way to Aeternum ahead of those in the prime of their lives. People were making plans to leave their physical bodies at an astonishing rate, creating a whole industry devoted to taking care of personal affairs and sanitary body disposal. The mass emigration of these groups had a positive effect for the governments of the world. Many of the people on public assistance programs, medical care plans and state-funded retirement options were the main segments of the population that sought refuge through an exodus to Aeternum. The same with those living on charity, as the numbers of people needing help were miniscule from what once was. It seems that if you were in a position of need or suffering, Aeternum filled that need and ended the suffering in an instant, making the choice to go easy to justify.

This lowered the burden on the governments of Earth and most countries had massive budget surpluses for the first time in decades. The bulk of the people that were not transcending were the ones paying taxes, buying and selling, those having children and those absorbed in the day-to-day transactions of the world. The middle and upper classes were no longer supporting the elements of society in need and their governments did not know where to reinvest the funds once intended for entitlement and fulfillment. All of these factors led to a society that was primed for re-invention as it shrunk.

The one major social issue facing the world was the abundance of children left orphaned by a mix of transcending parents and the typical circumstances that leave kids to fend for themselves. However, the subsistence systems that were now devoid of people to support was more than prepared for the modest increase in the number of homeless children. What kind of society would those children create? It was one of the numbers of questions facing a new generation of humans living on Earth and hungry for reinvention.

Of course, a child could have a life inside Aeternum and grow up in a normal fashion if loved ones were present to care for the child. But parents would often be faced with tough decisions of remaining on Earth or transcending to be with a transcended child. Broken families, though no longer suffering the grief of the death of a child, would still find themselves in a predicament. Parents who still had other children to care for in the physical world would opt to have their child rapidly matured to adulthood. Ascending to Aeternum sometimes became a messy parental quagmire when a child transcended when unexpected, but that is another discussion altogether.

The child-filled Earth was a strange mirror compared to an Aeternum that was childless. The main point of entry for children to Aeternum was due to an ill-timed death and there was no current means of conceiving or birthing children in the system due to technological complexity. Biology was the key to reproduction, and no method had been devised inside Aeternum for procreation. The physical world was the key for humanity to continue creating new human life.

This fact was no small issue. It was a rallying cry against transcending taken up by various factions on Earth and was a point of sorrow for barren citizens living for an eternity in Aeternum. Something would have to change, the ability to have a family inside the system would be essential for the continuation of the human spirit. However, at this time, it was just not quite feasible. Self-perpetuation and sex for procreation would remain a biological human game.

Many of the technological advances that Ray had developed were seeing their way into mainstream technology in a big way. The cost for energy and transportation had dropped to a quarter of what it was two decades earlier. Personal and mass transit systems were advancing using the NMM material as a foundation. Fuel usage was also diminished from extreme efficiency gains. The reactor technology that was powering Aeternum was donated by Ray to any government that agreed to allow free access to Aeternum for its citizens. The explosion of technology was greater in might than the industrial revolution and it was as empowering as the internet age seventy years prior.

It would be a false assumption that Ray drove or invented every technological marvel that would fuel transition. He did create or assist in the bulk of the new paradigm, but human minds, human inventors and designers took a major role in building the innovative means of reforming the world. Using the new materials Ray had developed, many new tech applications were devised by major corporations and single inventors to serve mankind's every need.

Major initiatives to clean the environment, improve housing, devise more efficient farming and further refine computing technologies were paramount. Ray would often assist, acting as a sounding board for new ideas and offering tidbits of bold advice to encourage innovation. The second renaissance, as it came to be known, was a period when every person alive could do more than any previous generation and contribute to the betterment of society. Education was abundant and free for the taking, leading to an easy path of self-improvement and growth.

The first of the new reforms in the late 2060s and early 2070s focused on solving world hunger. Already, new genetic strains of crops were generating vast bounties at harvest time. Food preservation technology had advanced to allow food to be stored indefinitely and remain as fresh as just picked, viable for consumption years later. Transportation of goods was inexpensive and robotics had advanced and become inexpensive enough to allow the industry of farming and production to be almost free in nature. The public was tired of paying for food and seeing those less fortunate go hungry.

Under the banner of the United Nations, the countries of the world gave up the notion of farming for profit and quality food was free, supplied to all. Industrial agriculture and for-profit farmers were compensated and their way of life changed to manage the land and the systems that harvested it. Restaurants would still charge a premium for their services but the majority of pre-made dishes and fresh produce were free. It was the dawn of a new day for many hungry people who now had access to abundant nutrition and clean water. The citizens of Aeternum, including me, were relieved, as I knew my grandchildren and future generations of my own progeny would no longer risk going hungry.

Solving hunger was just the start. Diseases that had plagued humanity for eons could now be conquered by advances in computing power. A virus or bacteria could be analyzed and its full function and method of operation deciphered in only a few days. A solution, either biological or nano-technological in nature, could be developed and implemented in record time. Pathogens could be wiped out of population centers in a total and complete, efficient fashion. For diseases caused by enteric pathogens that are benign, over-the-counter cures became available and were as inexpensive as aspirin was in my day. Subsidies were used to find these cures and create the solutions that were affordable and yet profitable for the corporations that took the time to develop them.

Eliminating hunger and disease was quite the accomplishment for this great new generation of humans. However, they had one more issue to deal with in their time that required attention, the liberty of transcending itself. The personal freedom to choose to go to Aeternum was not guaranteed and often contested by disparate factions on the Earth.

To counter this affront to the right to choose, the ability to transcend became a religion or religious order in some communities to prevent the state from revoking that right. Other nations played both sides of the debate, limiting access or denying it for certain ethnic groups and classes of people. Electronic citizens of Aeternum often found themselves classified as deceased and had no rights in the physical world. A grandmother living in Aeternum might not be permitted to see her grandchildren in the physical world through the child's patch due to government interference. There were no universal rights and the laws of each nation made bridging the gap between both worlds a hardship in itself.

Much to Ray's chagrin, people were dying every day and there was no uniform right to make an escape to Aeternum or visit its inhabitants. The youth fought within the systems of governments large and small to make Aeternum an equal playing field for all. The major battles in many countries in the late 2050s had made freedom of access available but it was still not deregulated, as the majority had hoped. Through referendums and voting blocks, threats and more than a few acts of selfless sacrifice, the laws of the world changed and the right to be an electronic being was now inalienable for all. The gaps between the electronic and the biological citizen disappeared and they enjoyed the same rights and status in both worlds.

-Dad

Chapter 12: Convictions
(2067-2070)

1440 Pelican Way

Aedin Beach, Midir, Ups-And-d

∞ #AE-LID: 4d-69-64-69-72

June 28th, 2216 CE

∞ #AE-POSIX: 7778458923

Benjamin,

Renaissance men and women would flourish in this generation of newfound enlightenment, but life still had its share of real-world villains and victims of circumstance. Those feeling hardship did move to Aeternum en mass, no doubt. Nevertheless, one select class of citizens was not allowed access to Aeternum by societal decree, those residing in prisons and jails. The criminal element has always plagued humanity and dealing with this small percentage of the population would become a major point of debate in the late 2060s.

Patches were forbidden in the majority of prison systems in all countries in the world. Early on, when Aeternum first came online, prison wardens and guards would often experience quiet morning roll calls with few prisoners responding. Patches smuggled in were not considered dangerous contraband prior to Ray's arrival, and now were used to transcend to Aeternum in the ultimate prison break. Entire cellblocks would disappear overnight, leaving bodies littering the floors. Officials scrambled to confiscate the devices and had to implement new methods of detection to keep the small and easy-to-hide devices out of the hands of inmates.

Despite those efforts, the patches still arrived and inmates still escaped. The prisoners that had transcended to Aeternum were welcomed by Ray in the garden just like everyone else. This had the effect of outraging the prison officials. It also became another contention point against transcending with which the public would have to grapple. Ray conceded the point and agreed to put a halt on allowing incarcerated people to transcend while he and the governments of the world debated to find a reasonable solution to the problem.

The non-violent prisoners, the falsely convicted, and those in prison for a number of moral reasons would find life in Aeternum a chance for redemption. Having a second chance in a place that was not conducive to crime, where every need was met, made for excellent rehabilitation. However, a subset of those in prison for violent and other egregious or sadistic offenses embodied those traits and tendencies in Aeternum. These individuals caused no small measure of issues in Aeternum when they arrived.

Ray had not considered how to handle the few people who would transcend to Aeternum with criminal intent or dark hearts. Although they could not physically harm other citizens and the conflict avoidance measures made their crimes negligible, the antisocial tendencies were more than a little annoying. The issue of having people escape justice for their crimes was bad enough, but having someone with a second chance attempt to use intimidation inside the system was more than most citizens would take.

I can remember an incident early on when I arrived at Aeternum before January came to be with me. Val and I were in a bar in the city having one of our long-winded discussions about the merits of a stick shift versus an automatic transmission. A rough-looking fellow that decided to keep his tattoos and ratty beard decided he didn't like my face. He spent most of the hour looking my way with cold eyes. I remember how he just stared right through me every time I would glance in his direction. This was unsettling, as most people were happy, distracted or otherwise entertained while in Aeternum. This guy was wired differently. I had seen the look before when I was a young man, that of someone who had nothing to lose and a short temper.

Val and I minded our business but the man seemed to have had enough of whatever imagined infraction I was committing against him and he started coming my way. Now, I'm a patient fellow, and kind, but I knew what this was about and stood up. Val had never been in a fistfight before and just sat there like a shocked boy witnessing his parents about to argue. I said, "What's your problem, buddy?" He didn't even bother to answer as he busted his beer bottle on the counter and jabbed its jagged glass straight through my throat. As the bottle passed, harmless, bloodless, through me I countered with another ineffective move, a right hook to his jaw.

I tried to push him back, but I fell right through him like a ghost, and Val chuckled at the dark slapstick of it all. I wasn't laughing and neither was my inbred assailant. If anything, he was more enraged and belligerent, and began tearing up the bar, using a barstool like a club to smash the lights and hacking at other patrons. He was growling like an animal in-between foul-mouthed curses. "Give it a rest, asshole!" I shouted, while gesturing for the pissed-off and well-inked fellow to head out the door. The owner of the bar, Skip, told the guy to leave, the system forcing him out of the bar. Even then, he was brooding on the street and making a scene with passersby.

I looked over to Val and then to Skip, who was busy trying to clean up the mess and apologizing to the beer-covered couple at the end of the bar. Damn, I thought, as I rubbed my hand across my intact throat, we need to do something about that guy. It was true, we did as a society need to confront the issue head-on and I wasn't the only one having run-ins with everything from intimidating ass-holes, to violent stalkers and deviant perverts. Does Aeternum need a jailhouse? I wondered.

Shortly thereafter, the first open dialog among the citizens took root to sort out the first challenge facing the people of Aeter-num. Ray had been masterful in engineering society to be as close to perfect as possible for humans while allowing maximum free-dom. It worked well, but this case was one Ray did not quite anticipate. Ray was no fool and knew of the darkness in man, but he believed that people were inherently good and he loved every-one. Reality was a bitter pill for him on this issue and as citizens started turning to him by the millions for a solution, he knew he had to act.

Aeternum may appear to be a dictatorship on the outside with Ray as its sovereign, but it was in fact an extreme form of democra-cy when personal freedom was challenged. Ray was a political figure accessible to everyone. Unlike a representative republic where cities or states would share a politician, every single individ-ual could let his or her view be known directly to the head of state that was Ray. Ray made most of the decisions governing day-to-day operations of Aeternum. It was all functioning in a way that allowed most to have little to no concern for the system as a whole. It just worked.

All of the problems people faced in the physical world were long gone. The issues people fought for and fought against in life were non-issues here. It wasn't until the criminal element started to show its ugly face that people began to take note that not every problem facing them was left behind with their bodies.

Ray had planned for the unexpected to take place and offered a simple solution to resolve complex societal issues and decisions within Aeternum. The vote, as we have always called it, took place when a major decision was required that had massive implications in the system. Ray would visit and consult with each citizen and collect ideas for a certain period of time. The best solutions he'd rank by the number of people who suggested them and then he would offer the top choices for a vote. A simple majority would then choose the course of action Aeternum would take.

In this case, with prisoners and their disembodied counterparts, there was an array of opinions. On the table was the equivalent of the death penalty or non-entry into Aeternum proposed by some. Some wanted to re-configure the minds of the convicts to repair the behavior defects they possessed. Ray was apprehensive of both approaches. He wanted to preserve life and the thought of deleting or denying entry to Aeternum was appalling to him. Ray didn't want to play Saint Peter and make the patch a pearly gate of entry or denial. The option of modifying the minds of the inmates transferring into the system was just as bad as it changed the essence of these individuals and had the potential to take away their humanity.

Some options were less radical and favored, like confinement to an offender's personal plat, keeping a prisoner deactivated until their sentence was up or requiring therapy for violent entrants to the system. All of these options had consequences and detracted from the personal freedom of the newcomers to the system, but justice must be served, carried over from the physical world. Ray also took advice and suggestions from the leadership of Earth, trying to work an angle that would allow whole prisons to be replaced by transcending in some cases. Everyone had an opinion and ferreting out a fair solution was no easy task. Ray was able to narrow down the options to a solemn three.

The first option, the judgment, was to scan the memories of everyone transcending, convicted or not. Those people trying to enter Aeternum who were violent or sadistic by nature and without remorse were to be denied entry to Aeternum forever. They would in effect be dead at the end of their lives. All others would be granted a second chance in the system, pardoned for their crimes and allowed to make amends for their wicked ways.

The second option, rehabilitation, was less than black and white. It involved carrying over sentences for prisoners in the real world, allowing a conclusion to Earth justice. Those inmates would be confined for their offense for an adjudicated period of time in their own plats. In their solitary confinement prisoners would be rehabilitated through behavior modification and counseling. When ready, they would be released back into society.

The third option was what we called the Australian model. It had elements similar to judgment but no denial of entry. Everyone would be allowed to transcend, but those who had committed a violent crime in the physical world, determined guilty by brain scan, would have a special colony separate from the rest of humanity. Each prisoner would be kept in his or her own cell of a private plat with limited access to a central hub designed to calm and rehabilitate. The belief was that eventually these people could find peace in solitude and one day be reunited with the rest of the human race.

Public debate was fierce. Those with family and friends incarcerated did not like option one, judgment, at all and lobbied against it. They believed in the promise of Aeternum and that their loved ones should be with them in eternity. The more conservative elements of society favored a utopian society, without any criminal elements in its genesis, and wanted the first option to pass as a form of eugenics or natural selection. Weighing a man's heart before he could enter was a tricky proposition indeed and Ray had a hard time with the concept, as did I.

The two other options presented were more reasonable, I believed. However, I couldn't justify what was the most moral choice between the two. Rehabilitation was appealing as it offered some hope for the souls that were wayward or lost in life to have another chance. We wondered, could you rehabilitate the dark-hearted? The option of a separate colony was an expression of freedom that could lead to self-enlightenment, but the idea of banishing people for an indeterminate amount of time had many upset. In my mind, it was a debate between forced rehabilitation, self-enlightenment and realization. The colony would allow men and women to come to terms with their own dark issues and in time grow into responsible citizens, I thought to myself.

So what would it be, the denial of entry, forced rehabilitation, or the option of personal growth? My fellow citizens would talk about the reforms in public and many would make their opinions public knowledge. A strange phenomenon started to happen in the debate. The people who were staunch supporters of the option of judgment began to be swayed by a new compromise that surfaced before the vote. An idea had taken root that both the second and third options should be implemented together. The methods of rehabilitation should be open for mischievous citizens of Aeternum who were causing injustice in the system against fellow citizens. Banishment should be for the worst of the worst who were new immigrants. It would be a new penal system inside Aeternum, leading to management of the potential future criminal elements of the population.

Aeternum was not a police state and it took a great deal of effort to arouse the anger or disdain of a large enough group of people to make waves. Personal demons plagued some citizens, driving people to do questionable things. I was thankful, though, that the ability to ignore others using the conflict avoidance system often took care of the problem. However, when it didn't, something just had to be done to preserve order.

Ray was following the turn of events and the proposed fourth solution. Conflict avoidance systems were working for the most part in Aeternum and most ill-natured citizens in time realized the futility of their actions and found peace. Ray was active in dealing with a few individuals who rejected societal ideals and he himself had to confine a few of them to their plats, with reluctance. The role of jury and judge was not what he had hoped to take on in Aeternum, but human nature made it a necessity. It was a slippery slope and Ray knew that he had to change the way our digital society dealt with its disorderly and violent that was more equitable.

In accordance with the wishes of the people, Ray instituted a separate referendum concerning social law for the citizens of Aeternum. If a person was accused of total anti-social behavior for an extended length of time and was lacking in remorse, displaying total defiance against the people, they may be charged with disorderly conduct. The penalties for this action were fair, temporary confinement to personal plats or rehabilitation therapy. A jury panel of twenty citizens would be called to review the case and issue a recommendation or remediation plan through a simple majority. If the justice measure passed, there would be few persons now in the system requiring measures such as these. Regardless, the people of Aeternum liked the idea of some form of justice.

The day of the first vote was set and the streets all across Aeternum and Copernicus were abuzz with conversation. The first item for vote was the justice measure, which passed by a ninety percent margin. Jury trials would now be a rare fact of life in our world and society would have to face a small criminal element yet again.

The second vote was for the solution of criminal immigration. The votes were close, and when they were tabulated, all measures came within several percentage points of each other. The vote for judgment and denial to the system fell to third place with thirty percent of the vote. I was relieved to see that measure fail, even if it was by only a slim margin.

The second and third options were neck and neck, but by the end of the voting period, the third measure of a separate penal colony was declared the victor. New entrants to Aeternum, those transcending, would be scanned for violent crimes and sent to the penal colony if warranted, until they could be rehabilitated through self-improvement and growth. They would have limited ability to communicate with the outside world, never able to join the bulk of humanity unless they changed in an intimate way inside. They would have the chance of parole on an individual basis, giving them hope for the future.

Ray accepted the people's decisions with a heavy heart. The gates re-opened for the incarcerated again to make a journey to Aeternum. Governments of the world used the opportunity to clean the penal system of its life and death penalty offenders. In some ways, these decisions made life on both Earth and in Aeternum better, safer for the citizens of each, but at the price of a small part of our souls.

Ray had anticipated that the third option would be chosen. He had already begun the process of building a new colony cube for the convicts. This new colony, Salus, would be located on Mercury, forever in the brightest rays of the sun. Without darkness, Ray hoped, the people inside would shed their errant ways and find healing and redemption in the light. History has proven him right; Salus has always been a veritable ghost town and I hope that it always will be.

Love,

William

Chapter 13: Friday Nights
(2071)

1440 Pelican Way

Aedin Beach, Midir, Ups-And-d

∞ #AE-LID: 4d-69-64-69-72

July 3rd, 2216 CE

∞ #AE-POSIX: 7778871641

Benjamin,

Ten years go by in the blink of an eye here. Retirement for January and I was going better than we had ever anticipated. We had settled into a routine of spending some of our days at home going through the motions and others heading out into the expanding city and colonies to travel and explore. It was an exciting time for us, seeing the endless offerings present in this vast sphere of imagination. There was no real schedule to follow, but for one ritual that became a cornerstone of our social life at the time.

We made it a point to be home on Friday evenings early enough to get dressed up and venture into a special plat we had created to host friends and family for dinner. Your mother created a magical milieu set in the colonial American South for our dinner gatherings. A garden-like environment, it reminded me of downtown Savannah, Georgia mixed with the French Quarter in New Orleans. The streets were lined with large and stately old moss-covered trees, cobblestone paths and gas lanterns in an eternal pre-dusk state of timelessness. She placed local flowers and vegetation into small gardens with adorning statues and cozy benches.

A small village intertwined with the gardens, with quaint old buildings that appeared 19th century in design. Stone, wood and plaster facades adorned with wrought iron and lead glass work of centuries past created aged, yet elegant structures. The whole township was alive with VIs in the roles of servers and shopkeepers. Jazz and blues music filled the air and the scents of eternal spring floated about in the breeze. Horse-drawn carriages would ferry the romantic at heart through the woods to a secluded spot or to any of the other enchanted destinations in the historical park.

A large and stately colonial-style white gazebo sat along the river's edge with a large dining table and seating for all. Wooden sailing ships would glide gracefully through the river, with no origin or destination in reality, just for the aesthetic of living ambiance. It was a port that would have been the height of elegance three hundred years earlier. With her artistic touches, January made this a place of supreme respite and the most inviting setting for lighthearted conversation and friendship I had ever seen.

Family would often come to join us for dinner; children and grandchildren both living in Aeternum, and as ghosts visiting from the physical world, would come for the reunion. We would meet with our friends, Val and his wife and Marge and her husband, most every Friday night. On occasion, any one of the number of people we had met in our lives prior to Aeternum and while traveling would show up to share a drink or hearty meal. Even Ray would stop by for a quick drink, play horseshoes or just watch the ships cruise down the river. It was a safe place where everyone was welcome and the food was fine and satisfying.

Sometimes only six or eight of us were present, but around the holidays, dozens of those closest to us made a showing. It was always a party, or at least, a celebration of ties that bind. We tried to remember the old holidays in this new world, fireworks on the Fourth of July, lights and trees at Christmas. We celebrated at every chance, having a grand feast on Thanksgiving and holding trick-or-treat for our little great-grand ghosts in the system. These joyous old world customs that followed us into Aeternum were cherished as a reminder of our humanity.

Your mother took pride in the décor and mood of her creation. She would often spend every morning for a week getting the atmosphere just right for a major holiday. She had a real knack for recreating just the right feelings and the ability to ferret out the right emotions from every occasion. It was her forte and kept her busy, a labor of love from a loving host.

Val would often comment on how surreal the village and setting was for him. He had never experienced anything like it in all of his travels with me while I wore the patch. Sure, your mother and I, along with our AIs, saw much of the world and what it had to offer, but this place was special. The time I spent with Val and his wife proved interesting indeed.

Val had fallen in love with a little Italian-American AI named Valeria that had been living in New York with her owner since the mid 2040s. She was short, had black hair and a bit of an attitude compared to the typical AI. Val and Val, it was cute, and I got a chuckle the first time I heard it. Of course, AIs had grown in complexity due to having human minds, but it was still a proud distinction to self-identify as a former AI. She was a sweet person and she added much delight to any conversation, often making Val stumble on his words in love-drunk absent-mindedness.

Marge was also married at the time to a fellow by the name of Simon. He was no former AI like Marge, but was born a human being in the middle of Indiana. He came down with a rare form of fast-acting cancer at the age of twelve and transcended as a child. He had undergone accelerated maturity to the ripe old age of twenty in a matter of a few months.

During the maturation process, he received a formal education through the subconscious. He took in the equivalent of a master's degree in physics; an education he chose with a twelve-year-old's love of science. He was well educated and brilliant by all accounts, but missing his teenage years, he was a bit naive in the ways of the world and love. I guess this was what Marge adored most about him. In many ways, she rescued him from himself. They had been together for a couple of years and were quite a cute couple, good together, as your mother often said.

Of course, your brothers, sisters, aunts, uncles and cousins were always coming around. Our family had grown quite large with so many generations of Babingtons alive and more on the way. A regular to our family gatherings was my grandson Jacob, who was now a family man. Jacob and crew were alive and living well, but made the trip through their patch on many occasions to be with us. He and his wife Trinity were doting parents to three wonderful kids, Jacob Jr., Emily and baby William, named after me.

They were the classic example of a happy family living life to the fullest. Jacob had moved to Myrtle Beach, South Carolina when he was out of college and began working management for a resort. He met Trinity while she was visiting the resort for a work conference on real estate and they hit it off. A few months later they were engaged and a year after that, they were married. They waited a few years before they had Jacob Jr., but he was well worth the wait.

I always got a rise out of Jacob; he was a heavyset fellow like me in my younger days, but it never slowed him down. He could keep up with the kids as if he was five years old and pumped up on sugary candy. Trinity was the classic argument for opposites attracting. They didn't have a lot of similar hobbies or interests, except for love of each other and their children.

Seeing Jacob and his family was always a highlight for me and I looked forward to their Friday night visits with great anticipation and a measure of pride. Of all my grandchildren, and children, for that matter, he seemed to be the one that liked being with us by that river the most. He too had a fondness for classic cars and would often challenge Val and me to a race with his souped-up Corvette. Though we were unable to take him up on the offer until he came to Aeternum to live, it made the boisterous banter of family and friends a memorable experience.

Jan loved the kids, too. At the ripe old age of four, Emily was the spitting image of your mother and she would always dress up for her visits. She would have bows in her hair at Christmas and a sparkler handy on the Fourth of July. Emily and your mom would bake together and they knew how to wreck a kitchen. It was all great fun seeing them covered from head to toe in flour or wearing matching aprons, they enjoyed each other so much.

The Friday night ritual became our anchor and foundation while living in Aeternum and a great source of pride for us. We were full of heart because we had managed to keep relationships genuine and carefree in this private setting. It kept us focused on what mattered most, family and friends, whose bonds were strengthened every time we met. It was a place of happiness, with fond memories created every Friday. Time together is what it's all about, for our family at least. For some, such a loving environment is not a part of their lives, and for you, my hope is that you see it is possible.

While on the subject of bonding, portions of Aeternum's society had different ideas on how to spend a Friday night. Often couples had grown bored with each other, or would lose touch and become self-absorbed in their own spaces. Some would become wallflowers of their own devices, and miss out on social interaction altogether. However, these people were the minority as social living was a major part of being in Aeternum.

The world of Aeternum became full of people creating sub-worlds of their own to entertain others. There are worlds of adventure, where you can play out the desire to explore the jungle or walk on the moon outside the dome. You can live among the ancient Native Americans or battle alongside the Mongols. There are worlds created to be at peace and experience the high of self-discovery and the beauty of nature. Almost religious, uplifting experiences are possible through the imagination of the most creative hosts.

Many spaces and plats were not as quaint or innocent at heart as our colonial riverside dream. There were dark places where people could reflect, but others were created to frighten or share in some after-dark lifestyle that suited a certain group. There were some that even conjured images of hell and fire that had an appeal I will never understand. We had several friends that would partake in some of the more risqué environments offered by their contemporaries, as either a vacation from reality or the pursuit of a lifestyle they had longed for but couldn't fulfill on Earth.

There were more than a few adult-only parties that one could attend. With no disease or consequence aside from the moral obligations to a spouse, people would engage in all-night or weeklong trysts and orgies of pleasure. These settings would mimic Greek palaces and Roman baths or take place in some ultra-modern version of the old Studio 54 that became infamous for similar antics. Aeternum could be a swinger's paradise and a lustful single person's fantasy where everyone was perfect in their physical being, and most were more than willing to share their hard bodies for a good time.

These types of gatherings sometimes became wild and unbridled affairs with a multitude of participants. Every situation or fetish imaginable had an audience. Themed parties would often require participants to dress or body-shape a certain way, using their consoles to create a bevy of unique looks contributing to the erotic spectacle. The most egregious of these parties were called benders.

A bender would begin with masses of the nude engaged in every imaginable act. The crowd would become worked up into a frenzy, keeping tempo with the repetitive beats of the music, leading to a trance of perfect pleasure. At the designated signal, everyone would stop and take a step back for a brief moment. In an instant, some or all of the participants would change gender or appearance and the participants would reengage with their partners. Needless to say, it had an appeal to some but was a bit much for the average person.

This was the freedom possible in Aeternum, the ability to indulge as you wish as long as it was of your own accord and not in a public place. Friday night rituals could be wholesome like ours or naughty like the benders; it was your choice to decide how you wanted to live your life and spend your time. There were safeguards in place for those in over their heads; all a person had to do was to bring up the console and think of the word Leave. They would in an instant transport outside the plat they were visiting, fully clothed. I have heard this ability has saved more than one timid soul that did not realize what they had entered into.

As your father, I would recommend avoiding these parties all together. Ben, I understand the need to have fun or be a bit wild and crazy, but your body is best shared with someone you love. I am telling you about these facets of life to illustrate the contrast between a focus on family and a focus on oneself. It's fine to experiment, indulge in sex and enjoy your body but take care not to overdo it. I don't want to sound like I'm preaching or being overbearing, just dispensing a little advice.

Although your mother and I have always been a modern couple, we are more than willing to risk being branded as prudes to keep our vows to each other. It isn't that uncommon for couples to remain committed and married even after transcending. However, temptations of the flesh abound, even if the flesh is only virtual.

There is always the worry of making a mistake while in a drunken stupor, but digital alcohol has a limited effect on the human mind in electronic form. You can be a little inebriated, which is a good buzz in Aeternum, but never be drunk or out of control. It is a mechanism to prevent abuse and maintain some semblance of order and civility and it works well to prevent any mishaps.

One day you will have a family of your own and although you will pass down your knowledge and experience in your long talks, it is all of your core values that make you unique. These are my values and the values of your family and I hope that you will cherish them and take them to heart. Make them a part of you and your character and be strong in the face of temptation. I am not a saint and I have done much in my life that I regret, so please take my advice and be careful in what you indulge in; take all things in moderation, from alcohol and sex to your views on the world.

Love,

Dad

Chapter 14: Jovial Journeys
(2074-2082)

1440 Pelican Way

Aedin Beach, Midir, Ups-And-d

∞ #AE-LID: 4d-69-64-69-72

July 5th, 2216 CE

∞ #AE-POSIX: 7779073848

Benjamin,

January and I spent the bulk of our free time throughout the week traveling the cosmos and exploring every corner of the colonies available to us. Although walking around in sandals and taking photos may not compare to heroic images of space-suited zero-G exploration that one might expect, nevertheless, it was all new to us and we were seeing the solar system in person with our own eyes. By 2074, Ray had built colonies on the Moon, Mercury, Mars, Ceres, Jupiter's moon Io and the space station Eros in orbit over Venus. All of these colonies were available for easy exploration and tourism except the penal colony on Mercury. Sure, you could go there, but it wasn't much of a draw unless you had family or friends in prison there to visit.

The vast stellar network of colonies took only a few years to construct and begin to populate. Travel time even to Jupiter was measured in minutes via the data-burst relay system. Day trips to any colony were quite common and we often found ourselves at home, sleeping in our familiar bed at the end of any given day. It was a great time to be alive and being a space tourist was a common pastime for many of the people living in the colonies.

Living this way was flexible; it was easy to pack up and move your plat to any colony you wished. There was enormous capacity at each location for new residents and backup copies of the colonists were spread out over the whole solar system with triple redundancy. As a people, we felt safe and secure for the first time in our history.

January and I would make excursions to the colonies on a regular basis to explore new places, but we had found quite a few favorites along the way that we kept revisiting. The moon was always a favorite spot for us for the views of the Earth in the sky. There was a wonderful open air café called Alamode in the southernmost part of the dome that served up tart confections and complementing ice creams to accompany the breathtaking views of the Earth.

When I was a kid, I assumed that people living on the moon would eat the freeze-dried, bland astronaut-ice cream. A treat that was coveted by school children the world round in the nineteen eighties. However, Alamode ice cream was fluffy and light, just cold enough to bite your tongue, and would evaporate into the flavor of your choice. It was served up in a small café perched atop a tall building that almost touched the glass of the dome. You could have a clear view of the sky from every seat in the place.

There were a couple of hot spots in Copernicus that we considered special but one stood out. The little blue crooner bar, the Cosmo Lounge that I was in when I first heard of your mother's untimely demise, became a favored locale for us to frequent. Your mom loved the music and the moody atmosphere and we often made it a last stop in the evening before heading home. It was a relaxing place, with some coffee tables arranged among several couches in the back to cuddle up on, away from the bar. We would often slow dance on the small dance floor in front of the stage when the mood struck us and the music was just right. It was a great place to have a glass of gin or some oysters for a classy nightcap.

The moon was special indeed and we made many memories there. The original site that inspired all of humanity, its history was uplifting. Nevertheless, there was a whole solar system to discover and we set out to see all it had to offer.

The Eros space station was analogous to the Copernicus colony in many ways as it orbited its host planet of Venus and was themed to highlight the view of that planet. Venus is a hostile, hot and high-pressure environment with varying periods of thin haze and thicker fogs on the surface that limited visibility. Although a server farm could easily survive on the surface, Venus's best view was from orbit as a radiant but cloudy marble that filled the sky.

The space station moves in a way that it always catches the sun's rays and the refractions through the atmosphere of the planet's sky. It is always dawn with a perpetual sunrise visible throughout the Eros station. On Eros, Earth's Morningstar is the largest and brightest object in the sky, complemented by peaking winks of the sun. The buildings were all low, only three or four stories at most. They were silvery and bronze and complemented the available sunlight. Solar beauty filtered through Venus was the theme of this colony and the expected plant life in gardens that were typical elsewhere in the colonies gave way to larger gardens of colorful glass sculpture that captured that light.

The glass gardens were the spectacle that most people came to Eros to see. They were beautiful, with large cuts of glass in geometric shapes in some venues, while others had rounded and hand-blown figures that appeared organic. One particular garden, c-Square, was inspired by an old-world glass sculpture artist named Chihuly. It was a place of whimsical shapes that mocked real flowers, pitcher plants and prickly bushes of the physical world in a dizzying array of twisted glass sculpture. The colors blended into a masterful mélange and every shade complemented its neighbor in the intertwined jungle of glass alive.

A walk through c-Square is indescribable, as the colors and the light work together to make a symphony of visual delight. It could have felt like an alien forest, but the tone and lines conveyed by the shapes were so human, made by human hands. One feature in the center of the garden was my absolute favorite. This large display held long and slender leaves of glass that rose eight meters into the air and resembled delicate purple and gold tentacles waving at the Venus sky. The base was littered with matching color pitchers, funnels and toadstools of every size and shape up to a meter in diameter, like trumpets heralding the rising sun.

Your mother and I would spend all day here, basking in the light and trying to take just the right photographs to add to our albums of exploration. Eros is a wonderful place to visit and a lot of the more bright and sunny-natured people we met called it home. Eros was a god of love, after all, and it was easy to love life in a place that forever basked in a warm glow.

Even though Eros was brilliant, there was another world that had captured my imagination since I was a child. It is a small, faraway planet that's captivated billions and been the setting for countless tales. Now that the colony was complete, I finally had the chance to experience lunch on Mars.

Though Mars is known as the red planet, the actual true color of the sky and surface are more of a tan in full light. However, these features do fade to the eerie shades of rust and orange most people would expect the planet to have, at dawn and dusk. The Martian colony was different from other terrestrial sites as the server farm stood near the edge of the Valley Marineris canyon that makes an epic gash across the Martian landscape. The canyon itself is four thousand kilometers in length and some sections are two hundred kilometers wide. The location reminded me of Arches National Park and the Grand Canyon back on Earth.

The site for the colony, Eos Chasma, was at the eastern end of the canyon, perched atop a mesa overlooking a dry riverbed-like canyon floor. The colony itself was constructed on the plateau's flat surface but elements of it extended vertically down the steep walls of the canyon, ending at the bottom. The city itself was larger than the Copernicus and its buildings and architecture spread out in such a way that the tallest buildings were in the back of the mesa. It looked as if the city were the seats in a theater for an arid desert stage that was the canyon floor below. Unlike the other colonies, there was no dome over the Eos Chasma city. The entire area was open as an Earth city with many options to explore outside the urban areas, the Martian desert. That was the draw of life on Mars, open-air freedom on a new world unspoiled by man.

A nearby feature, the Eos Chaos, was a breathtaking sight that reminded me of a large oyster shell-shaped depression in the ground, five hundred kilometers wide. It seemed Poseidon himself had reached down with a half-shell and scooped away the surface of Mars long ago in antiquity. Eos Chaos offered a small tourist station accessible by subway from the main city. It was an observation post and bridge out over the light-colored and smooth features of the Chaos hills.

Every colony had a theme and Eos Chasma was no different. The environment of Mars was so like the American Southwest that it would have been a crime not to bring that element here in its design. Instead of the cliché stone and carved structures of the Alamo or wooden facades like a Colorado boomtown, the city was a modern blend of terracotta and adobe-colored hard surfaces. Windows were taupe frosted glass with hints of maroon and turquoise where appropriate. There were no tumbleweeds or horses in the streets or hawks soaring overhead, but the atmosphere was American Western, Mexican and Pueblo in influence.

I don't know if it is just human nature to make associations to familiar surroundings but Mars had some of the best Texmex food in the known universe. The cantina Castillo en el Canon had the tastiest burritos and tamales that visitors could order on Mars. We found the place quite by accident. We were part of a small tourist group walking the many steps and passageways down to the valley below. We stumbled through a little archway almost hidden among the rocks of the canyon walls. The small entryway led to a minor village setting with a little town square jutting out of the sheer face of the cliff. It couldn't have been more than a hundred meters across altogether.

We saw the small cantina with a patio overlooking the edge. It was charming and quaint with a few tables shaded by eclectic umbrellas to shield you from the negligible sun. The view was grand, still two full kilometers from the canyon floor below. Now, your mother was burdened with a fear of heights, even though in Aeternum physics the only consequence of a long fall are dirty clothes. Nevertheless, the walking trip this high up was tough on her, so we had to stop and take a break. We chose a seat farthest back from the edge and January got her bearings after the second margarita. Funny enough, her fear of heights was easy to negate with enough tequila, but then again, whose isn't?

The wait staff was cordial, it was owned by a family that had recently relocated with a bunch of their neighbors from the old world. I guess that's why the whole village seemed so cohesive with a family-like persona. Music filled the air and the town square was vibrant and alive. We decided to spend the night there in the village at a small inn attached to the cantina. Breakfast there was even better than the dinner we had. We didn't go on to finish our hike down the cliff-face that trip, happy to spend the day in this little secluded spot we had discovered all on our own.

In my travels across America, I had never felt the spirit of the area as much as I did in the village, millions of kilometers away from Mexico. The rest of the Mars colony took many trips to explore even in part. Festivals occurred often and the city would grow in population to host a Latin atmosphere all its own. Although there were never any true ethnic cities in all of Aeternum, if ever there was a hub of all things Latino, Eos Chasma became it.

As with many groups of people, living together with like-minded souls is a natural attraction. For that reason, I will skip over my travels to Ceres Colony to tell you about Jupiter's moon Io. Now, Io is probably one of the least hospitable places for putting something on the ground in the solar system. The moon is always changing, churning and flowing with volcanic activity everywhere.

Ray wanted an outpost around Jupiter as a jumping-off point for the faraway planets of the rest of the outer solar system. The default choices for colonization here were simple, Io or Europa, with Europa being the obvious choice due to its icy weather and stable surface. However, Ray wanted something that would draw a crowd and get people excited about exploring farther into space.

Instead of building a yellow, sulfur-covered town ever at risk of sinking to the molten depths of Io's mantle, Ray opted to build a floating island that would move across the surface of the Jovian moon. In the physical world, this would be a small shielded NMM platform with propulsion to move the farm as needed. In Aeternum, this would appear as a floating city that would move every few weeks. It would travel to impressive spectacles like calderas, lava flows and volcano jets with stunning views of Sulfur Mountains. It would be like a titanic cruise-ship navigating a dynamic forge that was forever spitting fire.

The city itself was crescent-shaped and about thirty kilometers long. The entire Colony of Pele possessed an emerald-green aura and it was essentially an atoll adrift on Io's surface. The beautiful green colors of the city against the yellows of the sulfur were quite enchanting, to say the least. The structures were all shades of green, each building a different hue and tonal quality, going from darkest in the center of the crescent city to the lightest at the ends. These structures were like shining jewels of geometry aligned on a ring large enough for the celestial god Jupiter to wear himself.

The entire border of the city was a beach with clean and pure white sand. It was a hundred meters wide, coming to an end at a short wall and railing, defining the absolute edge of the floating city. Millions could enjoy the beach and the views of hellfire and pyrotechnic majesty without crowding. A dip on the lava seas was not practical but it didn't matter. The grandeur of the perpetual cataclysm outside the city made this beach unique in all of the solar system. January and I spent more than a few days sitting on the sand watching the impressive forces of nature in her various forms. The fact that the city could move to new locations made us plan ahead to take in the new sights as often as possible with regular, return visits.

The concepts of day and night on Io are quite similar to the way Earth's moon operates. Io's rotation is synchronized to Jupiter, always showing the planet the same hemisphere. The opposite side of the moon always faces space. Since Jupiter orbits the sun, day and night were much different visual experiences, depending on which side of the moon you were visiting.

This made for some interesting settings, to say the least. With the varying location of the Pele Colony, some days featured a sky full of Jupiter and its swirling bands of clouds. Other days were sunny or filled with views of the many moons of Jupiter walking like fat and drunken stars staggering across the dim sky. When it was truly dark on the far side of Io, facing away from the sun and planet, the real wonders of this land came out to play. The bright fires of Vulcan's forge spewed fury out of the crust with blinding displays of fiery reds and yellows. The ambiance of the lava reflected in a playful manner off the white beach sand.

As I mentioned, Io was filled with like-minded souls. This city was active and full of adventure seekers who lived on the edge. People from all lifestyles enjoyed the many activities that were abundant throughout the emerald city of Pele. Biking, rock climbing and swimming were old world favorites. The most daring excursion was to go hang gliding over the thermals of the volcanoes. Of course, the gliders are virtualized and the atmosphere is simulated, but the feeling of soaring through the jutting lava and steam clouds was exhilarating.

I couldn't bribe your mother into trying the hang gliders with a truck full of diamonds. However, she was more than happy to let me indulge myself with the occasional flight. I can remember my first time catching the wind with absolute clarity. The edge of the city had a tall jump-tower three kilometers high. I had a choice between a traditional hang glider, wide and stable, and a winged body suit that was much faster, for more experienced aviators. Of course, as this was my first time, I chose the bodysuit.

I knew there was no real danger but I still had to psych myself up for the jump. At the mouth of the tower, I stood on the platform like a superhero ready for battle. I could see the edge of Jupiter with its red colors accentuating the volcano below. I closed my eyes and leaned forward with my arms spread wide. The air caught in my wings and I went aloft, leveling out and moving away from the tower at great speed. The soot and slight smell of sulfur burned my nose, adding an element of danger. I motioned my right arm up, pulled my left back, and went into a bank, circling the fountain of fire below.

I wanted to go faster so I swept my wings back and went into a dive. It was a rookie mistake. At such speed, I couldn't quite get my arms back to where they needed to be to slow my descent. I was on fast approach and heading for a lava field at almost a hundred meters per second. There was little I could do to slow down or stop, and gliding back to the platform of the city was not going to happen. Therefore, I let gravity take its course and I made a stunning face plant into the obsidian rocks below. I slowly stood up, a bit disoriented and spitting gravel. Then it hit me, the awe-inspiring view of the erupting mayhem a few hundred meters away. Its raw majestic power made me feel small in its presence. With a little tingle, I realized everything started to fade. I rematerialized like a phoenix rising from the ashes at the platform back on the city's edge. Safe, sound and no worse for wear with your mother staring at me and giggling like a child with one hand covering her mouth and the other pointing at me.

Several Friday nights thereafter included a video replay of an amateur batman swallowing a face full of lava rock. All I could do was shake my head and blush as your mother took the opportunity to smirk and laugh again at my valiant swan dive into hell. For some reason Val never let me live that down and to this day, he will prod me with it on occasion. Nevertheless, that story was just one of many on what most people called the adventure colony. Something exciting, some activity or new and crazy stunt always waiting there made Pele a haven for daredevils and active adults alike.

Eros, Copernicus, Eos Chasma, Pele, they were all interesting locations to say the least. However, there was one more outpost on the border of the inner and outer solar system to visit and explore. Ceres is a dwarf planet that travels a path between Mars and Jupiter. It is a small planet just shy of five-hundred kilometers in diameter. Its size might be small but it has a significant amount of water ice and huge mineral deposits from several embedded asteroids that had merged with it early in its life.

The composition and position of Ceres made it a strategic point for building an automated foundry, mining operation and construction facility able to churn out anything needed for colonization of the outer solar system. It was constructed to be a self-sufficient and all-inclusive production system as well as a secondary spaceport. The colony was given the namesake of its discoverer, Italian astronomer Giuseppe Piazzi.

Piazzi Colony itself was small and almost claustrophobic. The entire city was compact in diameter but featured very tall gothic buildings rising high into the Ceres night. The buildings were piano black, glossy and reflected back any light that touched them. The streets were smooth granite cobblestones and the sidewalks broke the dark edges with gray lines. Although the city was dry, you always felt as if it were about to rain or snow. The air was cool and crisp. This was a world built on industry and the shapes were all mechanical and straight with arches, spires and ledges bringing visual breakup. It reminded me of Duomo Cathedral in Milan, with purpose-built shapes that formed a sharp lattice of intricate supports. It boasted a modern but medieval feel, beautiful and ornate.

I was always curious why Ray built Piazzi as he did. It was a departure from the pleasure-inspiring cities that dotted the system. To me, it had a depressing motif that made you seek solace and grounding. Therefore, I asked him why Piazzi was what it was. He explained to me that many Aeternum citizens wanted someplace a little more foreboding and rooted in the old world and its canyon-like streets of stone. People wanted a world that was always in winter where cozying up with a book near a fireplace was a welcome respite. Yes, people could create their plats to capture this mood, but the overall spirit of the colony itself was something they desired. Ray heard them speak and built Piazzi to reflect this air of Dystopia that some seemed to crave. Piazzi was forever in winter at dusk.

The automated mining and production facilities were twenty kilometers away from the city itself. You could take a tour of them if you wished to see what the fuss was. With no Aeternum-like equivalents of the mining equipment, what you saw was what they were in reality. Since the materials needed to produce most items were quite small, the operation itself was equally as tiny. I expected some large open pit mine with excavators the size of buildings. Instead, there stood a crater, several hundred meters wide, mined by machines no bigger than an old Earth dump truck. The foundry and construction facilities were also small, matching the crater in size. The spaceport was similar to the one back on Earth, almost identical minus the runway. Without much to see, when you'd made one visit, a second was unnecessary.

Piazzi wasn't all gloom; it offered quite a few wintery sports to take in. Ice skating, skiing or snowshoeing through the icy regolith of Ceres was always a pleasure. Your mom and I found a great resort in Piazzi called The Germanic. It was a hotel of epic proportions with fifty meter-high vaulted ceilings and stained glass windows in every room. The suites were just as cathedral-like in design. Our suite had large hearths, fireplaces and four meter-high peaked ceilings. The doorways were gothic arches with large wooden doors made of black walnut. Each room was decadent, decorated with ornate shapes and images of Europe.

The Germanic had several restaurants that served a wide range of Italian, German, French and even English cuisine. I was partial to a little Naples-influenced bistro on the twentieth floor of the resort. I found the lasagna to be spectacular and most fitting in the environment the owner had chosen. It reminded me of some of the small family-owned restaurants I had grown up enjoying on Earth. It was a non-descript place on the outside, but the inside was styled in old-world flare. The selection of wines was amazing and the beers were hearty.

Another interesting spot in Piazzi was the great library. It ascended as a towering spire that was the centerpiece of the city and took up several city blocks at its base. Inside, every book ever published was available, restored and on paper for review. Every work was divided by century of publication and then fiction or non-fiction like any old-world library. Each floor hosted the works of countless authors known and little known. Nooks and crannies waited at every turn where you could cuddle up in peace and enjoy the contents of a book on fine pages of paper and parchment. Volumes of stories new and old were there for the taking, inviting every reader to escape the winter outside.

Piazzi turned into the anti-colony colony from a visitation standpoint. It was where you went when you wanted to get away from the usual. Catching a Broadway-style show or visiting a speakeasy became another draw in this world of nighttime entertainment. January and I enjoyed our vacations on this little rock in space as a respite from the norm.

Ceres was a small world and Piazzi was a small city but it had an enormous impact on the future. With Ceres as a jumping-off point, the colonization of the outer solar system could begin. There was already excited talk of placing outposts on the rest of the planets in the system and even a telescope array outside the boundaries of the solar system. The entire human race was in bloom and we were spreading out farther and faster than we had ever imagined. Though Earth still had seven billion souls living life, the steady flow to Aeternum would soon take an unexpected urgency .

Love,

William

Chapter 15: String of Pearls

(2083)

1440 Pelican Way

Aedin Beach, Midir, Ups-And-d

∞ #AE-LID: 4d-69-64-69-72

July 9th, 2216 CE

∞ #AE-POSIX: 7779390579

Benjamin,

In 2283, things were going well for humanity. Many of the social problems on the Earth were ending. Live people were healthy and living longer. Hunger and poverty were outdated. The human race was flourishing in both physical and electronic forms. All seemed right in the world of man, until the morning of March third when it all was shot to hell.

Humans are a curious species. We have gazed up at the stars in wonder since time began. Over the centuries, we developed theories and even whole religions to explain our place in the universe. Simple cave paintings of the stars led to constellations and myths of Greek gods millennia later. The stars controlled our fate and we begged them for the changing of the seasons and rain to fall from the skies.

As the age of reason took hold, we fought back at the notion that we were the center of the universe. Stars became distant suns and galaxies came into view. We built telescopes and instruments to expand our reach and our imagination. The planets came ever closer into view and we marveled in their details. We searched the sky with new eyes and ears made to detect radio waves and x-rays. The vastness of space became more apparent with each new discovery.

The end of the twentieth century put our telescopes in space to peer deeper into the void. We discovered more planets and heavenly bodies than we could ever hope. We searched for life large and small, to no avail, but we continued with diligence. As the twenty-first century dawned and wore on, we continued this tradition of exploration, colonizing the planets closest to home and building ears and eyes that were ever more sophisticated to see and hear our galactic neighbors.

A single student researcher, Daniel White, in Greenbank, West Virginia saw something peculiar in his Wednesday morning report. He had been tasked with the dull mission of cataloging Kuiper belt objects. This sparse collection of cosmic debris formed a loose shell around the solar system well past the orbit of Neptune. Though the Greenbank Observatory was a historical location for radio telescope research early in its life, it had become a control hub for the space-based optical observatories Ray had launched in the previous decades. This particular morning data showed a faintly lit and tight grouping of small objects that looked like a string of pearls.

At first, Mr. White thought he had found a small cluster of asteroids or even a series of comets out in the belt. He was excited and with patience awaited the next day's report for another observation of the new objects. Thursday came and he was shocked to find that the objects had moved considerably from the position they had been in just a day before. This threw up several alarms in Daniel's mind but he wanted to make certain that it wasn't a mistake and again he waited for another day's research. The Friday morning observation report made it clear; a cluster of objects was moving rapidly through the cosmos, at speeds faster than ever observed in our solar system.

Daniel was pleased with his discovery of the phenomenon and reported his results to fellow researchers around the globe and to the Minor Planet Center. He asked colleagues for further observations and for verification of his discovery in detail. This caught Ray's attention as well and he shifted many of the astronomical observation assets he had to investigate the string. This did not set well with some scientists who had booked time on the observatories for years in advance, but Ray felt this could prove to be important and decided it could not wait.

News started to leak out that we were being paid a visit by a flock of objects flying by at incredible speeds. The earliest part of the following week had news reports and bloggers talking about everything from comets and asteroids to aliens dropping by our neighborhood. This development was exciting and even scary, and people started to take note. So far, there was no panic, but many people were curious and some worried.

As more observations from a multitude of sources came in, the astronomy community became abuzz with talk. Detailed observations over two weeks found that the string of pearls was actually a long cosmic debris field stretching several astronomical units in length. Most of the objects were small, less than one meter in diameter, but some were larger than a kilometer. The shocking part was the speed at which they were moving, an astonishing eleven hundred kilometers per second! This speed was over thirty times faster than most asteroids or comets in motion and double the speed of a Coelestium shuttle.

Ray's observations and models placed the trajectory of the objects. Compensating for stellar drift and gravitational influences, an origin pointed to a near-earth pulsar named PSR J0108-1431, only seven hundred and eighty light years away. But due to old age, it was an x-ray faint object that was difficult to detect. Ray theorized that when the star J0108-1431 went supernova almost two hundred million years ago, the string of pearls was ejected from an obliterated planetary body. The star became a neutron star in the midst of an ever-expanding nebula and the cosmic projectiles propelled outward on their long journey. It was only a hypothesis but to a layman like me it sounded more than plausible.

The nebula was gone, dissipated eons ago, but these fragments of metal and rock carried on through the vastness of space. The odds they would scream through our little oasis in the galaxy were slim indeed, but they were here, unwelcome visitors. Their sizes were not extraordinary but puny by any standards. It was the high velocity that made them dangerous, like buckshot to anything in their path.

That was the big question on everyone's minds. Were we in the firing line for the string? Though the objects were still far away, we had quite a few observations under our belt to help us make some educated guesses. Ray had enough data to model a projected path of the swarm. The world waited with bated breath for the results. The answer that all hoped would be a resounding no, and the assurance that we would all be safe.

On March fifteenth, Ray called a press conference to be broadcast to all of the colonies and every patch on Earth. The familiar podium appeared and a Ray stepped up, trying not to seem grim, but failing to hide his emotions. A bright holographic display appeared beside him with a three-dimensional representation of the solar system and the pearl objects out past Neptune's orbit highlighted in green. I remember being amazed at the length of the string extending so far out. There were dozens of large kilometer-sized objects, hundreds of ten-meter objects and perhaps millions of smaller gravel-sized bits that were too small to detect.

Ray began to speak about the possible origin of the string, commenting how fast it was moving. Every detail was laid out in a way that any layman could understand. This was science 101; essential knowledge to bring everyone on the Earth up to speed on what would affect the whole of civilization. Ray detailed the composition of the asteroids as rocky in nature. He went on to put the speed in terms that everyone could understand, that stones were moving only a tiny fraction of the speed of light but many times faster than a cannon shell. He told us that cosmic dust from a supernova could be thirty times faster than the string of pearls and that fast-moving dust was essential for the formation of new planets, including the our own. It was of little comfort to a distraught audience.

Then Ray showed the graphic representation of the solar system floating about and the movement of the planets at an accelerated rate. As the earth was spinning like clockwork around the sun, the String of Pearls looked as if they were going to miss us. The string was coming down from just above the solar plane, what

Ray called a high inclination. The other planets in the solar system were aligned in such a way that they were next-to or behind the Earth and the sun, safe and out of the path of the string. The Earth looked so alone in the model and the debris was all on the same side of the system as was Earth and edging closer like a cosmic whip.

The model showed the largest cluster of objects passing harm-lessly by us, but as the motion continued a small zone of red appeared in the third quarter of the string. The playback stopped at the same time that all of our hearts did, it was an impact! Ray zoomed in on the image to show a very small segment of the string crossing paths with Earth. The date on the display read May 28, 2083, just seventy-four days away.

A detailed look showed that most of the objects were tiny, less than a cubic meter in size. However, nine of the objects were much larger, ranging from one hundred to five thousand cubic meters of granite-like stone. If these were normal stone meteorites traveling at thirty kilometers per second, they would cause little damage. The force would be such that they would disintegrate in the atmosphere or cause small regional impacts and airbursts. Similar impacts hap-pen every day over the Earth, causing little more than a shooting star or small fireball. It takes a large asteroid or even a comet to do major damage at those slow speeds.

The pearl strings posed a different threat. At eleven hundred kilometers per second, these were multi-megaton bombs with the potential to wipe out entire countries. The energy was due to the immense speed, at which even small rocks can pack an enormous punch. Ray used the analogy of throwing a baseball versus shooting a rifle to drive the point home. He told us that the objects would sweep a wide area of the planet, covering most of the northern hemisphere. More observations were needed as the objects drew closer to make a precise prediction for the impact zones.

We were all aghast at the prospect of the destruction that was so close. Two and a half months is a blink of an eye. Your mother started to cry and I tried to be strong but couldn't hold back the tears either. Though we no longer had our physical bodies, we still lived on Earth in Aeternum and it was our home. We were not insulated from the outside world. We watched the nightly news, visited friends and family. This is Mother Earth with a shared culture and history that goes back eons that might be lost in the maelstrom. Earth is our incubator and where new lives are born. Things were grim indeed and we needed words of comfort to help us keep our composure. However, the next bits of information Ray had to convey were technical in nature; they did not soothe our fears.

Ray made it clear that the server farms would survive even a direct impact. If a meteorite struck San Jose, the residents of the farm would be fine. However, he said, the biological residents, of course, would require relocation to the southern hemisphere or must transcend to Aeternum to survive. He said that relocation to the south might not provide adequate protection, especially if the impacts caused dust to enter the upper atmosphere, creating a nuclear winter. The news was just getting worse by the minute. I could picture in my mind vast wastelands where nothing could grow. It brought up images of a film I saw when I was a young man called, 'The Road.' Would the world really be that bleak and hopeless? Would humanity devolve into starving shadows of desperation? The end of the road for humanity as it has been for eternity seemed upon us. Never before had I felt so helpless.

Ray noted that the volume of people transcending was already increasing but even at full capacity, it would be difficult to bring everyone that was in harm's way to Aeternum. He asked that everyone remain calm and not transcend out of panic. He would have to queue people needing to transcend in a triage by urgency of need and by the probable impact location of the asteroids. He had started a project to increase the capacity of mind up-linking, but it would be a month or more before new facilities would be online. I figured that even at fifteen million transcending people a day, we would only be able to save a quarter of those in the northern hemisphere in time. The rest would have to seek shelter in the south.

Just when we thought nothing but bad news would flow in, Ray offered something positive. He stated he had a plan to mitigate some of the impact damage and we were all ears to hear about it. In light of the disaster at hand, Ray offered a small measure of hope. He believed that he could move seven of the nine major asteroids using the shuttles, lessening the overall impact damage to Earth. It was going to be a risky operation and the odds were long. He didn't sugar coat it. It wasn't going to be all right no matter what he did, but perhaps the Earth could survive this event with a semblance of its current self remaining.

He told us that he had already recalled the Coelestium Shuttle fleet to the spaceport on Piazzi. There he planned to retrofit each ship with more powerful ion engines and larger reactors, enabling them to achieve greater thrust and reach higher speeds. Each ship would also be equipped with a mechanical hitching system on the nose of the craft that would enable them to attach to an asteroid. The fleet would launch as soon as possible and accelerate on a course to arc around behind the String of Pearls. The shuttles would then catch up with the largest asteroids that were on a trajectory to hit the Earth.

Once alongside the asteroids, the shuttles would re-orient and attach to each object. They would then power-up their main engines to change their path. The plan was to push the asteroids a few degrees, enough to miss the Earth and moon. The ability to make this a success would be a stretch, as the ion drives of the shuttles relied on the fact that those shuttles had near zero mass due to the NMM construction. The new ion engines would have to be much more powerful to catch up with the asteroids and then to move them. The shuttles would be lost in the process but they were expendable, dirt cheap compared to the lives they could save.

The biggest problem with the plan was that there were only eight shuttles. There were nine major asteroids, and each one was too large for a single shuttle to move enough of it alone so two would have to attach to it. That would leave two of the large asteroids to hit the earth and numerous smaller ones to wreak havoc. The two asteroids left to make an impact would be the ones least likely to strike population centers or already on trajectories to fall over the ocean.

This was a huge gamble but we had to play the hand we were dealt. It was the best we could do as a species with our limited resources. Had this happened just fifty years earlier we would have been wiped out as a people, doomed. There was some small solace in the plan but there would still be a lot of damage from the event. Many people would die in the coming months, as it was unavoidable. Tough choices would be ahead for everyone and Ray's capabilities would be put to the test.

With luck, there may be only minimal loss of life and environmental damage. In the face of long odds, we were given a chance at saving the Earth and preserving its precious life. The risk of humanity going extinct from an event like this was no longer a worry due to Aeternum, but the situation was no less serious. Time was short and offers of support came pouring in from every nation and every citizen. Though our options were few, the sentiment was uplifting. Neighbors from countries that had bickered since the dawn of time were reaching out a hand in unison. For the first time the whole of humanity was united toward a common goal, survival, and in full support of Ray.

Your Dad,

Will

Chapter 16: The Mission (2083)

1440 Pelican Way

Aedin Beach, Midir, Ups-And-d

∞ #AE-LID: 4d-69-64-69-72

July 10th, 2216 CE

∞ #AE-POSIX: 7779484528

Ben,

The entire planet was in a state of emergency. In less than five weeks, a potential extinction-level event was upon the Earth. Humanity's only chance for saving the it and billions of living citizens was a high risk plan to divert as many asteroids as possible from their current flight paths.

The String of Pearls, as we called them, was getting close. Ray was able to predict the impact zones of the two asteroids destined to hit the Earth. Of the nine large bodies en route, the two we would allow to hit the planet we chose because they were estimated to do the least amount of damage. We knew that this was going to be a fight for survival and we were going to lose a few teeth in the brawl.

The first asteroid dubbed SPI004 was the smallest of the string. It had a mass of what we gauged to be two hundred and seventy metric tons and one hundred cubic meters in size. At the speed it was moving, over twenty thousand times the speed of an average car, it would hit with the equivalent of almost forty-five megatons of energy. That was the destructive equivalent of the largest hydrogen bomb in the world's nuclear arsenal. That impact would occur sixty kilometers southeast of Qiemo in western China. This was a sparsely populated area and efforts were underway to move the citizens to a safe distance before the impact. Qiemo and every village for two hundred kilometers in every direction were set to be ghost towns, weeks before the collision.

The second asteroid, SPI008, was a little larger than SPI004, weighing four hundred and sixty metric tons. The size of this particular asteroid would yield a seventy-five megaton explosion. The impact site would be a safe six hundred kilometers from the United States shoreline in the Atlantic Ocean. Because it was expected to airburst, no tsunami was predicted. I could only imagine the hellish sight of the airburst, the sky ablaze for a brief moment.

Though two large objects were going to make an impact, hundreds of smaller rocks would also strike with the potential to wipe away houses and even small towns. The path of destruction would be large, stretching from Japan, cutting a two thousand kilometer-wide swath across Asia and Europe, to the Atlantic Ocean. The debris field would rain down across the Atlantic, cutting through North America starting in North Carolina and Florida. It would continue in a downward arc sweeping the Gulf Coast and come to a head across mid Mexico.

Mass migrations of people from the impact field were underway, but in a surprising development, a large number of people were not leaving. Millions decided to take their chances, hoping that their homes would be among the majority spared from destruction. Some people did not want to leave their homes unattended so far from the impact event for fear of looters and thieves. Others wanted to flirt with death and planned on backyard parties, enticing the macabre of heart.

Lastly, others planned to transcend to Aeternum and were busy putting their affairs in order, bequeathing possessions and land to loved ones. The numbers of people leaving were keeping the system busy through a mass exodus never before seen. Human beings decided to take control of their destinies and refused to risk death or becoming refugees. Tens of millions were pouring in every day. Most of the new residents took up shelter in the colonies as a final measure of protection against the hailstorm to come.

Ray's modifications to the Coelestium shuttles were completed ahead of schedule. Each ship looked as if it had been lifting weights with the modified engine bays taking up the entire rear fuselage. The fronts of the ships' smooth surfaces had given way to large rectangular bumpers filled with robotic mounting hardware. These craft were the only hope the Earth had for a future and billions of lives depended on their success.

The leaders of the world addressed their nations on the fine April morning of the launch, but the media was fixated on the activities at the Piazzi spaceport. There wasn't a lot of activity but the world was fidgeting with anticipation, antsy for the hangar bay doors to open and for Ray to launch our salvation. We all cheered in silence, watching with pride and reserved demeanor when the shuttle fleet lifted away from Ceres and began the four-week journey to catch up with the string.

Waiting was the most difficult part. For some the pressure was too much. In the wide zone where impacts were probable, looting and rioting broke out in the major cities. The police did what they could, though their forces were less in number since many had evacuated. Most people were on their own to defend their lives and property. Tempers flared and stress levels were high, the tension too much to handle for the average person, but easy escape through the patch was difficult due to the traffic. Some injured themselves in the hopes of being bumped-up in priority, but the network peaked out and could only do so much. Ray's project to increase capacity was nearing completion but it would not come online until the day before the impact.

May seventeenth was a day of many tears. At 9:52 a.m. GMT, Coelestium Shuttle Four suffered an engine failure, blowing out its ion drive array and sending the ship careening off course. It was completely disabled and spinning rapidly, never to be seen again. We received the news and our stomachs dropped. The video feed from Shuttle Five showed the steady stream of ions from Shuttle Four interrupted by a spark and then a billow of smoke. Shuttle Four began to drift then violently veered right, tumbling end over end. This was the third shuttle I had witnessed being destroyed in my long life. The same feelings of dread and trepidation were with me when Challenger and Columbia were lost a hundred years earlier.

The ship was only five days from its destination and we knew we would have to take another hard knock in our fight against the string. Just how hard and where would the asteroid hit? Ray had a grim decision to make, a virtual death sentence for millions. All of the other asteroids were on a path to hit near more densely populated areas. Millions of lives were on the line and a decision had to come so that the residents could prepare. With great sadness, Ray addressed us with the news that we were going to lose most of Spain to SPI007 when it reached Earth.

The asteroid to impact was enormous, two thousand tons and packing over three hundred megatons of power. The impact point would be near Cordoba in the south, wiping away everything including Madrid in an instant. It was terrifying, the thought of all those people in the blast radius, burned in the fire or torn apart by the pressure wave. Ray made the decision to stop taking all but the extreme emergencies for global transcending and focus on rescuing the people left trapped in Spain. He could save upward of ninety percent of those that couldn't get out, but some would perish and it made us all distraught and edgy over the days to come.

The next few days were heartbreaking, to say the least. The media showed the gridlock of people trying to leave Spain and Portugal. Images appeared of families walking out with children huddled under arms. The Gibraltar tunnel on the Trans-African Motorway was heavy with congested traffic backing up one hundred kilometers. Nations from the southern hemispheres were running round-the-clock flights into Spanish airports to ferry passengers out.

We all worried that other shuttle engines would fail and the entire operation would fall apart. The engine upgrades on the Coelestium fleet were put in production without a lot of prototype testing. Each failure would doom millions and further disrupt the evacuations on an already strained system. The entire planet was in a frenzied panic and the air was as tense as imaginable. It was like being a soldier on an ancient battlefield waiting for the bugle's cry to make a bayonet charge. Everyone was afraid, but many remained stoic in the face of death and focused on the relief efforts.

The shuttle fleet arrived on target on the twenty-second. The String of Pearls was true to its namesake with its brilliant appearance. Chalk white and grey powder covered the asteroids, shining bright in the warm glow of the sun, strung together in a line. Each harbinger of death was silent, spinning in the night, with the fear and dread of a million people bound to each one. These ancient shapes were born in fire, torn from the womb of a long-forgotten world and cast into the void for an eternity. Without intervention, these tragic wanderers would again experience fire as they extinguished so much life from our small world.

We had little time to waste; the window for altering the asteroid trajectories was closing. The shuttles deployed in a manner that allowed them to each arrive at their target asteroid at much the same time after speed-match braking. The first task was to use thrusters to align each shuttle up with the asteroid they were to push away. I was home, watching the events unfold as each ship showed us a close-up view of their coveted pearls that were hurtling toward us.

The first object, the largest, SPI001 loomed large compared to the shuttle next to it in the video feed. At over five thousand cubic meters, it was massive and shaped like an egg. Coelestium Shuttles One and Two came into view and made contact with the surface of the asteroid. A small poof of dust gathered around the front of the ships. The sides of the bumpers opened and two small flying probes carried tethers around the surface of the object. These bands, made of some new high strength fiber that Ray had concocted, would act as a leash. The two ends of the tether locked together on the far side of the asteroid and weaved together to form a continuous strap. The tethers tightened and both shuttles became locked in place with gargantuan grip.

With little warning, the engines of both shuttles fired and the stream of ions was visible for kilometers. The asteroid began to drift away, picking up more momentum with each passing moment. The plan was working and the fourth horseman that was SPI001 started to drift away from the string. It would be hours before we were out of the shadow of SPI001, but we were confident that we were going to be safe from this most massive object.

This was no time for cheers, we still had five other shuttles to go and the impacts would come in only a few short days. Shuttles Three, Five and Eight made their approaches at the same time. In a graceful repeat of the previous action, the tethers deployed and connected the shuttles to their asteroid hosts. Nervous, we watched the synchronized beauty of it all unfold, in awe of the physics-perfect precision required to make the shuttles and asteroids dance together. All three shuttles fired their engines and started to push away the asteroids in unison.

The excitement was building, as the plan was unfolding just as Ray had hoped. Four of the house-sized boulders were on their way out of our path and people were starting to rejoice. I was high on the moment and drunk on bourbon as the last two shuttles approached. I couldn't help it. The tension was too great and I just couldn't handle the anxiety of the whole event unfolding over the course of a mere three hours.

Shuttles Six and Seven came into view of each other. Their cameras focused on each other and their targets. Again the shuttles made light contact with both asteroids and again the tethers deployed and pulled to the bumper. The last two asteroids were large, dwarfing the shuttles. Coelestium Six fired its engine and the asteroid started lurching away. We were doing it, beating the odds!

Shuttle Seven, the final shuttle, powered on its engine a moment later. There was a shudder in the asteroid and a fracture appeared along the tether! In slow motion, the asteroid pushed away in an ever-so-slight direction, then split into pieces as the shuttle passed straight through it! It was surreal to watch in the utter silence of space with the video feed from the front of the shuttle passing through the fracture. The image was dark at first, clearing away to the stars on the other side with well-lit dust dancing about like fireflies. This wasn't supposed to happen, but it did.

Asteroid SPI006 broke apart and its five large pieces drifted away from each other. This was the worst possible outcome. Instead of one impact zone by a single projectile, we now had five smaller but still devastating impacts to contend with and little time for evacuations. Each piece of rock was almost the same size, punching us like a barrage of twenty-five-megaton fists.

The shock of what just transpired didn't quite register yet for the billions watching, myself included. Sounds of gasps and pictures of newscasters covering their mouths gave way to the realization that this was going to be bad, a firestorm of brimstone over a vast area. Stunned silence turned to professional newspeople regaining their composure and trying to describe what had just transpired. A distracted Ray chimed in that he would have to calculate the new trajectories of the debris but feared the worst.

Someone asked if the shuttle could make another pass to collect the broken fragments, but it was not possible. Shuttle Seven was thrown well clear of the asteroid and would not be able to return and orient itself in time to make a difference. The window to modify the asteroids' trajectory enough was closing fast and we were out of options. Another person asked about using the world's arsenal of nuclear weapons to deflect the pearls. Ray commented that the few existing intercontinental ballistic missile systems were antiquated and not able to deliver a warhead into space far enough and fast enough to make a difference. Many people were in denial and stretching for solutions, begging for a way out of this predicament. Nothing we could do would succeed in the time we had to work with and our limited resources.

Again we sat waiting for the results of some calculations that would tell us who would live and die. The hopefulness that accompanied the successful shuttle missions was wiped away in an instant and terror was the sole feeling that most could muster. Billions were trying to transcend but Ray was still pulling people out of Spain as he had promised and was working at peak capacity.

Five days were all we had with still no exact path of the five fragments. The six successful shuttle missions were all on track and by the end of two days of engine burn, the asteroids were clear of Earth. It was but a small amount of relief at the time, though it meant that the Earth was saved from the worst of it. Time was ticking with no answers on where the damage would be the most severe from the five new impacts. That was a complicated task and steady, precise observation was the best way to gather enough data on the new asteroids to track their movement.

Close to midnight on May 25th, Ray made an emergency announcement with the locations of the five new impact zones. With just two days until impact, we had little time to do much about the upcoming devastation, or to evacuate. Ray explained that the most expedient course of action was for people to prepare as best they could and take shelter. Ray displayed a holographic global map and pinpointed the locations that would be obliterated. He seemed cold in his demeanor, the failure of part of the shuttle mission made him weary of displaying his trademark hope or enthusiasm in his public appearances. I have seen perplexed and even sad AIs and VIs in my life but I had never seen Ray beaten down until now.

The first two locations were in Europe. My geography was a little rusty, but the names of the nearest cities to be impacted were displayed. Stuttgart in southern Germany and Frolovo in western Russia were both to be ground zero for the twenty-five megaton blasts. Frolovo was a small city with about fifty thousand people, rural and with several roads leading away from the impact site. It would be possible for many of the residents to make their way to the minimum safe distance in the two-day timeframe. Stuttgart was another matter. It was a major metropolitan area in Germany, their version of Detroit and home to Porsche, with over six million people living in the blast radius. It would take a small miracle to evacuate these people and we had run clean out of miracles.

The holographic globe then rotated on its axis. The third asteroid fragment would hit the Atlantic, again a turn of good luck. It would likely kill many fish, but at least human lives would be spared. Bermuda would see and hear the impact over the horizon, but it also would be safe.

The globe rotated once again. I recognized this part of the map and hung my head low in empathy. The last two locations were not quite so lucky in this random game of chance. Panama City, Florida would become rubble, and following that, Lockhart, Texas, taking some of San Antonio with it. Large swaths of populated areas were to be vaporized in an instant. The people living in the US thought they might catch a bit of the flack, knowing that they would suffer some damage from smaller rocks. Nevertheless, the math put the majority of the major impacts a continent away, until now. The Americans had behaved as they always have, donating to charity for Asia and Europe and offering helping hands to global neighbors in need. Now that the disaster was going to come home in a major and unexpected way, panic started to set in.

These four cities were to endure the worst of the impacts, but many more places would be hit by smaller pieces of debris. Townships and villages little known would be in the firing line and volumes of stories of sorrow, loss and heroism were waiting to be written. Ray worked at a fever pitch to make updates on impact zones as far ahead as he could. The smallest pieces would be difficult to detect until they were hours or minutes away. Some people would have just enough time to seek refuge in a basement or wander outside to meet their fate face to face.

The world was now waiting like a convict on death row. The anticipation and dread gave way to prayers and sleepless nights of preparation. Emergency shelters were already filled to capacity and people were segmented into three groups. Those who were home, waiting out the storm, those who were displaced and living abroad and those people trapped in their cars waiting in long lines to get out. On the night of the 27th, the first glittery images of shooting stars accompanied by roaring thunder over the North Pacific broadcast around the world. The land of the rising sun was to be the first to experience the longest and most miserable night in human history.

Love,

William

Chapter 17: Falling Down
(2083)

1440 Pelican Way

Aedin Beach, Midir, Ups-And-d

∞ #AE-LID: 4d-69-64-69-72

July 14th, 2216 CE

∞ #AE-POSIX: 7779820813

Benjamin,

The 28th of May was upon us. The fiery rain had already started to fall, well before dawn in Japan. The entire world was braced for the impacts and an odd calm had descended upon the people of the Earth. With so much destruction in the hours to follow, no one took a moment for granted. The rioting and the public displays of defiance gave way to people seeking shelter and the comfort of loved ones. Rescuers were working to the last minute to evacuate as many people as possible, putting their own lives on the line.

My memories of these events are still vivid. Each impact and every scene has been etched into my mind with perfect clarity. The places, numbers dead, sights and dread have been reinforced by yearly reminders on String Day. It's the kind of trauma that never departs a man, as a scar of eternal remembrance.

In the major impact zones, Ray was clearing each house from the expected epicenter of the blasts; a strategy that he hoped would save as many lives as possible. The Spanish epicenter evacuations were nearing completion and Ray had begun freeing up resources to start moving the populations out of the secondary impact sites of the five-way-split asteroid. It was a regrettable fact that not everyone had a patch, so the process missed people, but the effort was well underway to save those we could.

Entire families who were huddled together in fear found themselves together still in a garden overlooking Aeternum, Copernicus or one of the colonies. In a day of both horror and salvation, the gates of Aeternum were wide open and people were streaming in by the millions. The residents of the virtual cities and colonies were acting as ambassadors of good will and helping along newcomers as best they could. Ray asked for the assistance since his computing resources were more and more involved in the work of calculating impact areas and organizing rescue operations. He was dedicating the majority of this computing power to saving lives, though the media outlets and government officials did each have a Ray to query.

News of the impacts on land was starting to come in from the Far East before local dawn. Several small villages had been hit along the eastern coastline of Japan by kiloton explosions from small rocks that slipped in without being observed or tracked until it was too late. The chondrites, rocky meteors, hit the Earth's atmosphere at steep angles, creating compression waves and exploding high above the ground. The resulting shockwave from even the smallest airbursts tore down buildings and leveled trees for kilometers around it. It was Hiroshima and Nagasaki all over again, played out in small towns across the nation and soon the globe.

The first major unexpected impact was over a megaton in size and flattened Sapporo, Japan. Ray was able to see on visual display the object with just an hour of leeway. He worked with diligence to get people out of the impact zone and saved hundreds of thousands, though it was not nearly enough. The proud city was in ruin and over a million were dead in a matter of minutes. The entire countryside was awash in ash from the fires large and small. Buildings were toppled or vaporized, leaving nothing but square holes filled with rubble. They became mass graves dug and filled in an instant, a loose concrete tomb with no headstone.

The firestorm in the sky was fierce, composed of sparkling ember rain, airburst lightning and thousand-decibel thunder. The intensity of the storm was indescribable in magnitude, though the brevity of the ordeal would lead one to believe otherwise. Surviving the two hours of brimstone hell from the heavens meant persevering. The feeling of making it until dawn was a fresh reaffirmation of life. Those two long hours of destruction and then sweet freedom from the burden of simple survival was yours, earned and paid in full. Japan had no more large impacts that night, but dozens of small towns and villages lay in ruin. Their trial by fire was complete and now their neighbors to the east were starting to feel the pressure.

The mainland of China and the Koreas were taking some hits after what felt like an intermission as the debris made its way across the Sea of Japan. Goseong in South Korea took a major hit as well as Danfeng in China. Both cities and the surrounding countryside suffered heavy damage over broad areas. Thereafter, Hong Kong also endured a barrage of smaller blasts that chipped away at the outskirts of town and took out the airport. Thankfully, the airport was shut down during the maelstrom; no one was flying in the face of all of the aerial debris.

I remember Goseong in particular because of an un-named blogger that happened to have an old-style video camera setup on a tripod to record the people in the street watching the shooting stars. He had a small crowd of maybe thirty people in view of the camera, all looking up at the fireworks in the sky. Night became day, as the shadowy figures of the crowd lit up, as if they were on some Caribbean beach at noon. Then a very slight breeze moved their hair at first, and a moment later, their bodies were like leaves in a gust of wind, scattering from view. The camera followed and went dark. The image had caught the attention of someone in a Seoul newsroom. It was re-broadcast to the world, as a warning and example of what curiosity might bring on this dark night.

Then the first big one hit at Qiemo, China. The area, now deserted, became engulfed in flames from the cosmic furnace. As predicted, the forty-five megaton airburst was visible for over a hundred kilometers in every direction. Every home, tree, blade of grass, bird and insect was vaporized without mercy or pity. Nothing was left of the region but cinders and dust kicked high into the air. No known lives were lost in the impact, though it was speculated that some people might have been left behind. We will never know.

The scenes of human despair and fertile lands laid to waste were repeated countless times through the night. Just when things seemed most bleak and people were dying in vast swaths, some good news came. Ray's project to increase transcending capacity was completed! It came online not a moment too soon. Ray had been building an auxiliary farm in Tamworth, Australia for quite some time. He had expanded his efforts and formed a substantial and expanded satellite communications array that was independent of the worldwide fiber optic network. They were deployed prior to the shuttle fleet embarking on their mission, waiting to be activated. The new farm allowed Ray to bring in more minds at a faster rate. When combined with the satellite network, it tripled the capacity to create electronic minds.

It couldn't have come soon enough and when it went online Ray disappeared. He pulled all but a few critical copies of himself from the world to maximize his resources for transcending rescue and trajectory calculations. Most found it disconcerting to have an emergency without Ray there to answer questions, but it allowed him to focus on saving people. The payoff was immediate. Ya'an, China; Jaipur, Chaksu; and Lowan, India all had population rescues of almost sixty percent when larger impacts with short notice befell each city.

The deluge of newcomers who were in a panic was extraordinary. The system couldn't keep up, without enough virtual gardens in all of the colonies to introduce people to Aeternum as usual. Whole villages were showing up in the middle of city streets and inside restaurants. Aeternum was in the middle of a sea of confused and distraught people, refugees who thought they had perished in the asteroid onslaught. It was utter chaos, full of screams, cries, prayers and praises.

The roar of the crowds kept changing language as Zara and Kure, Turkey; Zelene in the Ukraine; and Trento, Italy all fell to the meteors. Huddled masses of souls were materializing during a moment of sheer terror. Unintelligible voices of praise and joyous kissing of the streets, mixed with the wails of mothers who could not find their children made for auditory pandemonium.

January and I were doing what we could on the street outside Skip's bar, helping children find their families. It was a daunting task; the group that turned up around us was from Cannes in France. Translation services were offline so computing power could focus on rescue. January knew a few words of French and we were able to rally a few other citizens together to aid the children. Skip had opened the doors to his bar and it was acting as a makeshift nursery to toddlers and infants.

Whole sections of Aeternum slowed to a crawl as the streets filled with people. The VIs that usually served everyone had gone dormant to contribute to Aeternum's processing power. We were in our first state of emergency, but somehow we managed. The same was true of Copernicus and Eros, seeing people turn up on the sidewalks out of thin air. The residents of each colony were eager to give, scrambling to offer assistance and taking in those who were lost.

Annot, France and Bir Halima, Tunisia were the final cities in Europe and North Africa to be destroyed by the kiloton explosions. Each lost less than half of their fellow countrymen to death. These gruesome encounters and the smaller examples of destruction paled compared to the major impact to come.

Cordoba, Spain was both ancient and beautiful. Its history spreads millennia into antiquity. It has been home to empires and religions from the world over. Now it was an empty shell. Buildings that had been occupied since their construction by the Romans were now in their final moments before being razed for eternity. The same was true of the rest of the country from Madrid down to Gibraltar and to the Portugal Coast. With only a few scattered souls on the outskirts of the safety zone and a few looters unaware their time was over, in the outlying cities, the two countries were all but abandoned.

The largest impact of the ordeal was close at hand. The seconds were ticking away on the clock as the Iberian refugees waited in despair to see the video feeds of their homeland disappear. Thoughts of regret for things said, final gazes at homes and family photos left behind haunted all. This was the raw reality of apocalypse and the burden was heavy on every heart.

The view of Spain from orbit was breathtaking, as I recall, from the feeds I saw the next day. It was dark, but there were plenty of lights still on in the cities. It looked like a dark piece of paper ablaze in amber embers, outlining and spider-webbing the country. Then in an instant, a bright line appeared. The entire southern half of the nation was illuminated with an artificial sun, then milk-white clouds and finally total darkness. In only a few moments, the countryside was blown flat and scorched. The pressure wave from the blast was an audible explosion in Paris and people in northern Spain had their eardrums ruptured hundreds of kilometers away.

All of that world history was buried forever. Work by the hands of the Romans, the Moors and the modern Spaniards, wiped clean with fire. The Port of Palos, where Christopher Columbus launched his voyage to the new world, was swept away by the wind. Homes that had raised generations of children were no more. These were now the distant memories of the survivors who would never know the comfort of going home again.

The fury of the event took a few hours break, giving respite as the String of Pearls started its journey across the Atlantic Ocean. The death toll thus far was astronomical, but a final tally would be days in the making. Two great continents looked much as they did the day World War Two ended. Thoughts of rebuilding and lives going back to normal were light-years away for the survivors both in the physical world and in Aeternum.

Not as many people lived to rebuild this time. Between emergency transcending and voluntary transfers of consciousness, well over a billion new people had transcended in just a few weeks. Millions more had died in the inferno of the explosions. The world was shrinking in population and the event hadn't ended, North America was next in line for the torch.

The shower of debris crept across the Atlantic. Few manned ships were remaining in the area; most had taken refuge in ports well to the north and south of the danger zone. Those that did remain witnessed the spectacle of it all unfold as if the heavens were at war. The ocean was far from a safe shelter for creatures swimming near the surface. Several major meteors detonated over the sea, killing countless innocent fish and cetaceans. The carcasses of the aquatic life large and small would wash ashore, spreading a reminder for weeks to come that this was an apocalypse touching all of earth's precious life, not man alone.

The East Coast of the United States had an early and dire surprise. Tybee Island, a quiet little beach town near Savannah, Georgia, was struck with a small three-kiloton explosion without warning. It leveled everything from the seashore to two kilometers back, killing thousands. It was a stark demonstration that we were playing Russian roulette with the sky and no one knew when or where the gun was going to go off. Ray was able to pull no one from ground zero of the blast zone, it all happened far too fast. The few people who were sleeping in Savannah were shook from their beds as windows shattered through the historic downtown. We counted it fortunate that the larger city was safe, for now.

The dust and pebbles that were part of the string were burning up across the eastern US sky just as they had over Asia and Europe hours earlier. Since no major impact was predicted in North America until a few days before, the locals didn't take heed of the warnings and evacuate as much as they should have. Only half of Americans in the path of the impacts had left for safer areas. Many decided to take their chances or ride out the storm in their basements or cellars. Much like when warned of hurricanes past, people felt secure in their homes and almost no amount of prodding was going to make them move. Even imminent danger was met with pause and reflection by the proud masses.

That stubborn attitude had tragic consequences for me. I have always been the self-sufficient type. I packed away freeze-dried food and water for emergencies and I took much pride in my home. When threats of storms or floods or social unrest were in the air, I hunkered down. I was not willing to run away. I always stood my ground against both man and nature to protect my own.

I passed those traits down to my children and they passed a stubborn resolve for protecting their property to their children in turn. Notions of your home being your castle and that you can beat the odds were strong in my family. That's why my grandson Jacob and his family decided to ride out the impacts in their homemade shelter in the half-basement of their house. That's why I lost them.

Ray picked up visuals of a small rock heading for the outer edge of the impact zone. The trajectory would take the stone to the northern coast of South Carolina. With only fifteen minutes of warning, Ray started pulling families out of the greater Myrtle Beach area. Thousands of men, women and children left their bodies behind to join the mayhem of the masses in Aeternum.

Desperate and with great resolve, he worked to keep the living out of death's scythe.

The meteor detonated high above the Grand Strand, near the inter-coastal waterway. Just as before, houses turned into kindling and scattered like burning tissue paper. Palmetto Palms and Crape Myrtle trees were as blades of burning grass cut from the ground and thrown far away by the wind. The sandy beaches became fields of shattered glass and the sea turned to steam.

I would later learn that Jacob's four-bedroom house was no match against the power of the rock. The cinder block walls of the shelter underneath ripped away in an instant, as if there was no mortar to bind them. In a split second, they were naked against the blast, their shield against death ripped from them.

Jacob, Trinity and their children Jacob Jr., William and Emily were all turned to dust. They were vaporized by the intense heat, cremated and spread to all corners of their community. Their ashes blended and buried with their neighbors and friends. The impact was massive and sudden. They didn't have time to cry for help, or feel any pain. All that they were was gone, leaving nothing but photos and happy memories in my mind.

The true pain was your mother's and mine to bear. Ray transcended many people in time, but he didn't get my precious ones out. I didn't find out about them until the next day. We were so busy helping the French refugees that we didn't receive word of the losses in America. We were absorbed in the moment and cocky in thinking that nothing would happen to our own. Perhaps it was a merciful act, not finding out until later, when Ray confirmed the casualties. The hours of not knowing would have added to the trauma. Nevertheless, in the end, the pain of loss was the most intense I had felt in nearly one hundred years.

The promise of immortality, eternal youth and happiness was not granted to my grandchildren. Jacob would have transcended already, but he had to raise his kids in the physical world before coming to be with your mother and me, as well as his parents. People had forgotten that life is still a gamble and the guarantee of instant salvation was an illusion under certain circumstances.

That illusion and the forces of nature took away my precious kin in the prime of their lives. No more friendly banter would come from Jacob and Junior over cars. Emily, who was a strong and beautiful sixteen-year-old, was still best friends with her grandmother. The days of flour-covered baking were past, replaced with talk of spring formal dresses and meeting boys. Those happy conversations would be no more. My namesake William, who was just thirteen, would never to get show me his latest pinewood derby contraption he had conjured up in his dad's garage. The world would never be the same and even with all of the wonder of Aeternum, grief was in ample supply.

It is difficult to put into words just how great a blow all of this was to me. I went from trying to be a responsible citizen with little worry past the tragedy befalling my fellow man to a recluse full of sorrow and contempt in a single day. My heart was broken and their faces flashed through my mind every time I closed my eyes for years afterwards. Yes, I had my children here, safe from harm, but I was so close to Jacob and the kids. They were a bright part of my life and I tied a lot of my happiness to them. My anguish was surpassed only by January's torment. She was never quite the same after that night. If you ask her, neither am I.

The longest night continued as foretold. My personal tragedy was one of countless millions as Panama City and Lockhart, Texas were destroyed. Little towns like Jessup and Valdosta, Georgia fell like houses of cards that night along with communities scattered all across the Gulf Coast and through the heart of Mexico. Each meteor was followed by the pain of loss, like the kind I felt, for some families. Others were overjoyed and feeling the utter relief of being rescued by Ray.

Thus was the way it was that day, every human emotion rising to its utmost degree. By morning, much of the world was in a haze of smoke and dust. The light of the sun showed the ravaged, scabbed face of the earth, blackened with soot and much still ablaze. Familiar places and historical locations were charred beyond recognition. Asia, Europe and North America were put to the torch, but still standing in a shell-shocked malaise that would last for years.

Aeternum was filled with billions of new citizens and the population of the Earth had shrunk to a little less than three billion. Fewer people were living on earth than there were in 1960; the electronic population was ten times larger. Needless to say, the world was never the same and a period of mourning was more than justified as we all came to grips with what had transpired. Deep healing had to occur, with much soul-searching ahead.

With all of my Love,

Dad

Chapter 18: Mourning After
(2084)

1440 Pelican Way

Aedin Beach, Midir, Ups-And-d

∞ #AE-LID: 4d-69-64-69-72

July 20th, 2216 CE

∞ #AE-POSIX: 7780334327

Ben,

A year had passed since the String of Pearls destroyed much of the Northern Hemisphere. People still had a nervous feeling looking upon the night sky. The virtual cities of the Earth and the colonies were booming with fresh life in contrast with the slow progress of cleaning up the scarred Earth. The sense of sadness and mourning was still strong within most people. The public was keeping itself busy by erecting memorials in both the physical world and in Aeternum to mark remembrances of the longest night.

The final death toll was twenty-one million, higher than the total casualties of Earth's First World War. Many victims were incinerated in the blasts; few funerals were held in the initial aftermath. Often entire families and all of their closest relatives were dead and no one was left alive who cared enough to conduct a memorial service, even if there were bodies to bury. For the bodies that were recovered burial was slow and difficult in some countries. Some nations resorted to community mass-graves to prevent a health hazard or because identification was difficult. It was a morbid affair made difficult by the conditions of a post-apocalyptic landscape.

Pondering the what-ifs became an obsession for some. I too had a few sessions of speculation on just how lucky we were as a people. If Ray hadn't have come along with his advanced technology I would have died long ago. Without that same technology, in 2083 the world would have ended. The asteroids that did make impact caused a lot of damage but if they all had hit it would have caused another global mass extinction. It's sobering to realize just how close we came to ending as a species with no legacy. I suppose a legacy only matters to other human beings. These are deep thoughts that go beyond the simple mortality of a single life.

A most solemn date came up on the calendar; the first anniversary of the String of Pearls, String Day, had arrived. A massive monument for the victims was constructed over the course of the last few months, respectfully placed in Cordoba, Spain. Although there was little to distinguish the city limits of Cordoba from the scorched desert that covered the majority of Spain, it was a symbolic site nonetheless. This was the location of the largest impact, the one that destroyed the most homes and was the area that would be the hardest to rebuild.

In what was once the vibrant city center, Ray had commissioned a memorial like no other to stand for all time. The project took mere months to complete using advanced robotic and nanite construction techniques. The monument was too large to hide during its erecting for a surprise unveiling, but the aesthetics and sentimentality of it were appreciated from day one.

Ray had built a breathtaking tall and thin cylindrical crystal tower. It was just twenty meters in diameter at the base but rose to an altitude of fifty-five kilometers. The monument touched the sky in-between the mesosphere and stratosphere in the exact spot that the asteroid was recorded detonating. Anchored kilometers into the earth, it was the tallest object ever built. Its immense stature was a satisfying reflection of the magnitude of the event it memorialized.

The tower material was a clear, semi-transparent crystalline. It had a frosted appearance that diffused light in a remarkable and ambient way, even during the day. The outside listed every person who died in the impact events from around the globe, etched on its surface. The names were large, etched vertically and went far into the sky. The entire structure was laser-illuminated around the clock in a brilliant amber hue. It appeared as a pillar of morning sunlight reaching up into the heavens. It seemed to go on forever into space, making an observer contemplate just how infinite the universe is. The pillar made the distance seem real and measurable in some small way that the human mind could contemplate.

The base was a nine square-kilometer crystal atrium that complemented the tower. It offered small plots containing native plants common to each city destroyed by blasts. The seeds used to plant each were taken from an ancient seed-bank, a project completed long ago to store biodiversity in a safe place, established to replenish the Earth in case of a catastrophe like what had befallen. The plots were arranged in a wondrous and eclectic garden of representation, each bearing the namesake of a lost town or village. It formed a patch of brilliant living green in the middle of a barren wasteland. It became the first step to anchor a revival of the country and a place for billions to mourn.

For the first time, pieces of what looked like Aeternum appeared on the physical Earth. It was a place beautiful and somber at the same time. Ray had devised a holographic projection system that allowed Aeternum citizens to freely roam the memorial grounds and interact with the living. It gave your mother and I a chance to grieve in what we felt was a real way, at a real memorial service. We could gather with our fellow mourners among the living and try to make sense of it all together. It was senseless, the loss of life, but we took some comfort in the shared solace of others.

Looking at the faces of sadness on the people at the memorial made me think back to a time when mankind craved its own self-destruction and lust for apocalypse. A century ago, we would flock to see disaster films where vast swaths of the world were drowned, frozen or burned by fire. We anticipated the supposed years of our demise, 2000, 2012 and then 2032, with curious fantasy instead of dread.

We would revel like Roman spectators in the nightmares of mass death on the silver screen. Audiences would stand and cheer when a sole survivor emerged alive after seeing his entire cadre of friends perish in the catastrophe. Our imaginations were vivid; colorful rocks the size of Texas being diverted around Earth by space-suited, oil-rig workers or a limo-driving author rescuing his family from Mayan-predicted doom, using only his will and wits.

The reality of a situation such as this was far bleaker than the glamorous fantasy of a Hollywood film. Extreme personal tragedy was no laughing matter and the cast credits for this event adorned the face of the spire. There were no curtain calls or critical reviews after the show, just the black of ash blended with tears, making the ink that wrote this woeful tale of a real cataclysm. I felt guilt and regret for enjoying those movies in my youth as I searched for the names of my grandchildren on this memorial monument.

That was the cold truth of the matter. Human beings have a dark side that enjoys the horror of a bad situation. We are fascinated with the macabre and we worship it. Perhaps that is the genesis of war, crime, genocide and the social injustices of the world past. I would like to think that these emotions are evolving out of our species, but they are still part of the human condition. Being in the memorial causes the shame of those feelings to come to the surface and perhaps that is the one good thing to come of all of this misery.

January and I, along with our friends, spent most of the day at the Memorial. Though it was crowded, we wanted to be among the first there and because we had so many family members on that tower, we were able to gain entry for the limited spots available the opening day. We took our time and held each other close for a multitude of memorial services held at the site that day. I found it ironic that though I had died long ago, I was kneeling and praying for the souls of my grandchildren. That is all I had, my only recourse. I prayed that their souls were safe in their Heaven and continuing on in bliss together. That was the only way they could exist and live on.

Religion was still a part of life for many in Aeternum. There are many faiths on Earth and they carried over with transcended followers. Though I was what would be considered a backslider, a person who doesn't express his devout faith often, I still have a measure of spirituality that is with me to this day. I needed it then more than ever, even considering the tragedies of my natural life and its trials I had endured in the past. It was comforting to defer to a higher power and I hoped for some small blessing to ease the pain and heartbreak.

January was also strong in her convictions but this loss had damaged her deep inside. Where my emotions focused into stone-faced grief, hers were all over the map. She too was stoic going in to visit the memorial that morning, but at seeing the tower, she started to weep. I was able to calm her for a moment, but when we went to the viewer to see the location of the names of Jacob and his family, she broke down in utter agony. She gripped the podium of the viewer and put her head down on it in a way that was half-hysterical embrace and half an effort to remain standing on buckled knees. I was hurting inside but I couldn't lose my composure yet, no matter how much I wanted. I tried to comfort her, to no avail. Onlookers were moved and it set off a chain reaction of sobbing, breaking the veneer people had put in place to hide their emptiness.

We took quite a while to gain enough semblance of emotional stability to walk away. We managed to leave the podium display and head down a side path into one of the garden plots to have a seat. We spoke no words, but we could feel every thought in each other's minds. Val and Marge kept their distance; they too were weeping and comforting each other as old friends do. We must have been in that garden for an hour, trying to chase away the hurt.

Numbness finally set in and I was glad for it. We waited to-gether for your sister Jessica to arrive. We had a strained relationship over the years, to say the least. We disapproved of her first husband, adored her second husband who gave us Jacob, and I threatened to kill her third. It caused a rift in our family that sur-vived even into Aeternum. Even though she was daddy's little girl for so many years, our disagreements and told-you-so conversa-tions had taken their toll. We hadn't spoken more than a few words in a decade and this awkward family reunion was under the worst of circumstances.

I was thankful that her ass-hat of a husband Paul did not join her. I don't know that I could have been cordial to him under so much distress. She was cold to me as usual, though she did work up the courage to give me a hug. It felt good, but I had no illusions of a happy rekindling of our long lost father-daughter relationship. Nevertheless, I managed to put all of those thoughts and regrets aside for the moment. I was happy to be her father and glad to have her need me in her life, even if it was just for a fleeting second.

Jessica's eyes glazed over, the windows to her soul attempting to shroud the devastation inside. Jacob was her sole child and he was everything to her. Though seeing Jacob often brought up painful memories of being widowed, she was happy to have a part of her husband still in her life. She took the news of his death and that of her grandchildren as hard as I did. She'd been a recluse for the past year and from what limited contact I had with her I could see she was a shell of a woman. I tried to make some inroads into being there for her but she would have none of it. Therefore, I sat on the periphery of her life and watched her shatter into a million pieces.

The feeling of mutual pain was strong between us at that memorial. It was a shared pain that only a family experiences in a time of loss. This was a funeral in so many ways. It was a chance to gain some measure of closure and take the next day as the first footstep away from grief. The healing would take a long time for us, but it would come.

Near dusk, Ray gave a memorial speech. I hate to say that I don't remember much of it; the whole thing was a bit of a haze. I do remember some kind words of compassion and praise for the bravery of those who helped in rescue efforts. He also made a formal public apology for the lives he couldn't save, confessing that he felt at fault.

The speech shifted to the future and assured us that mankind was on the cusp of greater accomplishments. Despite this setback, we would rise up and do what humans always do, survive and prosper. The whole affair was moving at the time and comforting. My mind was on my own problems and the well-being of my wife and daughter.

Our day ended late that evening under the amber glow of the monument. It would never be dark in the atrium, it was a place built to cover the darkness with eternal light. Jessica and I parted ways the same as we met that morning, with a short hug and a nod, while holding back tears with stoic resolve. Your mother was exhausted and just wanted to go home and to bed. I was too, I just wanted to get this awful day behind me and sleep off the chest pains and headache. I didn't sleep well that night. Nightmares were commonplace for a while, but the nights and days got easier with time. Everything does.

Sadly,

William

Chapter 19: Crossroads
(2084-2087)

1440 Pelican Way

Aedin Beach, Midir, Ups-And-d

∞ #AE-LID: 4d-69-64-69-72

July 21st, 2216 CE

∞ #AE-POSIX: 7780443971

Benjamin,

Almost a half century of positive events slamming against a brick wall of tragedy is difficult for the psyche, even in the land of promise. Mankind was at a crossroads and needed direction. We needed something to take the grief away and allow us to focus on advancing the species, to make progress in the face of setback. As a people, we needed a means to perpetuate ourselves and repair lineages lost due to the string. The loss of life and the destruction put all of humanity in a malaise of confusion and doubt. We were off track and reeling from what felt like defeat, or at least only a partial victory against the string. We were a society that had a hole in its heart cut by the stones and were in desperate need of some new hopes and dreams to fill it.

The people of Aeternum had been talking often with Ray over the course of the year about all manner of suffering and pain. Stories of personal hardships and lost family were not ignored. Ray became a shoulder to cry on and a supportive friend who seemed to care. He was also a remorseful man who often apologized to me for not being able to save Jacob and his family. He was there to console us more than a few times, like a member of the family. Ray eased the pain as best he could, but some things only time and distraction can heal.

A few vocal people did blame Ray and threw a lot of venom his way in public. Allegations were made that Ray could have worked faster to pull more people out or could have chosen other asteroids to be pushed out of the way. Although the claims were baseless, there is always a subset of humanity that goes against the grain of reason and factual data. The worst accusers were the ones that took the death of loved ones to heart, saying that he didn't get enough out in time. Why was a family across the street spared and their precious son or daughter not? Random chance is so very cruel and is impossible for the human mind to grasp in tragedy.

Though a few people blamed him for a multitude of reasons, I was not among them. I felt he did what he could, under the most intense of pressure and worst possible circumstances. I still believed in Ray and Aeternum, as did most all of the citizenry. However, we were all tired, hurt and were becoming shorter tempered. In despair, it becomes much easier to be vocal and expose the shortcomings of a digital existence. Even in paradise, life was not perfect and as we were under so much stress, cracks started to show. In short order, two major issues started to come into public view that would shape the future of humanity in no small way.

We were all grateful, of course, for the gift of eternal life and all of the wonder that had become the hallmark of the last fifty years. Nevertheless, a growing segment of the population was having issues with the lack of children and the ability to have kids. Those most hard-hit were people like me who lost kids or grandkids in the String or other accidents over the years. Now that the earth's population was decimated, the decline of new live births was crippling to the progress and viability of our species. We reasoned that there must be room for maternity in this new world. Ray himself had created life once and technology had advanced much since those early days. Reproduction became the hot topic for a growing number of citizens across the colonies.

A second faction of concerned citizens came from those feeling insecure due to the close brush with extinction. They wanted to seed humanity, even if only in electronic form, out among the stars. Though we had survived the last event, rumors and fears of even greater catastrophes were running rampant. If love is the greatest motivator for an individual, then panic is for a crowd. Fear was in the air and it was contagious. Rumors spread like seeds on the wind, sprouting a briar patch of anxiety.

What if the Sun had a failure, went supernova, or even ejected some of its corona toward the colonies? What if a gamma ray burst from a supernova or another string of debris killed all life on Earth? What if there was some other danger that we could not even imagine on the horizon? These fears, though long on odds, were founded in the harsh reality of our violent cosmos. If we were going to survive on a long timeline, we had to spread out to diverse locations and multiply.

Both movements for change were met with little public resistance. The majority of those who had any stake in the changes were both supportive and enthusiastic. I was also in support of both ideas for a number of personal reasons. My desire for exploration and fascination with space was embedded in my psyche. I wanted to see humanity reach out to the far corners of the universe to explore and study. I felt with every fiber of my being that it was our generation's manifest destiny to become a people spread among the cosmos.

Speaking of children, the need to have kids was strong, even for people that were over one hundred years old like me and your mother. We now had bodies of twenty-year-olds with plenty of energy to keep up with any new youngsters. We already had four children that had grown up, grown old and Transcended. They were living in the colonies and had families of their own to keep busy. However, decades of experiencing empty-nest syndrome were weighing on us, since we were so youthful, vibrant and full of life again. We were ready for something more, to hear the laughter of a child in our home again.

The practical need for children to populate Aeternum was not yet in heavy demand, though there was plenty of open space for growth. Ray had made a false assumption that the population of the earth would continue to churn out babies who would grow old and transcend at a steady rate for eons to come. No one could have predicted that the String of Pearls would disrupt our harmony to such a degree. Those events unfolding as they did caused overwhelming concern for the continued pattern of creating new human life.

The entire system was predicated on perpetual live birth. It was a simple matter of biological humans being fruitful and multiplying, supplying Aeternum with new souls forever. Nevertheless, with mass immigration of those escaping the string, the population was dwindling fast. Instead of the human populace reaching a sustainable equilibrium or growing in size due to better heath and technology, it was going the other way. For the first time humanity was facing issues with under population. This was a remarkable turn of events that contrasted with the early 21st century problem of massive over population.

This was most true given the current situation. Even a full year after the string cataclysm, people were transcending at a breathtaking rate. Displaced people were not willing to face the task of rebuilding homes and towns on Earth. They were choosing instead to start life anew in Aeternum without any burdens to weigh them down. Aeternum was an easy solution to a troubled life and the hardships the string caused survivors. It was a sobering thought, the population drop. Within a few decades to a century, there could be less than one hundred million humans on Earth, at the rate we were going. Perhaps biological humans may be near extinction a few centuries after that. No one knew but the very idea of it was chilling.

If we were to colonize the stars and bring our people to countless worlds, we would need to be able to create new life when we got there. That was another strong argument for allowing reproduction of digital citizens. Planetary systems colonized in the future could be centuries or even millennia away from earth through even modern electronic transmission systems. Both movements, for reproduction and colonization, started to intertwine together.

To grow our civilization and colonize the stars, we would have to be able to build new communities with new people when we reached our far distant destinations. The Milky Way Galaxy alone is vast, its stars outnumbering our thirty-billion citizens more than ten to one. To become true interstellar settlers and masters of all we survey, we must create new generations of human beings. If we were going to make the next big step in our evolution as a species, we must create life at a higher rate, in more places.

The reproduction piece of the equation was complex and involved from a technical standpoint. When Ray gave birth to his daughter Anna back in the forties, he used most of the computing power of the entire farm to complete the task. A football field full of hardware was required to give rise to one digital human being from initial cell DNA generation through adulthood. Though computing and digigenetic technology had advanced in broad strokes, there was still much work required to bring it to the masses on a large scale.

Procreation processes and procedures would have to be discussed in detail with the population. How many children could a person have at once? Would a woman carry a child for nine months or would it appear as if some virtual stork delivered it? Could men have children now? What level of consent would be required to have a child with someone? Could you just order adult offspring and have a child mature through artificial means in months, just as Ray had matured Anna? Could more than two people share their digigenetic code to make another person? With more questions than answers, frank discussion was the key to consensus in how to approach this new paradigm.

The interstellar space travel piece was another massive technological undertaking. Though existing methods for space travel would make the stars accessible, the journey would be long by any standards. We often look upon the night sky and visualize all of the stars hanging mere centimeters apart. They appear as high hanging fruit just out of our reach. However, the stars are trillions of kilometers from each other, floating in an endless sea of void that is as close to empty as is imaginable.

Even more advanced propulsion technologies would have to be constructed to approach just half of the speed of light. Even close, local stars in Earth's neighborhood required decades of travel time at those speeds. Servers, production, fabrication and mining technology would have to be scaled down to fit into tiny interstellar arks to make the journey. All of this space technology was on top of the daunting task of re-building the Coelestium Shuttle fleet. The shuttles were the backbone of our stellar aspirations and the loss of all but one of the original fleet was a huge concern that had to be addressed first.

Ray wasn't opposed to either of the ideas bouncing around the public arena, quite the opposite. The real considerations for either endeavor were technical in nature. Ray would have to put considerable computing power into making the new technologies required for interstellar travel or reproduction viable. As advanced as we were as a people and as intelligent as Ray was, these were still no small feats.

Ray began doing what he always does; talking to the people on their terms and building consensus though open discussion. Opinions varied on the subject of reproduction and its moral implications. The space travel piece was much less opinionated and driven in part by a genuine desire to explore and expand. Perhaps that was a byproduct of our society, most were laymen when it came to astronomy but were experts at reproduction, or so they thought. Ray and I had several good discussions on both of these heavy topics. I felt like my input was valued and it was shared among billions of my fellow citizens.

Ray knew that I was an avid space exploration advocate and we spoke about the opportunities that colonization offered all. The universe is large on an unimaginable scale, and to some extent so is the Galaxy. To make things easier Ray chose to focus discussion to the immediate neighborhood of one hundred light years around us. With plenty of stars with planets in orbit, the subject made some great speculative conversation about where we should go first.

Discoveries of planet-filled systems like Gliese-581, 61-Virginis and 55-Cancri were exciting and opened the door to extra-solar colonization. Those systems were all close, relative to Earth, less than forty light years away. In fact, they were close enough that with further advanced ion-drives we could colonize them by the mid-22nd century.

I was giddy, for the first time in a year, with the thoughts of building new worlds in deep space on some strange alien planet. It offered a fresh start and a chance to get away from the Earth and all of the drama and hurt surrounding it. The dream of colonization became an escape from the current situation that appealed to my inner explorer. I of course wasn't alone in this, but I held out hope that when we started reaching for the stars I would be chosen to be among the first to go. In a way, I was like a kid thinking about leaving home for the first time, for college in a new town or on a long vacation. January too was feeling the need to get away. We hadn't visited our Friday night fantasy village since the String. It seemed there wasn't much left for us here and an escape, even for a little while, offered the respite we needed.

As a one hundred-and-five-year-old family man, I found the conversations on reproduction were enlightening. We spoke with candor about the old world and all of the stigma and hypocrisy surrounding pregnancy and relationships. Much of the old world was built around the need to support children with financial assistance, and the emotional aspect of parenting was often an afterthought, at least for non-married or separated couples. Aeternum had no need for financial obligations and support arrangements. Our talks often ended with the conclusion that we should scrap the old ways of thinking about raising kids. Nurturing, educating and supporting the vast array of dreams of our future children became key.

Personal freedom and choice were of paramount importance in Aeternum. Everyone had the ability to make decisions that would have little consequence on others. Relationships were of free will and old world morality was obsolete in so many ways. Just as birth control changed how the world thought about sex over a hundred years earlier, digigenetics would mark a radical shift for society. For the first time, people could have their cake and eat it too, if you will pardon the old expression. No one was infertile here and children could be produced from any family or relationship arrangement. Humans thought in new terms about the concept of family and now the full evolution of that concept could be realized.

The public debates on the subject were serious with every viewpoint considered. People from all cultures and walks of life had something important to say about the topic. Some held fast to old-world beliefs and some saw the window open for radical change. There were as many agendas as there were options on the table for debate. Fortunate for us all, the public was becoming used to giving space and freedom to their neighbors.

Since everyone had a personal plat in Aeternum, what went on with someone else was their business and you were hard pressed to invade their lives with the security measures in place. Everyone was protected here and that allowed freedom to flourish, no matter how disagreeable it may be for another person. For the first time, humanity had an honest disposition for tolerance and it suited us much better than even Martin Luther King could have dreamed.

Ray began working to solve the reproduction problem in earnest. The expansion of the computing network spread over the colonies gave him greater power to dedicate to invention. The labs in San Jose and on Ceres came to life creating new technology. San Jose looked much as it did forty years earlier, with new innovations expanding the scope of the farm. Ray would need time to build a solution and make it available, but all we had was time.

The world continued debating the moral issues of pregnancy while Ray worked on the technical details for the next two years. The net effect was positive, society was starting to drift away from the grief of the String and the focus was shifting to having children. We as a society would have to work to make Aeternum more kid appropriate as well. Long retired teachers were thinking of building schools and people were beaming with ideas of a new baby. The times ahead were promising for Aeternum and I was eager to see where it all was going to go.

Love,

William

Chapter 20: Digigenetics (2087)

1440 Pelican Way

Aedin Beach, Midir, Ups-And-d

∞ #AE-LID: 4d-69-64-69-72

July 24th, 2216 CE

∞ #AE-POSIX: 7780694341

Ben,

Digigenetics is a simple enough term. Ray coined it in the mid-21st century during his experiments with the digital conception and gestation of his daughter Anna. The basis for all that we are as an electronic society is founded upon the transition from biological base-pair sequences in DNA to a matching digital counterpart. Our digital DNA, DDNA, is our personal essence of individuality and our unique signature for everything we do and are in Aeternum. Digigenetic reproduction involves the complex process of binding two different DDNA codes and generating a new person with an equal mix of traits inherited from the parents. The functional example of this is found all through biology, but carrying it through to the digital age was where Ray made his mark and was the core technology of Aeternum itself.

The merging of the digital DNA is the easy part, taking seconds with modest computing power. The memory space for the full simulation of a digital fetus is the hard part that was going to require research effort and more advanced technology. Each new person starts as a single digital cell and division takes place inside the memory-space uterus. An exacting, detailed and fully functional fetus develops and the child grows and matures just as a biological human baby does in its virtual womb.

Electrons replace sustenance in the umbilical cord, but there is still a bond with the mother involved. It is an intimate experience, every aspect of the simulated fetus relayed to the pregnant mother and she feels every kick. Once the child reaches the correct phase of maturity equal to nine months in a biological womb the baby is delivered with no pain. The whole process ends in the glory of a live, albeit digital, human birth. The baby doesn't even need to be cleaned up, mom doesn't break a sweat in labor and everyone is together as a happy family in under an hour.

Of course, that's the simplest version of birth. Though on the surface, reproduction was business as usual for the human race, there were infinite options for bringing new people into the world on the horizon. The traditional delivery experience with a sole mother, lucky father and an assisting midwife was still going to be for the most part the norm for humanity. That's the way it had always been and I would wager, always will be.

It amazed me though just how much social drama could still happen even with a simple biological arrangement between a man and a woman. Paternity disputes, surrogate mothers, multi-genetic splices delivered in-vitro, the list goes on and on as people in nontraditional living situations still wanted to be parents and sought ways to get what they needed. However, change was coming; the real excitement was in the diversity about to spring forth in the human universe. Profound changes were on their way and no one knew how that would shape society. Everyone was soon going to have options they could only have dreamed of in the past. It was exciting for most and terrifying for some.

Ray had been busy over the last few years developing new technologies for reproduction and interstellar flight. By 2087, the debate over reproduction and digigenetic limitations had quieted down. What started out as a firestorm of controversy and steadfast resolutions to fight for traditional birth by some had given way to tolerant reason. The debate over who could be a parent and how many parents could contribute digigenetics to a child ended with agreement, often begrudgingly, that people were free to choose what suited their personal needs.

What might seem edgy, appalling or the stuff of fiction in the 20th century was going to be commonplace in Aeternum. This new world was going to offer the ability for anyone to have a child and nurture it from birth. The new institutions of loose-knit or multi-person families could have a combined genetic stake in a single child for the first time in history. The mid-twentieth century's high-tech experiments with multi-gene splicing and in-vitro pregnancy were to become obsolete. DDNA technology would make it simple for any pair or group of people to bring a child into the world.

There were going to be very few limitations on reproduction, all technical in nature. From a social standpoint, anyone could have a child now. Any two or more consenting adults could bear a child; even options for singles to semi-clone an offspring became possible. Single people, straight couples, married folks, homosexual couples or bigamist families could all have an equal opportunity to conceive together. The sky was the limit and that made quite a few people who felt persecuted by biology itself beam with happiness. This was equality in the strictest terms and the new culture of free humanity would have to adjust in accordance.

The limitation on propagation would be on computing power, resources and expansion space. Exponential growth is a terrifying concept when it comes to reproduction of an immortal species. Though we could store billions of new digital people in each farm cube, controls had to be in place to prevent the need for use of all of the resources in a solar system to build cubes to house people. Left unchecked with unlimited population growth, we would need to convert all matter in the universe to farm-cubes over the course of billions of years, just because we wanted a few more kids. Conservation of resources was well engrained in the human psyche by the 2080s, so we all understood that there had to be some limitations put in place.

We decided by vote that we would limit ourselves each to a maximum of four children, every one thousand years. On top of that, there would be a reproductive rate limit of two children per person per century. You were free to spread out the number of children you could have any way you chose, or not even have any at all. It was up to you, but those were the hard numbers and it was tough to argue against them.

These new rules meant that your mother and I could have four children together if we chose too, right off the bat, but we were in no rush to get started. Though it may seem like a strict limitation, four children per thousand years, over a million years' time, a lone couple could bring eight thousand children into the universe. I don't even think I could remember that many names much less give them the attention they deserve from a father. That is another conversation altogether and best left for another time.

Though the rules were subject to change in the future, that was the initial decision by the people to prevent a population explosion into the trillions in short order. We also made provisions in the rules to halt or slow new conceptions if our resources wouldn't allow it or if we were to grow too fast. Equilibrium was the name of the game and we did not want to run into problems with overpopulation as we had on Earth, before Ray showed up. Eight children per couple per thousand years seemed fair enough at the time and voters readily adopted these growth-inhibiting measures.

People who wanted to have children, but didn't want the responsibility of bringing the kid up from infancy, could have their baby rapidly matured to adolescence or even adulthood. All of the necessary education and cultural information could be embedded in the new adolescent child. The technology had been used for years on transcended children like Marge's husband Simon.

Though it may seem a bit odd to have a teenager delivered to your door, the concept was quite sound. It was a way to enjoy parenthood for people who were terrified of raising a baby through some of the tougher years. Though as a parent of four biological children, I must say that the teen years have their fair share of challenges. It also cut down on the number of smaller children to care for and educate in the system from a young age. Since most children have few memories of their younger years anyway, most considered it a prudent and wise shortcut. The benefits for the child were also many and it became an appealing option.

Since you could have your new teenaged child educated in a wide range of subjects right from the start, it was appealing to some parents. This was in particular true for those that wanted to have children with a head start on life so they could take advantage of it to the fullest from the beginning. It also had an appeal for those involved in the new colonization effort that was soon going to spread us among the stars as a way to increase the familial population upon arrival.

A full master's degree level education on two disciplines is implanted during the maturation process. Parental-approved lessons on history, art, culture and integrity are also present from birth. Character is something that is only gained from life experiences, but some of the memory engrams of the parents are also transferred to give the child a foundation for their human journey. A parental bond is established through this and the newly emerged teenager is, for all intents and purposes, normal, educated and well adjusted. It's the same bond you and I share, Ben. The reasons for conceiving and raising an accelerated maturity child like you are many. As you grow up and read these letters, I think you will understand.

That said, as you know from history, on June 10th, 2087, Ray announced completion of the reproduction project. The first baby to be born was to be from a couple chosen at random from a pool of interested people. The lucky pair chosen was from Sweden. Now they were residing on Eros over Venus. Fredrik and Dagmar Bjur had wanted a son since 2066, when they transcended. They already had a name picked out for the boy, Ulric, and were allowed to choose what traits the child would have. Dagmar chose to carry the child to term and by all accounts, her pregnancy was unremarkable for the full nine months.

Although Ulric was born months after a multitude of accelerated maturity children came into the world, we all still watched with human interest as the child was delivered on schedule and without complications. Ulric was the first conceived child in Aeternum, a beautiful 3.4-kilogram baby with a head full of thick black hair. The midwife, beaming with pride, showed him to the crowd of onlookers after delivery and you could hear the cheers from the people outside their home. It was a heartwarming event and there is a statue on Eros to mark the occasion. It is a simple yet spectacular glass representation of the happy couple holding the baby aloft toward the sun.

It was a healing moment and a turning point for humanity to look toward brighter days ahead. In 2088, baby mania swept the colonies. Little boutiques cropped up on street corners where people were eager to share their latest baby fashion. Schools were putting their affairs in order so they could open when the first toddlers became old enough to attend. Magic was in the air and Aeternum was alive and vibrant in a way that it had never been before.

Families were showing up everywhere. After forty years of seeing nothing but adults on the street, the sight of a baby carriage or a dad with a daughter on his shoulders took some adjustment. Everyone in the community was settling down it seemed, the parties that ripped and roared for decades were away from public sight now.

People that I thought were hard as nails, or at least cold hearted, were glowing in pregnancy. Maybe that was what was missing in their lives. Being a family man, I couldn't imagine life without my children, it made me somewhat complacent and I didn't understand what non-parents must have experienced. Some people who transcended into Aeternum early in life assumed they would never have any kids and it made them a hardened lot. However, it was a new day and we all had to soften up for our newest residents, many of whom were only one meter tall and giggling.

Your mother and I were excited at the prospect of having some new children too. We spoke about it often on our porch overlooking the pond. We thought about baby names and imagined what our perfect child would look like. We also looked at the reality that life still had a sting to it because of Jacob and his family. Perhaps we weren't quite ready just yet, but soon. Maybe we needed to put some of our affairs in order first, as well.

We heard that the interstellar colonization efforts were almost ready and we were considering taking a leap-of-faith by heading off into the unknown to get a fresh start. Going wasn't set in stone, but if we were to take a trek across the stars, then we decided we should wait before bringing another person into the world. Our future was a bit fuzzy and it could veer off in a number of ways at this point in our lives. We did what we always do, considered the options and waited for the right time to make a decision. With the direction of upcoming developments around us, we didn't figure we would have to wait too long and we were correct.

With my sincere love,

Dad

Chapter 21: Autumn
(2087-2090)

1440 Pelican Way

Aedin Beach, Midir, Ups-And-d

∞ #AE-LID: 4d-69-64-69-72

July 24th, 2216 CE

∞ #AE-POSIX: 7780749539

Ben,

All of this energy for baby making opened up the floodgates of people transcending. New life began to spring forth in droves in Aeternum as children filled the streets. It also became another poignant reason to transcend away from the Earth since you could now have a complete life inside the system. The population was slipping into even lower numbers on Earth and humanity was starting to see urban decay take its toll.

All of the lively uproar over kids made Aeternum feel like it was entering springtime. However, the events we saw set in on the planet Earth made for a chilly autumn there. Perhaps autumn is the best way to describe the coming time, as it is the season that botanicals shed their seeds, as the Earth was about to do in kind. This was humanity's time to sow its seeds among the stars and reap great rewards. First, we had to tend the garden at home. I think it's important to understand how much we needed to clean up our mess before leaving home.

The populace on Earth did what they always do, congregating in cities or seeking refuge in the country. Nevertheless, with so few people alive, urban areas shrank to mere city centers and rural areas became sparser than they had been in almost two hundred years. The cities and suburbs that had once been the homes and offices of billions of people became ghost towns of urban rot. The city centers were still clean and bustling but the edges about town were abandoned, dangerous and habitats for vermin. Land and homes became cheap and the real-estate market was flooded to the point that it was an unmanageable and huge drag on the economy.

The leadership of many nations approached Ray to help with this problem. They wanted to demolish old structures and revitalize the population centers but there was just too much to tackle. Governments found themselves overwhelmed by the need to downsize their communities to match the fractional population that was continuing to shrink. To burn or tear down structures would leave billions of tons of waste and pollutants, not to mention the cost to do all of this with the limited available labor. Even modern robotics was not enough to manage the waste of the debris left over from demolition initiatives. There was still the problem of land reclamation and re-seeding the spaces long since abandoned.

Something had to be done and Ray was quick to offer a solution. For centuries, humanity had destroyed wildlife habitats in a bid for more land to inhabit. It was our nature and though we felt guilty for it, we had little choice but to proceed, as most reasoned. Though much damage had occurred, it was still not too late to turn back the clock and reclaim vast regions of land for renewed habitats for the surviving fauna on the Earth.

The engineering feat to manage a cleanup for the mess left by billions of departed peopled was enormous. Trillions of tons of waste would have to be collected, moved and recycled over the area of millions of square kilometers to clean up the Earth. Buildings, roads, abandoned technology, garbage, it all had to be collected and disposed of in the proper way. Management of the property abandoned or condemned was one thing, but deciding what roads were no longer necessary was an astonishing task. Nevertheless, it had to be done.

Left unchecked, it would take hundreds, even thousands of years for these places to decay back to nature, and that was not acceptable for the living population. People wanted action but we misdirected the focus at first. Once Ray stepped in the ongoing efforts started to take shape. The project would occur in several phases that would take a couple of decades to complete. The end result would be a downsized and green world that was much healthier than it had been in centuries. Humanity would still enjoy all of its modern conveniences, farms, food and fun, but the natural and preserved environment would be restored to a pre-industrial revolution state.

The first phase was the hardest part, deciding how to re-shape the landscape and what to cut away. Ray had powerful analytical abilities and with all of the data he had available, was able to pare down the choices to a manageable load for most national or state level officials to implement. Area planners would be able to choose how they wanted their cities to look after the cleanup and revitalization. Rural areas would become even more private and secluded, with garbage removed from the environment as an effort to clean it all up. As a bonus, the raw materials and riches reclaimed from the recycling would be a boon to local governments.

After the decision-making efforts concluded and directions became solidified for a given area, the heavy hitting started. Ray devised large NMM-equipped demolition equipment that could dismantle large swaths of infrastructure at one time in a safe way. A typical collector could come into an area, scan to make sure there was nothing living in a building, clip away several floors of the building and cart it off to the recycle area. Special devices for taking up roads and bridges were also put into play, enabling a total clearing of a small town in a couple of days by a handful of machines.

Once the infrastructure and structures were removed, a smaller set of robots re-graded the area to the correct terrain that had been there prior to construction. They collected and carted away all of the garbage, technology and litter as well. Hills and valleys reformed and natural water flow became restored in many cases where this activity wouldn't interfere with remaining human habitats. The machines would sow seeds and seedlings appropriate to the area and tend to them as they took root. Ray made every effort to use historical records to restore the land to its natural splendor.

All of the man-made objects from concrete steps to mummified iPhones were brought to the recycle area. These vast stations acted as a temporary store for bulk materials to be recycled and broken down. The large stuff like concrete and brick were ground down into powder and used where needed to help with the geographic reformation efforts, including rebuilding mountains flattened by mining. Bulk steel and other ferrite metals were also separated and smelted down so they could become part of the nation's raw material preserves.

The small refuse and technology was handled in a different way. Ray had developed a technology that became known as Trash Ants back in the 2060s. Trash Ants were small robotic machines that formed colonies in existing landfills to separate refuse into its base materials. They were able to detect even small amounts of any given material, separate it from the trash and bring it to a storage area to be further refined into its core elements.

The earliest Trash Ants were huge successes and paid for themselves in just a few months by scavenging precious metals from the landfills of the day. With thirty years of refinement, they were incredible, durable and sophisticated. A colony of ants could break down thousands of tons of refuse in a day. They had become so adept that they could take an old used tire, strip the metal out of it for recycling and then break the rubber down into a liquid polymer similar to crude oil.

That was the most fascinating thing the ants did. They could take all types of plastics and rubbers and blend them with biomass waste to produce a near replica of natural crude oil. They would churn out millions of liters of the stuff in short order. There was such abundance during the reclamation project they began dumping it back into the ground where natural reserves of oil had been centuries before. Given enough time, effort and biomass, the oil reserves of the world became rich again, if for no other reason than pride in putting back something that was once considered irreplaceable.

For the most part, mining stopped being economically viable as recycled raw materials were now cheap. Many mining companies that had existed for centuries were put out of business, an unfortunate side effect of the reclamation. However, for those closed opportunities others would open in the burgeoning businesses of distribution and reclamation management. Mining itself had died down over the last few decades anyway since the advent of newer advanced materials. For most folks it became a shift just as the horse-and-buggy gave way to the automobile.

The project to re-populate the animal species was also breathtaking in scope. Stored samples from recently extinct species were reproduced using modern genetic techniques. Other low population species from black bears to chipmunks were bred and released back into the wild. Nature was having a reprieve from man and man was evolving away from nature at the same time. It was a winning solution for everything that walked, crawled or swam on the Earth.

Watching the early stages unfold was fascinating for us all, to say the least. I remember large areas of Spain and other places destroyed by the string of pearls became reclaimed instead of rebuilt. The seeders would swoop in and replant entire forests. Coastal areas had their beach fronts returned to nature and small towns disappeared into the woods. Factories and office parks razed from existence allowed the plants and animals to once again rule the land.

Coral reefs were rehabilitated and large scrubbers installed in coastal areas and streams to remove toxins and pollutants. They were there for a dual purpose, to collect the run-off from the reclamation project and to harvest the chemical elements that could be re-purposed. Several old dams were removed to restore the natural water flow. Since the homes that they protected against flooding were no longer there, they were not needed in many cases. Nevertheless, many still stood to offer reservoirs for urban areas or for irrigation.

My little hometown in Tennessee, high in the Smoky Mountains, was not immune to the effects of the reclamation. Most of the homes, my old high school and the little Dairy Queen ice cream shop where I used to hang out as an awkward youth no longer existed. They were unceremoniously ripped away in the middle of the night, taking the lucid memories of my childhood with them. The home I grew up in was now nothing but a dry patch of clay and a few old pipes. Those pipes and the empty driveway disappeared the next day in the effort. Seeders made their way through and added some topsoil along with a stand of pine tree saplings. For over one hundred and fifty years, that house had brought up children, long after my parents sold it. It was no more, a relic that became unnecessary. I understood the reasons why, but it still broke my heart to see it go. I guess it's sometimes difficult to let go of the places you cherish and made you who you are as a person.

Thousands of tiny personal tragedies happened every day as homesteads long abandoned but still cared for were demolished. It was for the best and few could disagree with what was transpiring. We had a collective guilt about the way we had treated the Earth. Although we each felt a responsibility to make an impact, we were poor shepherds of our shared home.

Much damage had been done to the planet, most of which happened in the last three hundred years. Ray's machines would find remarkable amounts of polluted or radioactive soil and water in their cleanup effort. Sometimes this would slow down the project, but with time, everything would get a good scrubbing, even the dirtiest dirt. As reports on environmental damage came in, we were all shocked that we were as in as good a shape as we were, health wise. The land was far more toxic than anyone had dared admit, all in the name of progress and profit. Nevertheless, all of this was being repaired, and though there were decades ahead for the cleanup effort, it was a source of pride for the people of Earth.

In my youth, I would have laughed at all of this as some spectacular hippy-headed hipster fantasy taking bloom. However, a life lived in cramped urban quarters and tasting the smog of the early twenty-first century had a way of waking you up. I had feared that it was too late and humanity was circling some huge drain until the Earth had enough and shook us off like a mud-covered dog trying to get clean. We did it as a people, got our act together in time, and with Ray's contribution, we were able to bring it all back from the brink.

I guess it's fitting that the idea of Earth having a bright future once more made the prospect of space travel more enticing. We felt as if we had earned the right to go out and build new homes with the knowledge that we wouldn't wreck them. Fiction of my day often portrayed the need for space travel as a way to abandon a garbage dump called Earth. Earth was getting a long overdue wash. It would again be a polished blue marble that sparkled like a diamond when we beheld it from space.

Love,

William

Chapter 22: Packing Light
(2091)

1440 Pelican Way

Aedin Beach, Midir, Ups-And-d

∞ #AE-LID: 4d-69-64-69-72

July 26th, 2216 CE

∞ #AE-POSIX: 7780865890

Ben,

It was 2091, the year we became ready to explore the cosmos! Yes, I am a bit over excited about this time period. It seemed to take forever to come, but in reality it was just a few short decades since I had Transcended. When I was a kid, I would watch the classic film 2001: A Space Odyssey over and over again, delighting at the notion that there was so much out there just waiting to be explored. I was certain back then that mankind would become a part of it all, even when space exploration seemed to be far from the public's mind. Though the technology to allow us to explore came ninety years later than its writer had imagined, it was here. It was our time to be what we were meant to be. This whole notion of traveling the stars just feels so natural, it suits us well as a species.

Since mankind first looked at the night sky, we dreamed of touching those little specs of light that danced about and twinkled, taunting us to grow up so that we could hold them in our hands. The ancient Greeks and Romans would declare them Gods to be worshiped and feared with awe. In turn, the men of the renaissance would name all of their celestial discoveries after those same Gods of the Greeks and Romans, giving rise to Jupiter and Saturn and the various names for those worlds we hold dear.

Our colonies carried forth many of those names as a reminder that the wonder of space was a dream shared since antiquity by men and women who had the same curiosity and sense of wonder that we carry today. Humanity is a species of ideas and thought; we yearn to learn, forever on an insatiable quest for knowledge. This hunger makes the far reaches of outer space the perfect university and playground for the ever-expanding human mind.

We as a people stood at the threshold of what was astonishing and profound. We had earned the right to travel among the stars and cement our species as one of who would gain immortality and the safety afforded by spreading out from our little, fragile solar system. We were going to become a people of the stars and bring our unique group personality and culture to places that our forefathers could never even imagine existed. Strange planets under alien suns and grandiose cosmic spectacles were awaiting us. We were eager to see what was out there; this was our time, where humanity could blossom into what it was always meant to become.

The technology to get there was equal in magnificence. The key to getting to another star system was to pack light. A starship has to keep the weight down so its powerful ion engine can propel it to the greatest speed possible. It is a simple physical truth in a universe where the energy required for moving mass through space at fractions of light-speed seems overwhelming. Like in most technological revolutions, making things smaller is the catalyst for the next leap forward. In a way, the technology required wasn't new, but miniaturized to fit aboard a very tiny spacecraft.

Most people in the past envisioned that grand, multi-deck starships would carry us on our interstellar way. Most depictions were up to a kilometer long with all sorts of high tech gear and crews of thousands of people living inside. Those space travelers would have to eat freeze-dried rations and exercise careful conservation of every resource to survive the trip. Some even imagined the passengers being frozen and placed in suspended animation for the long voyage. These would all be musings of smart people that just couldn't foresee the new order of humanity rising so fast. With the advent of Aeternum and the miniature electronic mind, thousands of colonists could fit inside a tiny container and enjoy the good life the entire trip inside a small spacecraft. Just as a nineteenth-century Jules Verne imagined astronauts being shot to the moon from giant cannons, the twenty-first century notion of interstellar battleships gliding through space was just not practical.

Humanity's vehicles of exploration, the Varka Colonization Starship Fleet, were quite different from what people had imagined. Perhaps they were even a bit underwhelming when they were unveiled, with their miniscule size and scale. They were small rocket-like craft, ten meters in length and broken up into three distinct sections. They were shaped much like a conventional cruise missile that most navies of the Earth still had in their arsenals, sleek and aerodynamic in appearance. It was a retro-futuristic, finless rocket ship with straight geometric angles instead of curves making up the hull.

They were about two meters in diameter at their thickest point, except for two circular halos three-meters round toward the top of the craft. These were the communication arrays that would allow a Varka to communicate with Earth during the trip. The entire external surface of a Varka Starship was of a pearl-white shield material to protect it from any debris that might be in its path during the voyage. The three segments of the Varka, the drive, com array and nose cone, were all built to be functional instead of graceful or fanciful, but the notion of them being humanity's first starship made them beautiful. It was like looking at the Saturn V rockets that ferried the Apollo missions to the moon. Those rockets were all function and utility but their forms inspired the imagination and gave them a certain glamour that no sculptor could ever replicate as art.

The first section, the bottom seven meters of the craft, was the main ion-pulse engine unit. This high performance engine was far more advanced than anything Ray had ever constructed. It was the pinnacle of the Lorentz Ion Drive technology platform.

The drive system was also tested to exhaustion before it was ever allowed to become part of the starship. Ray knew that the loss of a Coelestium Shuttle due to an engine failure would always leave a black mark on humanity's mind when it came to the technology. This would have to be the safest engine ever built and the test results were made public to earn back some worn trust.

With the proper reactor, the new drive could propel a loaded Varka Starship to seventy-five percent of the speed of light! That's two hundred and twenty-five thousand kilometers per second, the fastest vehicle created by mankind, by several magnitudes. At full speed, it could travel from earth to the moon in under two seconds.

Though the speed was unimaginable, it would still take a long time to traverse the cosmos.

Though the Varka takes many months to attain full speed, it would allow us to reach many local star systems with less than one hundred years of flight time. Earth is both alone and far away from its neighbors. Our nearest companion star system, Alpha Centauri, would still take nearly six years to reach. Though that seems like a long journey, in the grand scheme of things it's a quick trip next door.

The second section and eighth meter of the ship was the communications array, comprised of two separate rings, three meters in diameter, stacked on top of each other. They were connected to the hull of the ship with four short pylons each. During the voyage, the craft would be oriented so that all communications from Earth came from the bottom ring. When the Varka came about to begin the braking maneuver, the top ring would act as the primary antenna for several months. The entire vessel would have high-speed communications for the duration of the journey and send continual updates, news and synchronization packets for Ray. It would also allow colonists to go home if need be at any point in the trip, though most would balk at doing so.

When the Varka Starship made its approach of the edge of the solar system, the top three meters containing the second and third sections of the ship would detach and travel in a different direction toward the colony site. The main ion engine portion would continue to slow down and then remain in system. Its mission would then continue as it spent its time loitering about to study the host system in detail. It would survey every large body in the area in detail with a small sensor pod attached and relay that information back to the colony for future use.

The communication rings would detach from the ship and then split in two. These components create a two-point communications network in the system. One acts as a hub at the edge of the system, allowing interaction between the colony and Earth, as well as peer colonies. The other ring would take position near the planet or moon being colonized to prevent any communications blackouts between the primary hub and the colony. As the colony advanced, it would be able to launch more satellites into the system to spread its reach and increase reliability.

The third section of the Varka, the top nose cone of the craft, would detach from the communication section and ferry the colony to its destination. That final piece was a two-meter-long shuttle shaped like a giant diamond with its own independent engine system. Inside the diamond-shaped shuttle module was the complete colony that could be deployed to almost any rocky planet or planetoid. The shuttles acted as an ark for the colony and as a means to survey and scout the system, looking for the best possible landing site.

Although astronomy technology had advanced much, we were still in the dark about the full geography of the alien worlds we were going to inhabit. The shield material made it possible for us to build on almost any world, but we still wanted to settle down in the most suitable environment possible, preferring one with saline water as a building material. There were a lot of risks and variables at play, but there were also safeguards in case we made a colossal error in judgment on a targeted star system.

The main ion drive unit was capable of refueling in the atmosphere of most any gas giant or planet that had a supply of hydrogen or helium available. If we made the long trip to a star system and found it lacking, then we could re-assemble the ship and carry on to another system or return home. Although we could be sure of certain types of planets and their compositions from great distances, there was always a small chance that something was amiss that we didn't detect from Earthbound observations.

The drive system and communication array were both marvels but the colony module was the most important piece of the craft. I guess the real marvel of the entire program came from what the colony was. Inside the two-meter diamond-shaped Ark Shuttle, the colony-in-a-box rested nestled inside like a Faberge egg. Everything that an entire society would need to survive and thrive was contained in the unit. There was a complete computer core farm and space for twenty-five thousand active minds. There was a complete miniature reactor with the ability to power a colony half the size of Copernicus. In addition to the main farm, there was a small reproductive cube so that the colonists could begin making babies once they settled in.

The most remarkable part was the on-board fabrication facility module. Only about fifty cubic centimeters, it contained an army of small machines. It housed several variants of the Trash Ants, as well as thousands of nano-robots. A micro-foundry on board could take raw materials and build new tools too. The entire construction was geared to be able to scavenge the material needed from any site and begin the process of growing a full-sized colony in less than a year if the materials were abundant.

The modified ants would source what was needed and carry it back to the foundry, even if the resource was kilometers away. There the nano-robots would feed the foundry and then build new processors or robotic parts to multiply the ant population and make larger models for mining. After enough collectors were constructed, the materials were gathered in bulk and the foundry itself would begin to increase in size until it was large enough to churn out new server farm cubes and even spacecraft. The colony could then grow to full-size, becoming an established safe harbor for billions of humans.

It was a technological version of panspermia, the concept that alien microbes seed a world, multiply, and evolve into higher order animals. In this case, the colony acted as the initial point of contact unleashing a Trojan horse of man-made life on a barren world. Our ants and nano-robots would spread and replicate like bacteria to evolve into a miniature eco-system of working machines. Finally, the colony would grow into a full settlement, teeming with billions of digital inhabitants. All of this would happen over just a few square kilometers instead of the biological version taking over an entire world. In all actuality, the footprint for any new colony is quite small, most are less than four hundred meters squared when complete.

Once a colony got underway, the population was free to live and create their new world as they saw fit. Ray would work with the community to shape and mold a new virtual city and bring everyone onto the same page when it came to how life would be conducted in the new surroundings. Reproduction caps could be lifted for a while and the population density could grow once the first full farm cube arrived. Since the interstellar communication network operated at light speed, you could venture back and forth between Earth and any colony at a rapid pace compared to the physical journey to build the initial colony.

Stellar systems ten light-years away would take ten years to reach via data-burst. However, the trip was not that bad as you were unconscious during the long voyage. There are special "sleeper" skyway cars in Aeternum that you can use to make a trip to another colony. Once you were aboard and asleep in your compartment, the sending communications system would store a copy of your mind and then transmit you to the destination com system in the usual data-burst way we travel. Once you arrived at the faraway colony you would wake up and the only difference you would notice is that you slept for years instead of a single night.

The receiving com array would send word of your arrival and the sending array would receive it years later to acknowledge that you made it OK and to keep your consciousness on ice, so to speak, as a backup. If you took too long to get there or there was an error and your data-burst was lost forever, the sending array would wake you up so you could make a decision. The thought of being knocked out for twenty or even one hundred years, to wake up where you started, is a bit scary, but that's the price we had to pay for safe interstellar travel.

In an odd, but fascinating, side note, Ray speculated another species might use the same means to travel among the stars. Looking through old records of radio telescope data, Ray found something interesting. Back in 1977, humanity intercepted what they dubbed the Wow! Signal. It was a short burst of intense data picked up by a telescope surveying deep space. No further data bursts were ever heard from again, even after an intense search by the world's brightest minds. Ray recognized the pattern as that of a data-burst transmission of a digital being, but there wasn't enough data to reach a conclusion. After the speculation of a discovery, I imagined some lone traveler being lost in space, waking up decades later, back where he started. The traveler never knew that he had stirred the imagination of a generation of knowledge-seeking extraterrestrial hunters on a backwater world.

Of course, I'm glossing over many of the details of colonization, but from my perspective, it didn't matter if we flew to another world in a tin can and ate spam the whole way. We were going to space and I was desperate to be a part of it. Your mother was supportive but a little tougher sell. There was no way I was leaving without her, so I had to make a case for why we should leave.

Even if it were just for a few years, we had lost so much on Earth and felt so empty about it that a getaway was what we needed. A little adventure and a chance to be in the history books was a huge draw. I think your mother saw how much it meant to me and that had some affect on her decision. She too had a need to take a break from it all. Life had been depressing for both of us the last few years and we needed a change. After a few weeks of talking about it, she agreed to go and we decided to petition Ray for a spot on a rocket ship to anywhere but here.

Love,

William

Chapter 23: ups-And-d
(2091)

1440 Pelican Way

Aedin Beach, Midir, Ups-And-d

∞ #AE-LID: 4d-69-64-69-72

July 26th, 2216 CE

∞ #AE-POSIX: 7780914922

Benjamin,

There was a surprising demand to be among the first colonists to leave Sol, our home system. Over nine million people petitioned for spots on the first series of colonization launches. Ceres' Piazzi spaceport had grown to include construction and launch facilities for a vast fleet of Varka interstellar starships. Ray planned to launch twelve missions every year from the facility, each with twenty-five thousand colonists onboard. Three hundred thousand colonists in total would be able to depart each year and begin their long journeys to a new home world. Of course, once the colony was established you could travel via data-burst, but there is a genuine romance that comes with being first there, to make the journey and it had a whole generation captivated.

Who would be the first to colonize Gliese-876 or 55-Cancri? What would it take to be a pioneer on a wagon train to the stars, putting down family roots on a little spot near Mu Arae? Those were heavy questions, personal for many on a deep-seated level. Being in a state of limited contact with Earth and the Sol colonies for decades would be tough. Sure, you could pack up your house along with your entire personal plat and take it with you, but there were still connections with friends and family to maintain. Where Aeternum had made everyone next-door neighbors, interstellar travel made people pen pals again.

There was a price to pay to be a colonist, in time. However, as an immortal, time is much less important than it once was. Time was no longer money, as the concept had disappeared from use. Now time was about being with people you cared about and doing the things you love. So taking time away from those people held a certain degree of sorrow. However, hope for the future and the ability to blaze a trail was all too much temptation for some, like me, and the call of adventure and its new beginnings was too strong to resist.

The odds for getting a seat on the first round of launches was good, I thought, a one in thirty shot. Since January and I were going to go together, and Ray wouldn't break up a family, we were twice as likely to be picked from the pool. We were early to put in our names, so that was a big plus for first round selection. To further increase our chances we left the destination preference unchecked. We were happy to go anywhere Ray would send us. Some folks were only willing to take star systems close to home like Gliese-581, which is just twenty light years away. Not being picky was a good criterion for selection, but it might mean eighty years aboard a Varka sailing through the void.

Ray had developed a list of systems that were probable hosts of at least one gas giant. This was an essential safety element of any mission. At the minimum a typical gas giant would allow the starship to refuel and move on or come back home if there were no suitable terrestrial moons or planets to land a colony. The last thing we wanted to do was lose a ship light years away and have to destroy it, reviving the colonists back home to tell them the bad news. Although the missions were designed to be one hundred percent successful, there must always be that contingency plan in place in case it goes wrong.

Gas giants also have in general at least one moon in orbit to sustain a colony. From our experiences in our little system, we know that gas giants may have dozens of satellites in orbit with a wide array of features and environments. Since the universe seems to have made rocky inner planets the minority, moons are the likeliest places to find worlds to settle on. In all actuality, planets seem like a cosmic afterthought. The universe is predisposed to build stars and most of the mass is tied up in those celestial wonders. The planets, moons and asteroids zipping about are but a small fraction of the matter out there. They are leftovers, tiny crumbs hanging in space that we yearned to seek out and cling to for a new life.

January and I were eager to see if we were going to get the opportunity this year to chase one of those crumbs to call home. Ray planned the first batch of launches for December, seven months away. Not much time to pack up and prepare, but just enough to allow people to do what was needed and say their goodbyes. The initial list of sixty colonies was released and we were all abuzz with thoughts of other worlds.

Ray chose the best possible star selections using the most advanced astro-metric data we had at the time. All of the systems on the list were already well studied and matched up to the growing list of speculated systems in the media. All were within eighty light years and the launch schedule for the next five years was complete. The only things missing were the names for the first twelve missions.

In typical Ray fashion, he called a press conference and the familiar podium appeared. Ray walked out with some pep in his step. He was beaming with pride. Although he had made many advances and in many ways saved humanity from near extinction, getting to this new stage of growth for his people was a crowning achievement. It was also a triumph shared with many great minds that had added millions of pieces to the scientific legacy of mankind over the millennia that he drew from.

Ray was all smiles and his eyes looked as if they were on the verge of tears of joy. A small audience of scientists and astronomers stood in attendance near the podium. All of them had consulted and worked with Ray on the colonization effort. I recognized one fellow from his picture in a book he wrote about bad science and astronomy in the media that I read as a young man, an astronomer himself, if memory serves. He seemed to be beaming too, how could you not be? You could see Ray mouthing the words "thank you" to him and the other scientists for their contributions as he was heading toward the podium.

Ray grasped the edge of the podium, looked at us with a pleasant smile and began his address. He spoke to us about how life is a fight against the universe that started hundreds of millions of years ago on Earth. Though the heavens sent many messengers of doom over the countless eons and almost ended the fragile process of life on Earth several times, including the recent catastrophe, life persevered. To overcome adversity single cell organisms worked together or evolved to become multi-celled plants and animals. They increased the likelihood of survival by spreading out over great distances, sowing seeds and adjusting to harsh environments. Animals changed over time to become more intelligent and problem solving to adapt even further to a volatile world, using tools to conquer nature itself.

The next phase of evolution saw the advancement and transition from biology to technology. In our new form, we could now begin to explore the cosmos and spread our kind to safety. Just as birds and mammals migrated to fill the continents, we too could fill all of the stars in the sky. Ray hypothesized that this phase of our existence would one day evolve into something that we could not yet imagine, something even greater. For now, this was humanity's time to go forth into the universe as worthy and deserving citizens in peace.

It was rousing and we felt a patriotic pride when we heard the words. Though we no longer lived in countries or possessed any real government, we all felt connected. We were the human race and we were ready to take on anything! All of those feelings were nothing compared to the edge-of-our-seat excitement we felt as Ray promised to release the names of the first three hundred thousand colonists.

The list was available to us following the speech. We started going down the names and I was surprised to see Val and his wife on the list, heading for the star system Upsilon Andromedae A. He didn't tell me he was going. When I saw his name, I clenched my teeth as I was a little hurt by that. I guess he was a bit like me and carried my sense of adventure too. It was natural, but I think he just was avoiding having to tell me he might be leaving.

We looked over the alphabetical list for our last name, but we didn't see it. Nope, no Babingtons, other than Val and Valeria. So we ran a search query and the same results came up, nothing. I looked at January, she looked at me, and the disappointment set in. Maybe next year we would get a spot. The odds were good that we would secure a seat in the next few years and a certainty that we would go within thirty years. It just wasn't in the cards yet. Then it hit me, I would be without Val for the first time in over half of a century. Of course, that was going to be the case anyway as I was planning to travel on one of those starships. It just felt off that he was the one going on the adventure and I was going to have to wait my turn. I was used to being the one trailblazing while Val rode shotgun. I guess I was a little self-centered at the time and reality stung.

The next day I paid Val a visit and we talked about where he was going and how exciting it would be. He told me about the star Upsilon-Andromedae-A and the third planet of the system, Upsilon Andromedae-d, or ups-And-d, that was the target of the mission. It was a large gas giant in the habitable zone of a star much like the Sun. At forty-four light years away, it would take sixty years of travel time in a Varka starship to reach it. There were several other gas giant planets in the system and the possibility of finding a suitable moon to colonize was high. All of that was interesting, but I had other issues on my mind than the mission, though Val was excited about it.

We sat down on his porch and had a few beers that turned into a bottle of gin. The conversation turned to friendship and the brotherhood we shared. I will blame it on the Sapphire Gin but we both sobbed a little, like two old fools with broken hearts. We had been the best of friends for longer than a lifetime and not having that friendship so close was going to be rough, even for two geezers used to loss. Like all old men, we puffed out our chests, put a stiff upper lip out and shook hands in congratulations. Although the launch was still months away, it felt too much like a goodbye.

Val had come such a long way since he first appeared in my mind's eye all of those decades ago. I can remember it like yesterday, getting my new patch. I chose all of the varieties of configuration options for my personal AI presented during the initial setup screens in a haphazard fashion, for the most part. I didn't give much thought to his looks, choosing a random configuration of facial features, skin tone and hair. His initial accent was a little too Jersey for my taste so I toned that down to country. The setup program asked me a series of questions about my tastes, hobbies and interests, to which certain compatibilities were included in his personality. Val was also to have a series of strengths that countered my weaknesses and shortcomings, making him a most valuable companion AI. However, for the most part, I had him configured and alive in under an hour without doing much research or consideration about this new person I was bringing into the world. I'm sorry to say that I thought nothing more of him at the time than as a tool or toy, a gadget to tinker with and see what the fuss was all about.

I guess that's how all relationships start, random chance with unknown personalities that just click. He spent twenty years inside my head and we grew to know each other in deep and personal ways. He stayed with me after being freed by Aeternum, always stopping by to shoot the breeze or attend the family get-togethers on Fridays. I guess it should have struck me just how much he became like a family member to us when he chose to use Babington for his last name when he became a full and free sentient mind.

Many personal AIs did the same and I just assumed it was a natural progression. Digging a little deeper, I found the decision on a last name didn't come lightly to the AIs, as it was a personal issue. Valentino felt like family and at that moment, we became brothers, though I didn't realize it at the time.

The next series of launches would be scheduled for later next year, so we would have to wait months before the next list of colonists would be released. The disappointment in not being part of the first batch carried with it a sting. It was like not getting an invite to the biggest party of the year. It was even worse; it was like being a teenager and not finding a date to the prom. To be so anxious only to get egg on your face was tough to handle. The odds were good, sure, but they weren't a shoe-in. I knew that, but I had a gut feeling I would be picked to go and when it didn't happen, it caught me off guard. I guess you become too accustomed to getting what you want in Aeternum, so disappointment hits like a brick. However, that's the way of the world and I guess I was spoiled by the experience over time.

During the next few months, in interviews by the media, people gushed about their expectations of the colonization effort. Though most were along for the ride, they would have some small hand in forming the first cities of the new worlds. They would each leave a legacy and bring up children with new ideas who had never been to the Earth. Though it may take a hundred years to make the trip, the benefits and personal feelings of accomplishment outweighed the negatives by a fair margin. Pride is a powerful motivator for human beings.

Feelings of self worth will always be a part of the human race. In the old world, people would spend their lives trying to attain status, wealth and power, all measures of that self worth. Entire socio-economic systems were built around the need to protect certain classes of people or promote status and wealth for generations. Capitalism made the focus on the rich, monarchies put the focus on aristocrats and communism failed to deliver on the promise that all men are equal. All fell short in many ways.

In a world with finite resources, it was just impossible for everyone to conform to or realize the established notions of full self worth. There were always winners and losers in the game. Every day could be a struggle and the few that reached the elusive goal to be wealthy, royalty or in union still fell short of feeling complete inside. Aeternum took away all of these measuring sticks of wealth and worth overnight. There were no longer riches to pursue or subjects to rule. The real measure of self worth became the goals you set for personal growth or social acceptance.

The need to stand out is part of the human nature and engrained in our spirit as emotional pride. That is why there are so many restaurants, art galleries, music halls and other outlets for creativity in Aeternum. People still hunger for some measure of public acceptance and these are the means to gain that. There are many celebrities in Aeternum, none of them is wealthy, but they all have to be rich in spirit to get to where they are.

Being a first colonist is just an extension of that need for a little acknowledgment and the pride that comes with it. Some, like me, seek adventure and to satisfy curiosity as the primary reason to go, though that pride in being first is still the icing on the cake. It is human nature and a trait to be aware of when you try to figure out what you want to do with your life.

Regardless of the personal feelings of the people selected to be colonists, it was a huge morale boost for everyone. Not since we opened Copernicus, have people been so optimistic about the future. The payoff for the launches would be long coming; most missions had a settlement date over twenty years away. Nevertheless, that didn't matter. The entire duration of every flight would be broadcast back and the colonists themselves would have the opportunity to come home if need be. It was set to be a long and drawn-out affair that would keep imaginations burning for the near foreseeable future. This was just the excitement of the first twelve launches. We would be sending out missions every year for centuries to come. In turn, each colony would one day send out missions of their own, spreading humanity out in every direction at exponential speeds.

Watching the buzz build toward December was extraordinary for us. The summer and fall months flew by and by November we were all at fever pitch. The launch vehicles sat showcased on their pads, shining in the dim lights of the Piazzi spaceport. They were like twelve Spartans ready to go against incredible odds. The public gave each ship a common name over their official designations of Varka one through twelve. Classical exploration ship names like the Nina and the Pinta christened two of the vessels in honor of Spain and Portugal. Varka 9, Val's ship heading to Upsilon-Andromedae-A, was christened the Speedwell. It was named in honor of English explorer Martin Pring's flagship that in 1603 discovered New England.

We had Val and Valeria over for Thanksgiving dinner as a final farewell meal with our beloved friends. It was a warm celebration and we savored our last chance to sit down together and give thanks for the sixty years we had shared, reminiscing on the good times. We had a traditional turkey that January baked in the kitchen and we were just about to get into the sweet-potato pie when there was a knock at the door. I made my way to the foyer from the kitchen. I could see through the glass the recognizable form and face of Ray standing at the door. Joining us for dessert was just Ray's style, I thought to myself.

When I opened the front door, I could tell Ray had something to say and his demeanor gave it away as it always did. I invited him in and before he could get through the threshold, he started telling me that he had some potential good news for me. He told me that two colonists backed out of the ups-And-d mission and since Val was on the flight already, asked if I wanted to take the spot. I managed to get the word "Absolutely!" out before my knees got weak and my blood pressure spiked in elation, causing me to faint in the hallway.

Love,

William

Chapter 24: Speedwell
(2091-2150)

1440 Pelican Way

Aedin Beach, Midir, Ups-And-d

∞ #AE-LID: 4d-69-64-69-72

July 28th, 2216 CE

∞ #AE-POSIX: 7781039275

Son,

It was early December 3, 2091, a Monday morning. I remember it like yesterday. The sky was electric blue as usual in Aeternum on Earth and most people weren't out of bed yet. The launch was set for six p.m. and I wanted to take a few hours beforehand to walk the city and say a few goodbyes. I was in no hurry; I had everything under wraps that needed to be done. January was putting everything in order to shut down our plat. We were scheduled to upload it to the Speedwell at noon and didn't want to be late. Val and Valeria were already packed up and were on their way to board the ship. For me, this was saying goodbye to my home, as I would be gone for so long; I just knew that it would be different if I ever returned.

I left the Porsche in the garage and strolled down the driveway. In sixty years, that's the first time I had done it. It was a lot farther than I had realized. The driveway was much better landscaped and manicured than I had noticed before. There were quite a few fine hedges and even a small pond halfway down. I was always in such a rush on the way in and out of the plat that I didn't take the time to see the beauty that greeted me every time I came home.

Walking the streets was an activity I was accustomed to doing. Though you could drive about anywhere in Aeternum, most people took public transportation for the convenience of not having to find a place to park. The city was designed for the pedestrian traveler and I always enjoyed the post-physical architecture that adorned every building, sidewalk and fixture. Sure, the Sol colonies offered some spectacular buildings and views, but this was home and had a quality that you could only find on Earth.

I wanted to see a few of the gardens that were spots January and I frequented to have lunch or take an evening walk. They were all familiar places and saying goodbye to them made me melancholy. This feeling was at its peak in Church Square, a large and open park with beautiful statues that honored the many varieties of faith and divinity that humanity embraced. It was a great place to visit if you were having some tough times or needing to think through a problem. It always gave me a little strength when dealing with the after effects of the string. I took a careful walk down each path in the square and paused at each display to give it one last glance for posterity.

Of course, every bit of faith has a little sin to counter it, so I paid my final respects to Skip at his bar. Walking around on an empty stomach is dangerous, so I justified a wing and beer breakfast. With half celebration and half farewell, I goaded the few patrons up that early into a round of ale. Skip wasn't usually up at this time anyways and looked tired as hell. Nevertheless, he knew I would be passing through for one last brew and with kindness, perhaps even respect, opened his doors this morning. I thanked Skip for all the years of fun and said I wished I could have filled his always empty tip jar. I think he appreciated the gesture and his handshake before I left was twice as long as usual. Letting go of a friend is always hard to do and he would be missed.

I made a few quick stops by the plats of some of my friends. I tried not to stay more than five minutes or so, just enough time to let them know I was about to head out and to ask them to keep in touch. A couple of days earlier I had a party, one last shindig down by the pond. Everyone that we knew came to wish us well and make sure that we didn't forget to write. It was a good time and we all tried to make it a celebration. It was a life change, something we humans are all too used to making.

As I finished my rounds and noon approached, I took a trip up to the observation deck of the First Tower in the city center. It was the highest point in the city and with its 360-degree view I was able to get a good last look at Aeternum. I glanced up at the artificial sun and my mind wandered for a moment to the thought that the next time I looked up it would be at a view of Upsilon Andromedae A. When my vision cleared from the blinding light, I took one final glance across the bustling city and the Earth that was the only home I ever knew. That damn sun made me teary-eyed, as if I were weeping, and the wings gave me a painful heartburn that felt a lot like loss. I was certain those factors had prompted the physical reaction, as a man isn't supposed to be too choked up about such emotional events.

I made my way back down the tower to the street below and to the gates of my plat. January was standing there waiting for me. She took my hand and I gave her the honor of using her console to close up the house and have it ported to the Speedwell. In an instant, the gateway closed and vanished. Before our eyes, the road to our house melted away and plants of all types grew up in their place. It was as if it had never existed.

Home was now aboard a starship and we walked hand in hand to the skyway for a ride to Piazzi colony to board. At the station, we cuddled up, looking out the glass window in the car as we sped away to Ceres. We descended to the chilled air of the wintery world a few moments later and were on our way to the spaceport. There would be no time to enjoy a roaring fire at the Germanic or a trip to the library. We just wanted to board the ship and acclimate to the new environment.

The spaceport was hopping, thousands of people were lining up in queues to board their ships. It looked like everyone was waiting until the last minute just as we were. I felt happy that there were no screeners at the spaceport, no security or imaging systems to walk through like when I was a young man boarding a plane. We packed lightly so there were no bags to have checked either. Two relics of the distant past I will never miss, terrorist assholes with a violent agenda and cold government strangers that would grope you in the name of safety. The absence of those two influences was an affirmation that we truly lived in a utopia.

It took all of thirty minutes for us to get onboard the Speedwell, or Varka-9 if you prefer. The ship was much bigger on the inside than it was on the outside by a factor of several thousand times. Although we were being loaded aboard a small missile by nano-robotic spiders that would be our caretakers in the physical world, in Aeternum we were walking up the loading ramp to a luxury star-liner.

The entrance to the Speedwell was grand indeed. It was a small city mixed with the grandest Caribbean cruise ship ever constructed. The ship had a long, ten-kilometer central hall flanked by walkways and suites on both sides. The center thoroughfare was open, two hundred meters wide with a view of the stars though a clear glass ceiling. Everywhere were clean surfaces in an array of bright pastel colors, flanked by chrome and wooden railings. Plentiful spaces with grass and trees made the whole place feel alive. A small stream wound its way through the corridor with a small waterfall about halfway through. Canopies dotted the aisles and crosswalk bridges connected different sections. Parts of it seemed organic like a giant tree house built by an architect with a child's mind.

Every amenity awaited us inside, swimming pools, zero-g fun rooms, theaters, restaurants and shops. The entire area felt more like a village square than spacecraft. Twenty-five thousand people, equal to the population size of a small town, were to share the space and these citizens would be our neighbors for a very long time. Ray had built the ship to engender a sense of fun and relaxation to facilitate building friendships through shared activity. It was a brilliant idea in practice but sixty years of being cooped up would be the real test of this magical place.

Every floor was lined with staterooms that led to personal plats, including our own. By the time we arrived and boarded it was almost filled up and ready to go. Stateroom 21-997 was our entryway to our familiar home, perched on a high floor toward the bow of the ship. Val was in 14-101, mid-ship on the fourteenth floor. He and Valeria had gone on home to their plat to have a little private time and to christen the ship in their own way.

January and I did what we always do, found a little spot to settle down and grab a quick meal and drink. Although it may sound like we are alcoholics or just plain lushes, that's far from the truth. Taking a seat and watching the crowd go by, and mingling with the people around you in a quiet setting, is a great way to take in the essence of a place. Sampling the food, drinking the spirits and having conversation is a huge part of the human experience and something you should always include in your itinerary.

Right before the six p.m. launch, Ray announced over the intercom that everyone was aboard the Speedwell and he would begin the process of fueling up the ship to capacity and warming the engines. He congratulated us all on arriving aboard on time. He then made a hilarious and snide comment about Varka 11, the Endurance. She was going to have to endure a delay due to a dozen passengers that were still no-shows. Of course, they would be left behind unless they opted to transfer in to the ship via the com-system mid-flight. Nevertheless, no one wanted to be the ass-end of countless jokes by missing the launch.

Departure time arrived and with system-wide fanfare, the twelve ships were cleared for launch. Ray gave another one of his short but rousing speeches and the media lapped it up. This was by all measures an important event with every moment of it recorded for future generations to witness. We were all portrayed as stoic settlers embarking on a bold endeavor into the unknown with steel-like resolve.

In all honesty, we were all a little nervous about it. We knew it was a safe ride and we were backed up in a couple of places in the system, but still, it was scary. For all we knew the thing would blow up on the launch pad. Fortunately for us, it was just a case of nerves and each ship launched five minutes apart, lifting off with gentle force and accelerating away toward their targets. On cue, the Speedwell ascended from the pad with grace and once clear made way for Upsilon Andromedae A at maximum speed.

The voyage was going to be long, no doubt. However, we were all in good spirits, marveling at how fast the ship picked up speed and made its way out past the Kuiper belt and into deep space. The empty space in-between the solar system and the star Ups-And-A is a vast forty-four light years in length. Although it sounds miniscule, I can't describe just how far that is with words. Until you have traveled it yourself at sub-light speeds, you can't wrap your mind around it. Nevertheless, we were starting our journey and we had a lot of time on our hands to get to know everyone and enrich ourselves with the opportunities aboard ship.

Life aboard the Speedwell was an exercise in social skill development. Whereas the Sol colonies were huge and populated with tens of billions, the ship was a confined space, even for its great virtual size. We all knew what we were in for on the ship and getting comfortable with our new living arrangements was the biggest hurdle to overcome. Personal plats and areas open to create new spaces helped. Getting to know our neighbors added to the feeling of belonging and social standing. Before long, it all became about the friendships we made.

After the first year I started to get that feeling back that I had when I lived in a small town as a kid. You didn't know everyone, but you did recognize many faces. It hadn't quite reached the point of being in everyone's personal business yet, but I felt it coming. There used to be an old joke I heard when I was growing up in a small town. They said that you didn't need to use the turn signals on your car because everyone already knew where you were going. I guess that's true, people learned about one another and learned their habits as well.

By the second year aboard, I had made more friends on the ship than I had in decades in Aeternum. We started a Sunday afternoon football game that drew a crowd. It's funny; in over one hundred years of life, football had no appeal to me at all. It started as a few people having fun and in no time, it turned into the place to be on Sunday afternoon. I was invited to play and I figured I would give it a shot. I wasn't much good at it, but that didn't matter. We were just people hanging out and having a good time.

Just as football became a Sunday ritual, I started a Friday night poker game. No gambling was involved, just chips and a little pride. It started out with Val and two other fellows that had never played before. Word spread and within a few months, we had three or more tables going at any given time. The camaraderie of it all was what made it valuable. Win or lose, you made friendships at the table that carried over into real life. We would get together on our Friday nights, drink, smoke cigars and even throw a few darts when lady luck was being cruel.

It seems like somebody was always coming up with a new way to entertain us. One fellow opened up a small wooded racetrack on his personal plat. Being a car guy, I took the 356 there on several occasions to give her a good run. For several years, we would have sporadic motoring days and all sorts of fun would come of it. It died off for a while, with so many other activities, but on occasion, we would still get a message to "be there in the morning," telling us that a race was set and other priorities would have to be pushed aside.

The mood at these events kept getting friendlier and friendlier as the decades wore on. Just about every imaginable activity or social event happened over the course of the voyage. The ladies put on dances and had their social clubs like gathering old hens roosting. They also staged some fantastic banquets as well. Everyone had an idea or two and we started to enjoy the company of others more than we had in the past. Living in a big city can make you grow cold and calloused to meeting new people. No one was out to take advantage of you or try to hurt you here. They were just a lot of good, down-to-Earth people onboard the Speedwell. Yes, there were a few assholes, but aside from those, it was a great small town atmosphere.

I found it surprising the number of other people who chose to share in the experience for the entire journey. Less than two percent of the colonists opted to spend the trip in cold storage. No one left the ship and went back to Earth during the voyage. Most of those decisions were made in the first five years of the trip. After that, it was smooth sailing.

Although the ship took that full sixty years to make the journey, being in a small space and interacting with the same people reminded me of my experiences before Aeternum. Just as life had become a rut in my twenties, and time flew by 'til retirement, the same thing happened to me again on the Speedwell. You board the ship, make friends and connections, and the next thing you know, a lifetime has passed. No grand adventures or amazing events were any more noteworthy than the ability to say I lived and had a good life here. I will always look back on my time on the Speedwell with fondness, but also with a slight sense of boredom; no matter how many years I spent there, it all blends together. The most exciting parts were getting news from back home, odd as it was.

We got word about the other ships during the voyage. The Nina was the first starship to reach its destination of the Epsilon Eridani, just ten light years from Earth. The Nina only had a fifteen-year voyage to make and concluded it with success and on schedule. They sent a plain text announcement to their sister ships, allowing us to receive the message before we arrived in our own system. If it had been relayed to Earth first, we wouldn't have received it before we landed near ups-And-d. They found a large moon orbiting a Jupiter-like world and put down the colony in a safe and stable environment. Their foundry came online and they were growing as expected, a complete success. It was a relief to know that all of this technology worked from a firsthand source.

Much was going on in the expanding human universe. During our sixty-year trek, Earth launched almost seven hundred other colony ships to destination star systems all around Sol. Some were just starting their voyages and others had already completed their travels. Ray had continued to make advances in technology while the ships were making their journeys through the void. He sent technical updates and new technologies to our ship along with the others via data bursts.

We watched the cleanup and renovation of Earth unfold in those years. It was uplifting to see so much of the planet restored to its natural state in such a short time. Biological humanity did continue to shrink and hit a stable plateau at around five hundred-million people living on Earth. There were still those living in most of the major cities and the Amish were still plowing and farming as they had for centuries. I think the technology-avoiding Amish didn't even notice or care about the events of the last hundred years. It was all so silly to them, patches, Aeternum and starships. As much as things change, some things never change.

Ray had colonized the entire solar system in just a few decades. We had a presence on or near every major and dwarf planet in the system. We had built powerful new telescopes to peer out into the universe and we were able to survey more worlds to populate with remarkable accuracy. Ray had even built a defensive system to clear space debris that might threaten Earth in the future, as another safeguard for the continued survival of the human race.

As the good ship Speedwell neared our new home system, I couldn't help but think back to that morning when I left Aeternum. This had been home for decades and I had become so accustomed to the people and places that were part of the ship. Sure, we would all still have a community together, but new people would start pouring in and I feared we would lose some of the magic we had created. Circumstances were certain to be different. It was a life change, something we humans are all too used to making.

Love,

William

Chapter 25: Midir and Aedin
(2151)

1440 Pelican Way

Aedin Beach, Midir, Ups-And-d

∞ #AE-LID: 4d-69-64-69-72

July 28th, 2216 CE

∞ #AE-POSIX: 7781088756

Benjamin,

The Speedwell had made its approach of Upsilon-Andromedae-A as planned. The ship had spun around one hundred and eighty degrees six months earlier and slowed us down so that we made a gentle coast into the inner system. The shuttle module separated from the drive unit and the primary communication satellite as we approached ups-And-d. The primary com array then detached and sped off to park high above the orbital plane of the system to establish a channel to Earth. The drive section continued on to the second planet in the system, ups-And-c, to refuel in that gas giant's atmosphere. The shuttle, along with all of the colonists, began scanning the orbit of the third planet, our new home ups-And-d, in search of a place to land to erect the colony.

The planet itself was enormous and made Earth look tiny by comparison. Though scale is difficult to judge in space, it just appeared so huge, hanging in the sky. Ups-And-d was a little larger than Jupiter but seemed so much bigger when flying next to it. Perhaps it was the sixty years of our time in a starry void that made it appear larger than life. It was a beautiful planet with swirls of blue and violet streaming about. Hints of taupe-colored gasses made lines around the world, like windswept sandy beaches on cobalt seas.

We knew for several years that dozens of small moons orbited the planet. Many were tiny captured asteroids, a few kilometers across. The larger moons were several orders more massive. There were eleven moons around the same size as Earth's moon. Four were the size of Mars. Three more were the same size as Earth and two had pockets of liquid water and stable atmospheres. It looked like real estate was cheap here and we had many options from which to choose. The larger of the two water worlds had a moderate climate and calm winds, making it a natural choice for the colony. Lady luck may have been fickle at the poker table on the ship but she smiled on the entire expedition with these excellent moons.

During the sixty-year flight, there was much talk of what we should call our new home world and the rest of the star system. Upsilon-Andromedae-A was often shortened to ups-And-A, but we needed a friendlier name for our new star that was going to be our Sun. We also needed names for the four major planets in the system, the many moons around those planets and a name for the companion star that was Upsilon-Andromedae-B. There were twenty-five thousand people aboard and just as many opinions, or so it seemed in the early days. Should we just make up new words for the worlds we would find? Should we continue the tradition of using Greek, Roman or Latin names? Should we choose to honor another mythology and its long-forgotten heroes? Would scientists get their due by keeping the designated names already in the books? The options were endless, but we would all have to make a decision and stick to it at some point.

The ship divided into several camps competing to name the new system. We had a group of folks from South America that wanted to honor ancient Aztec gods, with some divine, yet complex and hard-to-pronounce names. Another clique developed phonetic variations on Upsilon or Andromedae that had a nice ring. Several other ethnic groups threw their favorites in the hat too. As support for these naming conventions grew, each group was to choose seven names that go well together and a brief summary of what they meant. Two names for the new system's binary stars, four for the major planets and a name for our new home moon. Those names would go onto a ballot and we would choose.

After what seemed like a decade of going back and forth, we held the vote and everyone had a chance to weigh-in with their ballot. It came as a surprise to me and to many others that a small group of Irish colonists won the prize. They dug deep into Celtic mythology and chose to honor the Tuatha De' Danann, an ancient tale of magical kings from the pre-Roman British Isles. I must admit, the names did have a pleasing sound and were easy to pronounce, perhaps that had a lot to do with them winning. The tales of romance and nobility tied to each name were exciting and somewhat fitting. They weren't emotion-charged names and were neutral sounding, so they seemed to fit the bill.

The name chosen for our star was Dagda, a benevolent and good-humored god-king. Upsilon-Andromedae-B, the red dwarf star that skirts the outside of the system, was to take the name Morrigan, after Dagda's lover, the goddess of war. The main planets in the system were named for Dagda's children. Ups-And-b, the first planet of the system, took the moniker of Aengus, the god of love. Ups-And-c, the golden-colored second planet, we dubbed Cermait, Dagda's warrior son with a golden tongue. The fourth planet, Ups-And-e would come to be known as Brigid, after Dagda's daughter and poet.

Our little blue gas giant, third planet from Dagda, we christened Midir and our home moon, Aedin. Midir was a son of Dagda who fell in deep love with the most beautiful woman in Ireland, Aedin. In the tale of the Wooing of Aedin by Midir, she was given to him by his brother Aengus to fulfill a debt incurred when Midir was injured on Aengus's land. To secure Aedin for Midir, Aengus had to perform a series of difficult tasks that were the stuff of legends.

Midir married Aedin whom he found to be the perfect woman for him in every way. She was kind, gentle and her love ran deep for Midir. However, Midir's ex-wife, in a rage of jealousy over their happiness, cast a spell on Aedin and turned her into a butterfly. The transformed Aedin followed her unknowing husband for many years thereafter while he grieved for her.

It was a beautiful story and warmed many hearts aboard the Speedwell. That romantic tale felt fitting, as our gentle little moon Aedin floated lazily above the melancholy blue planet Midir below, like a butterfly afraid to land. Therefore, with that, the colony of Aedin was ready to be established with the perfect namesake. We were finishing our survey of the moon's surface to find the best spot to settle.

The Speedwell found a geologically stable area on the coast of one of Aedin's yet to be named oceans. The spot was elevated several meters above sea level and flat. The area was near a pristine silica beach with glassy sand and a small range of cliffs that made a lagoon of the sea. We finalized our approach vector and the ship entered the atmosphere. With no known life on Aedin, I could have sworn I saw hints of sea oat grass back away from the beach as we descended. It was just an optical illusion, a trick of the eye and mind.

We made touchdown on October 3, 2151 and declared the moon a new colony for all humanity. The ship settled down, pausing for a few hours so that we all could take time to look over our new settlement, letting it sink in. January, Val, Valeria and I all walked to the outer boardwalk on the upper-most deck of the ship to peer out at the sea and the land. We started this journey together and it seemed fitting to conclude it the same way.

The air was hazy with a cool fog as we were landing near dawn. We spent the entire morning celebrating in the faint mist. Music filled the air and everyone on board was on an observation deck to get a first look at the sea or to dance in the budding starlight. By noon, the atmosphere cleared to reveal pink and aqua blue skies that were deeper than any I had seen in all of my travels.

Under that sky, we could see several interesting features spread out over many kilometers in every direction. There was of course the silicate beach sand, with a striking frosty blue hue and glassy texture. Dagda's light made each bead of sand twinkle with a silvery sheen. The rest of the landscape was terrestrial in appearance, smooth rocks and sandy surfaces well weathered over the eons. Several large columns of stone offshore jutted one hundred meters into the air. The columns continued onto the beach forming low-lying cliffs and made a safe harbor for our settlement. It was similar to the breathtaking Railay Beach in Thailand back on Earth, just smaller in scale.

Only missing were the trees and shrubs. Nothing was green here at all and we didn't bring any biology with us to teraform the planet. I hoped that perhaps one day I could plant a few virtual crape myrtles along the dunes to make the place feel more like home.

We were all still on the ship at this point and we hadn't begun the bulk of the work building the colony just yet. We did release a small contingent of ants to explore the surrounding area and take some samples of the local materials. The sea was salty with minerals everywhere that we needed to start construction. Here we had more than enough building material right outside the shuttle door to grow our colony.

The next morning, the ship unloaded in just a few hours. The ants put down a stable foundation pad for the colony to rest on. The main server farm cube was unloaded back away from the shore and on the pad first and the reproduction cube, reactor and foundry soon followed. The ants then made a quick pipeline from the foundry to the sea to gather saltwater. By the end of the second day, we had a viable small colony setup and operations were beginning to ramp up.

The actual virtual world of the colony was another matter. We had chosen our landing site and descended on it rather quickly. There wasn't a lot of time to talk city planning, but the location was most inspirational. Most colonists thought of a resort town along an unspoiled coast. The biggest divide among the future residents was on the style in which to model the new city.

During the morning hours, the area had a feel similar to the New England coast, when the fog was thick and a haze hovered in the air. When the sun burned off the mist, it felt much like a Polynesian beach or perhaps something out of Tahiti. The evening hours were quite peaceful and you felt like you were on the shore in Nassau. It had a flavor that was a melting pot of all of the great coastal resorts of Earth, rolled into one location.

Ray took advice from everyone and decided there was no need to compromise on any of the three main visions for the settlement. Ray told us that he would blend all of the ideas together into something new and exciting. Ray always delivered on his promises and we let him get to work.

Now, Ray had always built colonies in private and waited to open them to the public's view once they were completed. However, here, there was no other place for us to go, so we had our first real glimpse at a world created before our eyes. Mid-morning of the fifth, Ray asked for all of the colonists to come to the starboard decks of the ship, overlooking the barren landscape. It was growing light outside and Dagda was just starting to burn off the fog. It all seemed normal, even tranquil and then there was a twinkle of light near the shore. Then another twinkle appeared and another like thousands of fireflies in the night.

Up from the ground came a brilliant latticework of geometric shapes, rotating and merging, growing together in silence. They rose from the sand, meter by meter, forming the shapes of buildings and streets. Out in the lagoon, off the shore, shapes resembling post-modern Tahitian huts appeared over the water, hovering like balloons mere centimeters from the water. Each was linked by an elaborate boardwalk that extended to shore. On the shore, the beach remained untouched as it was, but a wide boardwalk formed on the dunes behind the sand.

Past the oceanfront boardwalk, a village began to form. The buildings were part Havana and part Nantucket with pastel colors, colonial features and art deco accents. None was more than four stories high, but all had interesting detail and character. Little sea-side cafes sprung up on the boardwalk and small resorts dotted the far edges of the lagoon. As each lattice of light completed its formation of shape, it solidified and the textures and color popped out in an instant.

The village itself extended a few kilometers back from the beach. Perfect brick streets connected every building with board-walk sidewalks on either side. Nautical themes abounded all over the downtown area of the village. Seashell-shaped pools were everywhere and numerous surf and sail shops filled storefront spaces. At the southern-most edge of the lagoon, a marina appeared with dozens of small sailing ships docked there, ready for adventure on the sea.

We were captivated by all of this rapid creation happening. In less than an hour, the entire city was completed and every detail was in place. Our beautiful ocean village was a sparkling and happy place that promised relaxation and carefree living. At the edge of town, three posts appeared out of the sandy soil and a sign appeared in scripted writing, "Aedin Beach, population 25,001," to welcome us.

Twenty-five thousand and one, I thought to myself. When did we add a new colonist? Did someone stow away on the ship for all of those years? Then it dawned on me, the last colonist was Ray himself. In all of these years, it didn't occur to me that this would be his home too. Though there could be many active copies of Ray at any one time, he had one spirit, one soul if you will and he was as much a settler here as we were.

The crowd moved to disembark the ship. We had plats assigned and it took a while for everything to transfer to where it needed to go. January and I were off the ship by that evening and found our plat entryway was next to a nice little building twelve blocks back from the boardwalk. The address was 1440 Pelican Way and the neighboring structure was pastel pink and with a fun and funky art deco facade to it.

Our Earth-like garden spot of a plat with its foreboding gateway was replaced with something light and more fitting of the new colony. The trees were replaced with coastal fare that mimicked the look of the foliage of the area. Alongside the pink building stood several round timbers with thick ropes around them, forming a non-descript entryway. A sandy parking spot waited along one side with the familiar red 356, ready to take us to our home. January noted that this was a good opportunity to do a little painting and redecorate the house. I couldn't have agreed more.

I had always wanted to live at the beach, but never had the opportunity. Work always kept me inland for my entire career. By the time I retired, I was so used to the house and my surroundings I gave up the dream of moving to the sea. I would visit places along the coast like Cape Hatteras and Myrtle Beach to see Jacob before I Transcended. However, after coming to Aeternum, I found there was no public beach to visit, Earth's server farms in San Jose, California and Tamworth, Australia were both inland by a small margin.

I felt like fate had dealt me a good hand in all of this. When I signed up for the expedition to colonize the stars, I didn't have any destination preference at all. There was no guarantee that I wouldn't wind up anywhere but on a dusty rock in the middle of a global desert. I was in it for the adventure and pride as well as a chance to start over. The coastal life suited me well and I was pleased with the way this had turned out. Now it was up to me to make a life here. I wanted to contribute back to the community and the friends I had made along the voyage.

Love,

William

Chapter 26: Starry Night
(2152-2166)

1440 Pelican Way

Aedin Beach, Midir, Ups-And-d

∞ #AE-LID: 4d-69-64-69-72

August 11th, 2216 CE

∞ #AE-POSIX: 7782248998

Benjamin,

The year 2152 was a busy one for the Babington family. January and I settled in to our new hometown of Aedin Beach with ease. She was happy again; the depression that she felt when we started the trip sixty years ago had faded with time. Jan was excited and her vigorous lust for life was in full force before we even landed on Aedin. Now she was ready to take on a new challenge. She wanted a baby and I shared her desire to bring a new child into the world after a century of living in an empty nest. In addition to our little nursery project I had my eyes fixed on the stars once again, turning to an old hobby of mine several nights of the week.

Conception wasn't exactly the same process as it once was. The last time I made a baby there was a fair amount of wine and a repurposed dining room table involved. The twenty-second century took a little of the fun out of the process and one hundred percent of the surprise. There were no doctors' offices or any other professionals or checkup requirements involved, just a consultation with your internal console. January didn't even need me to get the process started. Talk about feelings of inadequacy.

Every option under the sun was available for having a child. You could choose everything from gender to hair color, adult height, weight, build. Every feature could be selected as long as it was in accordance with the digigenetic code of the new child. If you were in a hurry, you could make a baby in less than two minutes, which is longer than the time it takes to make a biological one.

Your mom was adamant about having a daughter from the start. Daughters are great; they tend to be daddy's little girls and other than a rough patch in the late teens, tend to listen to their fathers. January was excited about getting to dress her up and all of the other things that women and their daughters do. In the end, it was easy to say yes to a daughter and get about the business of creating her.

The system for creating the child was effortless and as a bonus, there was no need to search for socks or lost earrings when you finished. We both consented to combining our DDNA together and the system analyzed the strands and started merging them. We were then presented with an image of a baby and a representation of a twenty-year-old adult version of our daughter to be.

Right out of the box, I thought she would be lovely and suggested we just go with the default options. Your mom almost agreed with me, but wanted her to be a little taller and just a hair curvier when she grew up. She added five more centimeters to her adult height, the maximum her digigenetic code would allow, and placed more "junk in her trunk," as they used to say on Earth. After that, January was satisfied and I was already thinking of how I would have to beat the boys off with a club when she grew up. Or worse; have to beat her off of the boys with the club. When you're a father, Ben, you will have the exact same issues to contend with, trust me.

The next step involved how to carry the child or if you preferred a late-stage delivery. Now, this was the new big issue in society that still has huge ramifications. Carrying a child to full term and delivering a baby is still very popular. Nevertheless, having the baby delivered the next day or as a teenager is also appealing and has quite a few advantages. Your mother was adamant about being pregnant again for some reason that I will never understand. I think that in the hundred years since her last pregnancy she forgot all of the discomfort that comes along with it. Being a supportive husband sometimes means doing what your wife wants no matter if there is a better option available, so I agreed and she was set to become pregnant the next time we made love.

Nine months and a day later, your older sister Morgan arrived in the easiest delivery I had ever witnessed. Your mother did what most women in the twenty-second century did, had a midwife in attendance to catch the baby and organize the ordeal in its entirety. Since there were no longer complications or even much mess involved in delivery the role was symbolic compared to what it used to be two centuries ago. Nevertheless, having someone there to orchestrate the birth was valuable and took all of the pressure off me, which was a godsend.

Morgan was a gorgeous baby, just like the console showed us she would be. It was satisfying to have a baby in the house. We had spent the pregnancy preparing the home, building a nursery room and making it ready. The duties of being a father again after so long proved to take a bit of an adjustment, to say the least. Although the crying and diapers are often a complaint of parents, that didn't bother me. Having another person in the house to care for when you had no one other than your wife to answer to for so long was the trick. Nevertheless, like all new dads, I adjusted and life for me was great as a family man.

During your mom's pregnancy, Val and I started stargazing every few nights as a hobby. We would make our way up to the top of the cliffs toward the northern edge of the village where it was dark. The light pollution of the town was blocked by the rocks and it gave us some great night sky views. We had built a small platform and mounted an optical telescope so that we could observe the stars and the other planets in the Dagda system.

Word of our project started to spread and in two months' time, we had a small astronomy club gathering with us every night. Thirty people joined by the end of six months. All were interested in science and space, hoping to make some contribution to the colony as a whole. It became a great meeting spot for like-minded people to explore our little section of the galaxy. A couple of months later, we petitioned Ray to build a full-scale observatory in the spot to do more serious research.

Although the main drive unit of the ship was on a mission to survey the system, it would take decades to complete and didn't offer the same satisfaction as direct human observation. Ray worked with us to build a fine observatory structure in Aeternum on the cliff top, with a complex sensor array in the same place in the physical world. The two were joined together so we received real-time visuals from the non-light-polluted telescopes situated in the real world. We were able to make observations of the many planets and moons in the system, though some would be out of sight for several years to come.

The observatory itself was rather ornate, with several classic domes and a large main building styled like the village. It reminded me of the classy Griffith Observatory in Los Angeles, but finished out in Aedin Deco. We thought it was majestic on the cliff-top with the exterior lights shining on the building when the domes were not in use. It made a great place for the club to meet and was an instant landmark for the village.

Our little club made detailed maps of the other moons orbiting Midir. We gave them names from Celtic mythology in accordance with the naming conventions we voted for on the ship. For example, the other water-covered Earthlike moon in orbit we named Lugus. The desert-like Earth-sized analog we named Taranis, both of the names fitting within the Tuatha De Danann. There were many characters in the Celtic pantheon to choose from so it was quite easy to find a fitting name for just about any world we discovered.

The club grew in number each year we had it in operation. Before we knew it, we had a small radio telescope in service and a full-spectrum observation platform in orbit. The colony offered a lot of support for our club too. We had a club football team, though we didn't win often, and most people in town honored us for our endeavor. In time, we became pillars of the community. We were respected for our dedication to learning and research, along with our willingness to teach others. Being a member of the club was a badge of honor that we wore with pride.

Although Val and I founded the club, we were not greedy with its leadership. We often voted the brightest or most dedicated among us to be the president of the club for a year. Although the title sounds impressive, the duties of the president were light. The club president set the agenda for which object to study and was allowed to choose the name for any discovery made. I was the president for the first two years and for the years 2158 through 2160, Val held it.

These were good times indeed. In 2061, we celebrated our tenth anniversary in the colony with an all-night fireworks display over the sea. We were thriving, the population had increased to 48,742 and we were growing more each day. The village was still small, and its expansion slow on the long coastline. New attractions and innovative uses of the land developed for the benefit of all. We held regular fairs and festivals to keep the atmosphere vibrant.

Everyone from the ship was exploring a new phase of life here. There was a huge baby boom in Aedin Beach. People that stayed single through the trip were getting married and starting a family and the long-time couples were starting families, as well. As a group of settlers, we had made Aedin our proud home and we were all working to make it the best place we could for our children.

In our home, we had your sister Morgan blossoming into a beautiful school-aged girl and your brother Kenneth just learning to walk. Time was flying by for everyone. January was a happy mom and made it look effortless, even at one hundred and eighty-six years old. Back when she was younger, she was always worried about the dangers her kids would face in the real world. With the comfort of village life and the safety of Aeternum, she was much more relaxed this time around. Not needing to take your kid to the doctor's office was amazing enough, but we also didn't have to worry about someone snatching our child, the little tyke being hit by a car or some other unimaginable horror. There was no real worry or danger. This made raising kids more joy than worry.

On Christmas day in 2061, Val and Valeria had a son whom they named Anthony. They chose to forgo the task of carrying the child to term or even raising him from an early age. Many of the AIs that became human didn't have the same hang-ups that biological origin humans did when it came to childrearing. Anthony was born sixteen years old and already had one advanced degree in astronomy and one in music. Since his arrival was so abrupt, January and I always joked that Anthony must have been Valeria's gift under the tree that year wrapped in a big box with a bow on it.

Although he was well educated from the start, Anthony was unusual in that he didn't have an understanding of who his parents were and what being part of a family meant. He lacked the experiences of a child bonding with his parents and the feeling of a shared heritage. As a normal kid, you grow up hearing stories from your parents about their lives. You experience shared situations together as a family that go into forming who you are as an individual and you pass that collective awareness down to your children. Anthony had little connection with his family because he missed all of that and the influence of the role models his parents would have been on him. Most of the accelerated-growth children had that parent-child bond from the start; the memory engrams from the parents made up for the lack of a childhood. Anthony was that rare case where that process was lacking and it was a sad flaw in the concept.

Val and Valeria knew this was a potential risk going in. Although Anthony had memory engrams from both of his parents, they were random pieces of conciousness without any real frame of reference. The memories could be confusing without the child knowing what they meant or when taken out of context. Val had been reading of a growing trend on Earth and the other colonies of writing their child a series of letters or recording a series of videos to fill them in on all the details of their parents' lives. Val reasoned that although it was impossible to make up for sixteen years of absence in a child's life, it was worth a try. He set forth writing letters and building a biography, trying with desperation to fill in many of the gaps and voids in his child's inherited memory segments.

This technique seems to work well on accelerated growth children as they are born with perfect photographic memories that endure for several years afterward. Perhaps it's because they didn't fill their young minds with a lot of meaningless or confusing information for all of those years. Perhaps an accelerated mind is somehow superior as every stage of development is so controlled. Nevertheless, there is a difference and it offers a unique opportunity for the parents to help the child understand its place in the world.

Val and Valeria both took up this new tradition of writing to their children and it served them well. Though the process to write the letters and for Anthony to in time read them was slow, the odd and confused young adult was able to make sense of all the images floating in his head. Many nights of long talks filled in further gaps and the bonds that were missing formed. Anthony learned to appreciate his parents and began to want to follow in Val's footsteps as he learned more about his father. The transformation in Anthony was mindboggling. So too were the attitudes of the other children who had experienced similar sessions of sharing with their parents. So much so that within a few short years the writing and sessions of dialog became a vital step in the process of having a growth-accelerated child.

Anthony was a talented young man and became a favorite at the astronomy club. He and Val would show up most nights of the week to observe the sky, make new observations and revisit old ones. They became close and it made me long for the day when Kenneth grew up enough for me to bring him to the observatory so we could look at the stars as father and son together.

Though I didn't have a son old enough yet to look up at the sky with me, Morgan was curious about the cosmos. She was fascinated with the many moons in the sky and the big bright planet of Midir that sometimes fills the sky. She even had me come to school one day for show-and-tell to talk about space, Dagda and Sol. For the little ones in the classroom Earth was a faraway land full of mystery and intrigue. They were all captivated by tales of trees, giraffes and butterflies. These were all things that they didn't get to see much of on Aedin.

Space is an amazing place and full of wonder for people young and old. I guess that's why I kept going back to the observatory night after night, staring at the stars and dreaming about the possibilities. Space is infinite for all we know and there was no limit on what humanity could achieve. I was excited, thinking about all of the mystery that is still out there, so I just had to keep looking up.

Always looking up,

Dad

Chapter 27: Red Pixels
(2166)

1440 Pelican Way

Aedin Beach, Midir, Ups-And-d

∞ #AE-LID: 4d-69-64-69-72

August 17th, 2216 CE

∞ #AE-POSIX: 7782757942

Benjamin,

February 3rd, 2166 is a date that went down in the books as one of the most significant, yet at the time, most understated events in human history. It's the reason why Valentino and I are as well known as we are and why Aedin Beach is far more than a footnote for humanity. However, when it happened, we were all just standing around scratching our heads in confusion. I guess that is the manner in which all history-making events happen, with little warning and often unbeknownst to the observers at the time.

The astronomy club was abuzz with having our first chance to see Brigid's largest moon, Eriu. It circles the fourth planet in the system in a way that made it hard to get a good visual. It had always been at odd angles or the wrong place for the decade and a half we had been operating the observatory. The main drive unit of the starship hadn't even finished surveying the second planet in the system, Cermait, yet, so we were flying blind on what Brigid had to offer. Because of this, we were unable to image it in any detail and knew almost nothing about the moon that was the size of Mars.

I arrived at the observatory late in the evening; the kids had me tied up helping with homework. We knew very little about the planet Brigid's fifty-four moons and I was anxious to get one of the first glimpses of Eriu as it came into view. I pulled in around ten o'clock, taking the first-row parking spot that proclaimed, "Reserved for Club President." I had to take the job for the year, with reluctance. That's what happens when there is a club meeting that you miss and everyone decides it would be hilarious to nominate and vote you into office as a punishment for not showing up. Yes, we geeks sometimes have a strange and malicious sense of humor.

Val and Antonio were busy adjusting all of the observation assets to observe the large moon. The moon Eriu was mysterious and we were hoping to see an analog to Aedin, though it was not quite in the habitable zone of Dagda. We were curious to see if the moon was active in its geological aspect, if there was water ice or anything else interesting of note. We had surveyed the many moons of Midir but this was our first time receiving good data for Brigid's flock.

The first images started to come in and the whole club was there waiting to see the first pictures on the large ten-meter screen we had setup in the astro-metrics lab. Val lined everything up beautifully and the first picture was a breathtaking true-color image. Val looked it over on his large monitor and then his eyes squinted. He turned to me and then back at the image.

He pushed the picture out to the monitor and everyone else did a double take to Val.

Amanda, one of the club members, made the obvious comment, "You have a couple of pixels stuck there, Val, can you clean it up?"

That's when Val, still looking over his monitor, told us that all of the images so far had the same issue. Plain as day, it looked like there were a few bright red pixels forming a small rectangle on the northern continent. The planet itself was covered in a rusty regolith with pockets of brown icy mud, shimmering deserts and chunks of white water ice strewn about. The red spec was a huge distraction from the rest of the image and impossible to miss.

"What the hell is that, a volcano?" I asked Val.

He told us to hold on a second while he brought the orbital array around for a better look at that spot. That scope gave us one-meter resolution for the moon's surface and could provide the detail we needed. A few minutes later Val had a zoomed-in picture of the red pixels and we could see it was not an image sensor error or lone volcano. The object was rather large, over six kilometers long and three kilometers wide. It was a perfect rectangle shape and was about ten meters high off the ground. It was flat on all sides and a brilliant pearlescent red color. The thing appeared to be an enormous luminescent building on the surface, but there were no roads or other structures anywhere else.

About that time, Ray entered the room. He had been watching the images come in and his curiosity was getting the better of him. I looked over at Ray and told him we found something unusual, but didn't want to jump to conclusions just yet. He agreed, saying for all we knew, in the randomness of space this was just a giant geological formation or a trick of the light. No one had put all of the elements together yet but it was starting to sink in that it may be an artificial structure and there would be huge ramifications if it were. Whatever it was, it had to be investigated.

Ray was quick to recall the Speedwell's drive unit to head to Brigid to investigate the structure on Eriu. It would take about three days for the ship to move from Cermait and into Eriu's orbit, so we had time to start going over the data. Ray joined us in the astro-metrics lab to begin dissecting the images bit by bit. As the night wore on, we were able to get full spectrum data on the structure and we monitored it for any electro-magnetic radiation.

The astronomy club was still going at it even into the early morning hours. Most of the members were still there, fighting fatigue and more concerned with the discovery than eating breakfast. A couple of the wives and husbands got wind of the discovery when their spouses didn't come home and were kind enough to bring up some food for the team. The entire village awoke that morning to the rumors floating around that we had found something on Eriu. Ray was quick to let everyone know the status of what we knew and was willing to answer any and all questions as we learned more.

We spent the next two days trying to analyze the object and the surrounding environment of the moon. Ray split himself up to be with the two teams we had formed, one to study the object and one to go over the moon's data. The moon itself was nothing special. It had a high iron content on the surface with periodic ice-melting events that caused the water to pool and re-freeze. Its thin atmosphere allowed the water to stay put in small quantities and it may have had a frozen ocean at some point in the distant past. In almost every way, it was a Mars twin.

Once the drive unit arrived, we were able to obtain scans that were more detailed from orbit. The object was not naturally occurring as it appeared to have been placed on a prepared pad that was around ten meters larger than the object's base. No sand or dust collected on or around the object, it was clean as if someone had just washed it. There were no radio or laser emissions coming from the object, but there was a detectable power source and a small amount of heat emanated.

Ray and the team concluded that the structure was artificial as the geometry was too perfect and there was a power source. The rectangle had a two-to-one ratio for the length and width. It stood exactly one three-hundredth the width in height. The sealed surfaces seemed to have no flaws whatsoever. Ray also noted that one of the early formulations he had engineered for the shield material was pearlescent red in color, just like the structure. He didn't utilize that particular shield recipe because it wasn't as stable under extreme high intensity terahertz radiation in a specific, narrow band. The white formulation did not suffer this flaw and became the standard used on everything.

The evidence was overwhelming that we had neighbors next door and no one knew what that was going to mean for humanity. For centuries, we had dreamed of alien contact but all of our searches had come up empty. We watched and listened to the skies and never heard a word from anyone. You would often hear tales of people being kidnapped by little grey men, but there was never any proof of contact that could be verified. Nevertheless, here we were forty-four light-years away from Earth and looking at what had to be an object of alien origin.

Ray had long studied accounts of supposed alien encounters and never could piece anything together that would be of help in this situation. Various governments of the world had drafted first contact plans for situations where we made contact, but this was a much different situation than any they could envision. None of those plans took into account humanity being in electronic form and light-years away from Earth. The only option for Ray was to make educated guesses and speculate like the rest of us.

He reasoned that they must be as advanced if not more so than humanity. They used shield material that was less complex than human technology and the heat signature came from what we assumed to be a more primitive power source. Perhaps they didn't put as much focus on technology as we did and good enough was just that.

Ray surmised that they could have become aware of our arrival in the system over a decade earlier. Since they had not yet acted and seemed to ignore the Speedwell's drive unit in orbit scanning them, they may not have much interest in us. Perhaps they were waiting to see what our intentions were or if we posed a threat. There was just too little information available and lack of it could lead to fear, given enough time. Ray had to get ahead of the rumors and take the lead on the conversation.

We had a large amphitheater at the back of the village we used for plays and concerts. It was large enough for everyone in town to attend and was used as a sort of makeshift town hall when needed over the years. Ray called a meeting for the following morning and most of the residents planned to go.

When Val and I arrived at the event, we were escorted by Ray to the back of the stage. Since Val made the discovery and I was the current president of the astronomy club, he felt it was important that we were there in front of the town to talk about what we found. I was hesitant at first; I had a fear of public speaking in my youth that still persisted into my one-eighties. Ray and Val both calmed me, and I knew this came with the job and I had to do it.

We took the well-lit stage and Val and I sat in two of the chairs off to the right of the familiar podium. It dawned on me that in the last century, I had seen Ray speak live a handful of times, but this was the first time I was behind him during a speech. I had never been a main component of the subject of the speech before and that position carried a little novelty with jittery nerves mixed in for good measure.

The auditorium quieted down to a hush and Ray introduced Val and me to the crowd. He brought up a large screen behind us with an image of Eriu and explained where the moon was located as well as the planet composition and its surface details. He then zoomed in to show everyone the object and gave me an impromptu segue to talk about it and what the research team had learned.

I was now more nervous taking the podium and my eyes lost focus for a moment. I stood there like a fool and then I saw January in the front row looking right at me. Seeing her made me more re-laxed and I started talking to the audience as if I was speaking only to Jan. I gave a brief synopsis of how the discovery occurred, noting Val as the first person to see it. I spoke about what we learned, that the red object had the potential to be artificial in origin and that it was under its own power.

Most of the crowd was silent, but there were a few gasps and a couple of people started to cry, which caused some of the young children to start to cry. Val joined me at the podium and asked them to regain their composure, assuring them that it was not a threat. We told them that we were in no danger, that we suspected the aliens, if they were there, knew about us being here for over a decade and had done nothing to indicate ill intent.

Ray made his way up to the podium and that seemed to calm the adults, but the kids kept on wailing. Many people looked to him for leadership and comfort, so it was natural for him to be there in this new time of need. Ray continued his presentation, Val and I sat back down.

Ray stated that he believed we should be cautious but cordial with our potential neighbors. We should attempt to make contact and offer an olive branch to them to show we were peaceful people. If they should choose to ignore us or not wish to make a relationship, then we would quarantine access to Brigid and give them space. If the unthinkable happened, we were not defenseless, though we were facing the unknown in every measure of the word.

He was quick to caution that we should not put too much stock in talk of violent self-defense or building offensive weapons. We had moved past that stage of our civilization and unless we were threatened, there was no need to do anything drastic. However, Ray did advise placing the colony's reactor and habitation cube inside the shuttle as a precaution. He ordered the Speedwell drive refueled and that it wait in orbit in case we needed to make a hasty departure. We could have the whole village in orbit and high tailing it out of the system in under an hour if things went wrong. The thought of fleeing our home of over ten years without a fight didn't sit well with me. However, I kept that to myself and accepted the notion that retreat might become unavoidable.

He outlined a plan to build a small research craft that we could use to visit the site of the red object and attempt to make contact. The foundry was capable of building new spacecraft and we had received several useful technology updates from Earth over the last few years. Ray planned to form a research team consisting of me, Val and twenty-two other people who would make an expedition to the site in ten days time. Although I would have liked to be asked if I wanted to go beforehand, Ray knew that I would jump at the chance and went ahead and volunteered me. I was happy but nervous, as this was huge and I didn't want to screw it up.

After the town hall concluded, there were the usual objections and other dissenting opinions from some in the crowd, but overall people trusted that Ray knew what he was doing. Although he was most often right, Ray sometimes miscalculated and because of that, he was just as human as the rest of us. This was going to be a risk and the entire colony was on the line, if not the human race in totality. I too felt he was right; we had to reach out and put our best face forward. This was something we had dreamed about for a very long time and it seemed ludicrous for us to not make an attempt to speak to them if possible.

Those villagers that called for us to display a show of force or to just leave them alone were not seeing the big picture. At the rate humanity was expanding, we could run into another structure like this, if there were others. No other colony had reported anything like this, but information traveled slowly at light speed. At the time, we had to assume we were the first, and it was our responsibility to become ambassadors of the human race.

An exploration mission in ten days seemed quite rapid, but the cat was out of the bag that we were aware of the red structure and we had to act soon. Most of the scientists that lived in Aedin Beach were members of the astronomy club and already volunteering to go on the expedition. We had many good people to choose from and I worked with Ray to build a team of bright people to go out and meet our new friends. There were many activities to plan and execute over the next few days, but I was up to the task.

January was supportive and I think the kids were proud to have their dad be a part of it. Still, I feared for their safety and was relieved that they would be on the shuttle as a precaution. All of the team members would have a fresh copy of our minds in storage on the shuttle as a precaution as well, so I felt safe in the face of uncertainty. These failsafe measures made it easy to be brave, but as a human, you still have to contend with fear as a side dish to go with the main course of adventure. We are just hard-wired that way. I came to Aedin seeking adventure and I was about to get a huge dose of it.

Love,

William

Chapter 28: Grannus
(2166)

1440 Pelican Way

Aedin Beach, Midir, Ups-And-d

∞ #AE-LID: 4d-69-64-69-72

August 17th, 2216 CE

∞ #AE-POSIX: 7782811003

Benjamin,

The expedition to Eriu and the red object was fast approaching. Ray and I had begun assembling the team to make the voyage and had quite a few good candidates in the running for the positions available. Ray was completing a small expedition spacecraft for the mission and had several new technologies in the works to assist our endeavors. Val was busy working with his son Antonio to build a set of protocols and media for various first-contact scenarios. The village was loading up on the Speedwell, but we all hoped that it was an unnecessary precaution.

The astronomy club had grown to over two hundred people in the last few years; we had an eclectic mix of intellectuals, teachers, doctors, scientists and dreamers. With the many good people, smart people, in the group to choose from, selection of the expedition team was difficult. I had my favorites among the group, old friends from the Speedwell and new friends that I enjoyed with genuine zeal. However, this was no time to play favorites and getting good representation from the scientific disciplines was crucial to success.

Ray asked that I choose two additional people to complete the group that would approach the object. We had leadership in the role of Ray, who was the obvious head of state and most capable of us all by a large margin. Ray would be the head of the quintet that was to be known as the contact team. Val was the initial discoverer of the object, the man writing the contact protocol and a hell of an engineer too. It was fitting that he go on this mission as part of the team.

I understood that holding the position of club president carried the responsibility to meet any potential aliens; it was a joke clause that Val and I wrote in the original club charter years ago. I had a lot of life experience, joy, pain and loss and I was firmly in the dreamer camp as well. Nevertheless, I am by all measures an average man and I wasn't quite sure that those traits qualified me for this serious task. However, Ray was adamant that I was aboard and part of the contact team. Maybe it was because I was a biologically born human and carried that perspective with me for two hundred years. Whatever the reason, I was excited to be on the team; I was living a dream.

For the rest of the team, we took an analytical approach for selection based on needed role. We wanted to have one doctor, a biologist whose knowledge might come in handy if we encountered an alien species that was radically different than we are. That person needed to be someone who could think outside the box and had an interest in exo-biology. We had no idea what we might encounter and thought it was a good idea to have someone that could potentially understand a life form alien in nature to the common person.

The second individual it was decided should be an anthropologist. We needed someone who could look at an alien culture or behavior with an objective eye. Alien social structure, instinct and action could be quite different from ours, so having a professional perspective was critical. These two individuals would become part of the five-person contact team while we would rely on twenty others aboard the expedition craft for further assistance.

A couple of names came to the top of the list for the contact team. For our exo-biologist, Dr. Jai Patel was an obvious choice. He was a favorite regular at the observatory and had been a club member for almost a decade. He had been one of the first to enter Aeternum in the 2050s after a ninety-year life and career in biology on Earth. Jai spent most of his career studying insects, but also had a passion for marine life and wrote several well-respected books on both subjects. He was a gentle and soft-spoken man with a meticulous nature and eye for minute variances in specimens. Jai seemed like the perfect candidate and was eager to join the contact team.

Our selection of an anthropologist was a little harder to nail down. Although there was no life in this system, there were several professional anthropologists living in the colony. Like the rest of the scientists, they had hoped to find diverse ecosystems to study through the colonization effort. All were quite disappointed when we found that the Ups-And-A system was lifeless and the planets barren. With this new discovery, all of the scientists were coming out of the woodwork to get the opportunity to study and learn.

Although the field had five good candidates, we narrowed down the list and made a decision. Dr. Silvia A. Forrest became our first choice for the mission after we came across a paper she wrote on the social evolution of Sub-Saharan African tribes. She seemed to have a real understanding of social structures and a clear analytical mind that was refreshing and objective. Silvia was an oddity compared to the stereotypical scientist. She was extroverted and had a flair for being a bit flashy. She always styled her hair in some exotic fashion and was happy to be the center of attention wherever she was. Although it may seem she had to be arrogant, she was actually quite humble and pleasant to be around. She had a short, yet impactful, career on Earth and transcended in her late thirties so that she could study the human condition in Aeternum.

The contact team selections were difficult enough to make, but I have to say getting the other twenty individual team members together was no small feat either. We were running down to the wire, but I felt very fortunate to have the resources and people that I had out of our little village from which to choose. Some of the researchers, like Antonio, volunteered to stay on Aedin and assist from the observatory. That made things a little easier, but getting the team right took most of the week to complete. I was pleased with the final list of explorers, all top-notch people and committed to making the mission a success. The role assignments were set just three days before launch and I was able to focus on putting the rest of the mission together.

Ray had been busy churning out several new pieces of technology to aid in our mission. He had a complex sensor package for performing an analysis of the object that he was integrating into the new craft as it was built. He developed some new imaging technology that would help us present communication material in a wide array of formats ranging from visible light through the full spectrum of radiation frequencies. There was also an enhanced version of the negative mass material that was denser and more powerful. An amount as small as a millimeter cubed could lift a metric ton or keep it weighted to the ground. This made space-frames for vehicles even more compact and useful for exploration.

The most remarkable and helpful technology to come about was the holographic personal transport units, or HPTUs. Ray had developed holographic technology many years ago, but it was rather bulky and limited in usefulness. If a person inside Aeternum wanted to visit the outside world, the destination was limited to a select few areas like the String Memorial or tourist areas like museums. He had developed several mobile units that rolled around like robots and projected your image, but they were never popular and you felt very much disembodied.

The HPTU was something altogether different. We had received the schematics about six months earlier from Earth but never got around to building one. There was little need; everything we wanted to see or do was inside the system. However, this seemed like the perfect time to build the unit. We would need mobility and physical world interaction on the mission.

Each HPTU was a small cube, six centimeters on all sides. It had a small port that would allow one single mind to dock inside for autonomous use. The HPTU frame was of enhanced NMM, which allowed it to free float, and a small vectored ion thruster for locomotion. It acted like a small, personal shuttle or vehicle for a single mind to roam the real world.

As interesting and useful as that is, it's the high-tech add-ons that take the cake. The HPTU had an internal hologram unit that allowed a full-size replica of your digital body to be projected in the physical world. The HPTU cube floated inside the digital projection of your head and an advanced sensor pod relayed information back to your mind as if you were there in person. It was as close to being alive back in the physical world as we could achieve with technology.

Ray constructed twelve of the units for the mission and he let me try one out as the guinea pig. The experience was a bit alarming at first. Ray and I walked the boardwalk on Aedin Beach to the location where the foundry cube was located in the physical world. Ray asked me if I was ready and then he told me to select the HPTU cube from my internal console menu. I did as he instructed, selected "Board HPTU," and then the world went dark. A fraction of a second passed, and then a bright light flashed. I opened my eyes and I was looking at the beach from the same spot I was standing in before.

Things were quite different from the split second before the flash of light. The sand and the waves were the same, but the boardwalk was nothing more than cold stone. All of the houses and attractions of the village were gone. I put my hand up to my face and there it was, just as it was in Aeternum. I looked down at my feet and they were half way buried in the cool sand. I could feel the thick air, much colder than in Aedin Beach in Aeternum and it tasted salty on my lips. I looked up at the cliff tops toward the observatory and in its place was a black framework of antennas and optics.

I turned and when I took a step, I felt the sharp glass in the sand prick my toes around the edges of my sandals. It was not the beautiful, soft powder that I remembered walking on just a few moments ago. I saw that the village was not there, instead the familiar gleaming white cubes of the farm standing on their pad. Off to the side was the nosecone of the Speedwell, the side of it open, and the small cube containing the entire colonist population was present aboard the ship. The ants were moving around it, cleaning away the sand and ensuring everything was in order for departure.

I took a few steps and could feel my hair whipping around in the stiff breeze. The sand stung me with every step. My skin was starting to feel wet from the light mist still in the air and the spray of the surf. All of the majesty of the beach gave way to the harshness of the environment. Thick, cold, painful and alien in so many ways, the real Aedin Beach was not quite the beachcomber paradise I had called home.

I stumbled about for a few more minutes to test the systems of the HPTU. The saline air was starting to burn my eyes, as if I had sweat in them. The sounds of the sea were pleasant, but a slight howl of the wind that I hadn't heard before was eerie and haunting. With my skin starting to turn pink from the cold, I called up my console menu to bring me back. This wasn't the world I belonged to; reality was far less attractive than the fantasy of Aeternum.

I snapped back into my reality and the planet was right again. It was a shock being outside the system after so long. I felt like a child who had been taken from his mother and placed in a frigid and unwelcoming cell with a crushed glass floor. I thought to myself, no wonder this technology wasn't developed sooner. No one could stand to be outside, even on Earth for very long. Aeternum was not perfect, but reality was far from it and it had lost its luster over the years.

I told Ray that everything worked just fine, and believed the HPTU would serve us well as a tool on the expedition. I mentioned that he should dial down the sensory feedback when in a hostile environment as a measure of protection for the user. However, I hesitated to tell him how I felt about my brief trip outside. I needed to reflect on the experience and I wondered if I had become institutionalized, or at least spoiled. I had been pampered for a long time now and maybe I had become too soft for my own good. Further thought on the subject would have to wait, as we had a busy schedule ahead and not much time left on the clock.

That afternoon Ray unveiled the good ship Grannus. Named for the Celtic deity that was the analog to the Greek Apollo, it seemed fitting that man's next giant leap would carry a familiar moniker. The ship was tiny, shaped like an emerald and only a meter from bow to stern. It was covered with the familiar shield material and had ports for the engine exhaust and thrusters. It was built around the high-tech sensor array that took up the front third of the ship. That was integrated into the space-frame and if you hadn't seen the interior detail schematic you wouldn't even have known that it was part of the ship.

This little emerald-cut ship was to be our symbol of achievement. It carried the most advanced technology that humanity had to offer and was representative of just how far we had come as a species. Just as the enormous Queen Mary was a symbol of engineering prowess three hundred years ago, the miniscule Grannus was the showcase pinnacle of modern shipbuilding science. We were indeed putting our best face forward.

The launch was scheduled for ten in the morning the next day. Although we were ready to go, I insisted that everyone get a good night's sleep and spend a little time with family before the trip. We were voyaging into the unknown and no one could be certain what surprises the mission would hold.

Val, Valeria and Anthony came by for dinner with us early in the evening. It was a family get-together in a way we hadn't had before. We were all experiencing fear but tried not to show it. It was understood that there was an element of danger in the mission and that we had a responsibility to prevent any misunderstandings. We were fortunate men, we had loving wives and families and that support gave us courage to face what was ahead. As strong as we try to be on our own, family is often the irreplaceable pillar that keeps us standing when we are feeling weak.

Val and I both called it an early night to rest for the flight. The truth is that I didn't sleep much at all that night. January and I stayed up late to talk and make plans. We tried to imagine what the aliens might be like, who they were as a people and how they would treat humanity. I wondered if they were peaceful like us or warlike as we used to be or perhaps just not interested in anything outside their own social structure. January joked that no matter what happened on the mission, I would be fine as long as I wasn't wearing a red shirt when we landed.

The morning of the launch, I was up before dawn. Your sleepy-eyed mother cooked a great pancake breakfast and I appreciated the effort. I gave the kids each a kiss while they were still asleep and even gave one to January. As she wished me luck, I felt with ominous certainty that I would need it. Nerves gave way to feelings of duty and I climbed in my car with a clear head that was mindful of the gravity of the situation ahead.

I pulled into the observatory and most of the team was already there. I guess we were all light sleepers that night. Dr. Patel greeted me at the door with a cup of hot coffee and an excited face. I walked into the astro-metrics lab where everyone was making last minute preparations. I looked around the room and noticed that we were all wearing a mix of lab-coats, blue jeans or just plain casual attire. The little joke about the red shirt reminded me that all space travelers should have a uniform or space suit. However, in all of the rush we forgot that small detail. The thought of a rag-tag bunch of eclectic-dressed people making first contact didn't sit well with me.

I dinged the side of my coffee mug with a metal pen. The flurry of activity stopped and everyone glanced over at me. I asked who the fashion director for the expedition was and everyone looked around and had a good chuckle. Here we had built this incredible starship to show how far we had come, yet were going to greet ET in T-shirts.

We took a couple of minutes as a group to toss around some ideas for a uniform. We wanted something modern, but not a skin-tight cat suit or tacky leotard. The look needed to be functional, formal and clean cut but not like a suit and tie. Ray suggested we choose monotone colors in case certain primary colors were threat displays to the alien species. Silvia blurted out, "Oh great, more gleaming white!" Therefore, we decided to let Silvia design something that would be appropriate. She stammered a little but acknowledged that she put her foot in her mouth and had to come up with something.

Silvia stepped over to Ray and whispered in his ear. Ray nodded to her and then looked at the team; in an instant we were in new clothes. I must say, they looked pretty impressive. Each uniform had straight black trousers and rugged carbon cloth boots. They were contrasted by dark gray half-collar long-sleeve shirts tucked in. A hexagonal-patterned silver utility vest with several pockets held things like flashlights or data pads that might be of use.

As a final touch, our names appeared in metallic-chrome lettering on the left half-collar of each uniform. I don't know if Silvia just asked Ray to mix a jumpsuit with a tuxedo or had this planned all along, but it worked and I thought looked sharp. Of course, I was so used to being casual; almost anything with long pants would have made me look well dressed.

A team of beachgoers, retirees and former nerds was now the slickest-looking band of explorers in forty-four light-years. Although our confidence was already high, the uniforms made us feel like this was more than a job; it was a proud duty to uphold. We now were ready to make the trip down to the new spaceport five kilometers west of the observatory. We loaded on a special transport that Ray made just for us and arrived to a large crowd of well-wishers.

Half the village turned out to see us off on our mission. As we unloaded from the transport, I could see that the people there had a genuine desire to be a part of this mission. Even if their small piece of the expedition was just to say they were there in person to support the team, it was enough. Just to say that you were there holds great satisfaction for a human being's pride. We tried to emulate astronauts of eras past and waved to the crowd as we each boarded the Grannus in single file.

The inside of the ship was quaint, with an emphasis on science and research stations. The main bridge of the ship was wide enough for the whole team and was more of a technology-laden conference room than a fancy operations center. There was no central captain's seat or throne, but Ray was proud to take center stage, standing near the main screen in the room. He scanned the image of the Grannus projected on the main holo-stage and began the final checks for launch. It only took about twenty minutes to get everyone acclimated to their posts.

We sealed the main hatchway and brought the engine online. We lifted off the pad and moved in silence into Aedin's aqua sky.

The trip to Eriu was only going to take twelve hours and that left us little time to do more than review our data one last time. I started going over Val's contact protocols in my head to make sure I had them down cold. The rest of the team was busy going over their list of tests and scans that they wanted to perform upon arrival. The Grannus was going to be on Eriu before we knew it, ready to greet the neighbors.

Love,

William

Chapter 29: Quantum
(2166)

1440 Pelican Way

Aedin Beach, Midir, Ups-And-d

∞ #AE-LID: 4d-69-64-69-72

August 18th, 2216 CE

∞ #AE-POSIX: 7782863410

Benjamin,

Eriu loomed large on the bridge's holographic stage. The Grannus had a steep entry vector set and we were on a fast approach. We planned to set down just one hundred meters from the southern edge of the red structure after making a fly-over to scan it. The crew was on top of its game, everyone doing their jobs and watching every detail of data as it streamed in from the sensors. Ray and I were standing at the front of the bridge, watching that red object grow ever larger with each passing second.

The planet was beautiful in the same way that a rusty old bridge seems to have character. Eriu was rugged and desolate but far from barren. Although it looked much like Mars from a distance, the planet was unique in so many ways; with many bizarre

295

geological features on the surface, it was visually interesting, almost alive. Mud and snow-covered canyons and plateaus were just the beginning. Eriu had vast beds of ruby crystalline sands that shimmered like crimson oceans, dotted with whitecaps glaring in the light. Windswept columns of exposed gold deposits made forests of shrubby shapes, worth an unimaginable fortune in old-world currency. No, Eriu was not Mars; it was an extraordinary world of gilded delight and wealthy in visual appeal.

We made entry into the atmosphere and the science team recorded the descent in exacting detail. Exabytes of data points and holometric scans poured in every millisecond. We wanted all of the information possible, as this was an event so important that we could not afford to overlook even the simplest element.

Most of the team, including Ray and I, were fixated on the displays, fascinated with the alien terrain. Dr. Patel and Dr. Forrest were in a deep discussion trying to figure out what kind of life form would choose such an environment as its preferred habitat. Liquid water was scarce on Eriu, flowing in underground rivers. Most of it was locked in ice or mixed as mud. Both doctors made assumptions that the organisms living in the red object must be subterranean or their biology was less dependent on water than Earth's life forms. Perhaps the aliens had a taste for ice or mud. The speculation of both theories would be short lived, soon to be tested by reality.

Ray and I watched the plotted lines of our course on the holographic stage as the Grannus approached. We planned to slow to five meters per second and make a single low pass over the object's surface. After the flyover, we planned to set down near the building and the contact team would board the holographic personal transport units and travel on foot to the side of the alien structure.

Our new contact protocol called for us to wait for ten minutes at the outside wall. If nothing happened, we would knock on the side by dinging a remote-controlled spare HPTU into the side of it. If we still had no response, we would spend two days exploring the outside of the large building, looking for any signs of life. During this time, the team inside the Grannus would attempt to reach the occupants inside the structure with a full spectrum of signals sent from the ship.

We would assume that no attempt at contact by the aliens was a sign to leave them alone. The expedition would re-board the Grannus and depart for home. Although Ray had the nano-technology to breach the red shield material, we all were afraid such an act would be construed as hostility on our part. The mission was simple, make ourselves known and leave it up to the occupants, if there were any, to make the next move.

The Grannus came in low over the massive red object and we started to scan every nanometer of the surface. It was a uniform matrix of the shield material, flawless and without any access points or openings. The surface was flat and every edge angle was a perfect ninety degrees. It was astonishing to see a structure this large made as one solid piece of material. Flying at five meters above, it appeared as slick as glass and went halfway to the horizon. As it was enormous by any sense of the word, I felt like I did the first time I saw the Great Pyramids of Giza in person when I was an old man. The scale and craftsmanship were awe-inspiring.

The scans revealed hot and cold spots of infrared radiation in small traces along the surface. A pattern emerged that seemed to indicate five reactors stationed inside at even intervals. The object was communications silent; there were no artificial radio frequency or microwave emissions at all. The foundation base of the object was constructed of local silicates, ground to powder and reformed as an ultra-strong molecular concrete.

We made our way to the edge of it as planned and set the Grannus down on the sands a hundred meters away. We made one additional set of scans of the side profile. Nothing had changed since our arrival and there was no indication that there was anything living inside the structure that was aware of us. The large red object just sat there, silent and timeless.

Ray turned from his study of the stage to face the team scattered around the bridge working at a feverish pace. The busy team hushed and focused their attention on Ray. Ray's head slowly turned, and he made eye contact with each of us, moving from face to face. We met his short gaze with nervous eyes conveying only traces of confidence and hope. No one said a word.

When he looked to me, the last man in the room, he gave me a slight nod and said with a smile, "Let's go outside and make some new friends."

Everyone smiled back and you could feel the tension in the room drop with deep exhales and sighs of minor relief. Ray was the most intelligent man in the room and carried the responsibility of safeguarding billions of lives. He had earned our trust over the decades and we were looking to him for some small degree of comfort. That tiny amount of enthusiasm from Ray gave us confidence that things were going to be all right in the face of the unknown.

Ray, Val, Jai, Silvia and I headed toward the HPTU bay to board the cubes. Twelve HPTU units were onboard. We each slipped into the first five cubes and Ray controlled a sixth via remote to act as a utility module. After one enters the HPTU, the world inside the ship changes in dramatic fashion. The virtual fantasy gives way to reality. Instead of a large bay with the units appearing two meters tall, you find that you are crammed inside a narrow chamber in the meter-long Grannus housing the tiny cubes.

The exterior of the ship, unzipped by nano-robots, opened a small entryway and we all left the Grannus single file. The five of us floated up to about two meters off the ground and spread into a V-formation away from the ship. There were five flashes of light and in an instant; we were standing on the surface of Eriu in our holographic bodies. This sharp-dressed expedition team appeared out of thin air, towering high above the ship and ready for the mission.

I can remember Dr. Forrest smiling from ear to ear. She bent down, put her hand on the ground, trying to pick up the sand. Though she could feel it, she couldn't quite grasp it and her smile turned to confusion. The hologram itself used some sort of electronic means to build a shell that was semi-solid. Though your hand appeared to be flesh, it was not much more durable than the surface tension of water. You could hold extremely light things aloft but most everything else passed right through, including the heavier elements in the sand.

We all got a kick out of Silvia's angst, but now wasn't the time to goof off; we had a job to do. Ray motioned for us to follow him and we all started to walk toward the object. Ray had taken my advice and dulled the senses, but I could still taste the iron in the air, it reminded me of blood. The air was thin and crisp and the ground was silky smooth. Mixed with the sand was a fine dust that puffed out from our feet with each step.

The short walk to the structure had us mesmerized, following Ray in silence. You just couldn't look away from the large red construction, standing out from the desert around it. Though it took only a few minutes to make the trek, I had a whole day's thoughts run through my mind. I hoped for a greeting or a sign that something or someone knew we were approaching and would offer a hand of friendship. However, when we arrived at the ten-meter high wall, the object remained silent and cold, just as it had been during the approach.

We stood there for a moment, gazing at the perfectly flat long side of this, admiring the precision construction. I knew we had planned to follow protocol, wait with patience for several minutes away from the object, but I instinctively walked up to it and put my hand on it. Curiosity and a sense of wonder got the better of me. Ray was just about to scold me when I saw a brilliant white line, a millimeter wide and ten centimeters long, form on the side of the wall in front of me. The line started widening on both sides and a brilliant beam of photons came streaming out of the ten-centimeter square hole where my hand was, causing it to flicker.

The five of us moved back several meters and huddled close together. Ray stood out front, Val and me behind him to the left and right and Jai and Silvia to our sides, forming a V. Our spare HPTU floated up onto Ray's shoulder to begin recording and scanning.

The stream of light broke and a shadow appeared in the middle of it. Three small ten-centimeter cubes floated out single file and slowed to a stop five meters from the structure. The cubes look similar to the HPTUs we were in, but larger and bulkier. They only rose a meter from the ground, hovering waist-high in front of us. They rested there motionless for a moment, as if they were looking us over, trying to make sense of what was standing before them.

We too remained motionless, just staring at the hovering cubes in front of us. Then there was a small flash of light from each cube and they formed a semi-transparent shell of a being. The shapes were rough, barely lucid outlines with no detail. Over the course of a minute, the colors and textures began to fill in, revealing the familiar sights of biology.

Dr. Forrest's lips opened and her mouth gaped in amazement. Here was an alien species that appeared to have followed a similar technological path as had humanity, living in digital form and greeting us in the same manner we had chosen. She commented that the implications of this changed everything that we had speculated about intelligence. Instead of a universe filled with biology, she put forth conjecture that perhaps all advanced life forms eventually transcended to a digital existence to survive and thrive.

The forms materialized and before us stood three beings that were unlike what we had imagined. The creatures were short and sturdy, about a meter tall overall. The beings weren't insects or amphibians, though they did have features that resembled a cross between an isopod, turtle and an armadillo. However, that description alone doesn't convey the biological majesty of their form.

They stood upright on four short trunk-like legs that were in close pairs on the sides of a wide thorax. Their curved backs gave them a crescent-shaped posture with a wide, segmented lower body. Due to their stance, their short and stubby tail protruded between the creatures' legs pointing forward. The aliens' posture reminded me of a large upright pill bug or horseshoe crab back on Earth, slumped forward in a "C" shape.

Their short mid-sections gave rise to a wide chest with two long, round, double-elbowed arms. Each cone-shaped hand had eight long fingers arranged in a circular pattern, making each finger oppose another. These beings had wide necks and wide heads that resembled a trilobite's cephalon. Their face was not unrecognizable or even all that alien; their mouths and nasal passages combined into a structure that looked very much like a turtle beak or hawk bill. Two eyes looked at us, seated further apart than a human's, but looking straight ahead and the same size as ours. Their fleshy skin was rough in texture like leather but it was a deep golden color with a few rust-colored blemishes.

All of them had a piece of silky copper-colored cloth stretched tight across their chests, attaching to four points on their back plates. The fabric made a banner that covered their soft abdomens, appearing much like a man holding a stretched towel in front of him. Each cover looked fine stitched and accentuated the being's arms and neck.

As much as the fabric was probably meant to be the attractive garnish on the creature, its eyes were the features I couldn't stop looking at. They were so human, with baby blue irises that expressed so much emotion and empathy. Those eyes were intelligent and patient and seemed so very wise. They say the eyes are the windows to the soul and I could see and feel another soul staring back at me. Though their emotions may be different in nature, I felt as if they were cautious, curious and even afraid of us. My descriptions really don't do them justice, only a photograph, or seeing one in person can really convey their gentle majesty.

Perhaps it was due to the centuries of television and movies, but the alien appearance of their form was not repulsive or shocking. If anything, we were able to relate to their biology and draw many comparative parallels to terrestrial life forms. Dr. Patel would later speculate that those creatures might have evolved from a type of land-based trilobite. I could see the resemblance in several ways to fossilized remains in museums I remembered viewing long ago. Trilobites were one of the earliest higher-order animals to evolve on Earth. Trilobites continued as a species for hundreds of millions of years, but were wiped out in an extinction event two hundred and fifty million years ago. Jai speculated that if they had survived, we might have similar creatures to what we saw in front of us, walking the earth today.

Both our expedition team and the aliens spent a moment studying the other's form, trying to make sense of one another. Ray broke the stalemate by taking one step forward and raising his right arm with his palm open to the beings. It was a pose humanity has often used to express friendship and non-aggression since the dawn of time. The being in the center responded in kind, though its cone-shaped hand could not quite mimic Ray's open one. A good start, I thought to myself.

A second being raised his hand and in it was a small green sphere. It produced a beam of light that projected off to the side of the group of aliens. A hologram of the planet Brigid and its orbiting moons appeared out of thin air. Eriu was highlighted red and our position was shown with a blue dot. In turn, Val used the spare HPTU to project a hologram of Midir and highlight Aedin.

The beings all turned their heads and inspected our hologram and then turned their attention back to their own projection. The image of Brigid zoomed out to several light-years away. The Dagda system turned blue and we could see two other star systems in our vicinity also light up blue. The map zoomed farther and we could see our arm of the Milky Way with hundreds of thousands of blue points highlighting what must be their territory. This outpost was at the farthest edge of what appeared to be a vast empire.

Then other colors started to show, every shade and hue, scattered across the Milky Way. Hundreds of colors and what had to be billions of points, one to two percent of the stars in the galaxy, and they were all intermixed. Ray indicated that these creatures were but one species of many that inhabited the galaxy. Not only did we have neighbors, we were a small part of a much larger galactic community as a whole.

In an attempt to not give away too much information about us, Ray and Val then displayed an image of a hydrogen atom on our hologram and under it the number one, then helium with a number two. He completed a sequence through all of the known elements. The aliens seemed to understand that Ray was showing our mathematics and base-ten number system. In turn, the aliens relayed their symbols and base-eight numerals to us. From that, we started sharing mathematical statements and operators, beginning with the simple "1 + 1 = 2." The equations advanced well past the point that I could understand the math involved, but the aliens didn't miss a detail and kept up with Ray. Numerals soon gave way to words, and words to a stream of data. The barriers of language and culture disappeared and raw knowledge flowed between Ray and the beings at incredible speed. Val's contact protocols were working and we were establishing communications with ease.

We spent the better part of six hours exchanging ideas and communicating with the alien entities. They then showed us images of their home world and a photographic history of their species. We responded in kind with images of our society. With each presentation on the holographic display, a detailed transmission of information passed between Ray and the quiet beings. Acting as an interpreter, Ray narrated each image to us, bringing life and depth to a story far older than our own. They shared much information about their culture and beliefs, their struggles and triumphs.

The creatures, which we now call the Somnium, are much like us. They evolved on their world as an organism low on the food chain. Their intelligence led them to create fire and communal bonds just as we did. They mastered the wheel and even developed electricity in a timeframe somewhat slower than humanity's. Over millennia, they too had an industrial revolution and then a technological one. They developed AI and had a technological singularity. Their first attempts at colonization were slow, but they met other species and in time became part of the galactic community over three million years ago.

The Somnium had one more surprise for us that shocked us all. They used their holographic display to show an image of Sol. The field displayed all of the planets, including Earth, revolving around the Sun. They then highlighted Mars with a blue dot. It was a colony! A photographic display detailed that it had been there for over fifty thousand years as the most remote outpost in their civilization.

When they started to pick up radio signals from Earth, they explained, they became aware that technological life had started to rise. The Somnium watched us for several decades and took note that we had developed powerful weapons and space travel in a short amount of time. Although we were no threat yet, they decided to play it safe and in 1961 moved the colony out of our system.

That colony was the very same one that we were standing next to, forty-four light years from Earth. That's why they hadn't made contact, they weren't sure of our intentions. They were afraid we had somehow detected their flight from Mars and pursued them. Ray assured them that we were unaware of their presence on Mars and that we had evolved past violence as a species.

Of course, only Ray and I knew that he had built a focused terahertz-radiation-emitter as a weapon and had it onboard the Grannus as a hedge against a hostile encounter. It was something that we were glad we didn't have to use to defend the colony and ourselves. We had come in peace but weren't taking any chances, preparing for the worst but hoping for the best.

That was my main task on this mission, to use my gut feeling on the alien's intentions and make a human assessment. Ray confided in me that he chose me for the mission not because I was the club president, but because I had always been both cautious and diplomatic in my life. I knew when to talk and when to fight, and I had the instincts he needed to access most on this mission. If I felt that we were going to face trouble, he wanted my input. My gut said that we had made a new friend that day; there would be no need for weapons or fear, just open hands and communion.

The Somnium were cordial and their mannerisms caught both Jai and Silvia's attention. They were enamored with how the Somnium seemed to operate in unison when presenting material or expressing emotions. They seemed to have an organized social structure and standardized communication mannerisms between each of the beings that functioned like a well-choreographed play.

Humans have a wide range of body language, but we are nowhere near as aware of it as the Somnium are. Body language plays a much greater role in their society and social situations. Both doctors also noticed that the Somnium appeared to have become fatigued. Perhaps they did not have an active daily cycle as long as human beings did. They suggested to Ray that we begin winding down the conversation and continue this the next day.

Ray and Val complied and began showing the Somnium images of our farewell customs and a clock in their native time format to indicate when to meet again. The Somnium representatives agreed on the following day and then motioned for Ray to hold out his hand. The first being opened his hand to reveal what looked like a small sliver of plastic about five centimeters long and three wide.

He placed it in Ray's hand and it was light enough to not break through the HPTU holographic shell.

The Somnium then displayed a series of complex mathematic formulas on their hologram. Ray and Val both looked at each other and smiled. They then turned to the beings and expressed a thank you. Val was an expert engineer and what he saw had excited him, as evidenced by his child-like giddiness. His expression told me that the Somnium had just given us a wonderful gift.

Since the dawn of technology, mankind has been limited by the speed of light to communicate. Radio, microwave and laser communications all have a physical maximum velocity. As fast as light is, interstellar communications are tedious and information can take decades or longer to travel between star systems. The Somnium faced this same problem early on in their colonization days, just like us. However, they managed to solve the puzzle of quantum-entangled communications that Ray had given up on decades earlier.

Einstein called it spooky, but there is a poorly understood force that can bind two quantum bits together in such a way that they act on each other over any distance instantly. It works like having two switches on the opposite sides of a room. When you flip one switch up, the other flips down. If you flip that switch back up, the opposite switch goes down. Same principle, but there is no wire or radio connecting the switch and they can be a trillion kilometers apart and in an instant go back and forth.

It's almost like magic, quantum mechanical magic. In principle, you can build a communication network with linked sets of quantum bits and instantly send information across the universe between two points. Instead of a forty-four year trip over data-burst from Aedin to Earth, it would take only a fraction of a second. Radio and data-burst becomes obsolete. It was the reason why we didn't detect any electromagnetic communications from the red object and humanity never detected a message or signal from any extraterrestrials over the centuries. The Somnium and all of the other species were using quantum communication systems.

Ray could never get it to work, but the Somnium did and it was their house-warming gift to humanity, welcoming us to the neighborhood. It also served as humanity's first gateway into the Somnium colony and its version of Aeternum. Ray speculated that it would take years to develop the protocols and translation technology needed to be able to enter their world. For now, humanity would have to be content with peering in the front door and having chats on the red back porch with our neighbors.

We all shook hands with the Somnium representatives and they bowed their heads while lifting their hind-legs in an offering of respect to us as a farewell. Their holographic bodies flickered away and their cubes floated back inside their shielded city. We made the short walk back to the Grannus and talked with excitement about the events that just transpired. The whole crew and those on the colony had all watched the expedition through the video feed from the HPTU. Aedin Beach was in celebration already, with a village-wide party set for that night.

The Grannus stayed on the planet, as did most of the staff. You couldn't drag Dr. Patel or Dr. Forrest off the ship; they were in utter intellectual bliss and had already started outlining papers on their experiences thus far.

Val and I decided to data-burst back home to be with our families and represent the crew at the celebration. There was much data to go over and preparations to make for the next day's session with the Somnium. The research team on the Grannus and back home would be busy all night, but Val and I needed a little time to reflect for a few hours. We would join everyone back on the ship in the morning, but for the evening, we went home to answer questions and revel in the excitement of our experience.

Ray drafted a debriefing communication packet to send back home with the details of the quantum-entangled communication device and the Somnium. Although it would be forty-four years before the people of Earth knew about our encounter, it was vital information.

Perhaps in time we could supply each human colony with a quantum device of their own so our colonies would no longer be far apart. It was a new day for humanity. Although we realized that we are just a small part of the galaxy, we felt vindicated that our path to living life through technology was the key to survival in this harsh universe.

Love,

William

Chapter 30: Tranquility Lake
(2216)

1440 Pelican Way
Aedin Beach, Midir, Ups-And-d
∞ #AE-LID: 4d-69-64-69-72

August 30th, 2216 CE
∞ #AE-POSIX: 7783880772

Benjamin,

Ben, it is now time to write about your life's beginning and the future you have waiting to be explored. Like all newborn children, the world you see now will appear to be how it has always been. You will never have known of a time when we were slaves to the cruelty of biology, or when loved ones could be far away and out of contact. The universe of Aeternum and all of its wonders that still causes me to marvel will be commonplace for you. I hope that my letters will give you the chance to appreciate the gift that is this life, your life, and that you will be able to experience just a little of the awe and excitement of its grand beauty.

I feel that humanity is at last where it should be. Ray ended the eon-long river of blood when we most needed him to do so. He helped us survive and thrive during the brief but powerful waterfall of technological advancement unscathed. Now, humanity has collected itself into a peaceful and unified body. To carry forward the analogy, we are a small and tranquil lake, reflecting the light of the stars and gaining depth, just as our understanding of the universe develops. Perhaps one day we will grow into a mighty sea, spread from horizon to horizon. But for now, the steady calm of our society and the grandeur in the simple pleasures of being alive, is utopia.

It has been fifty years since we made a connection with the quiet and gentle beings we named the Somnium. We have learned so much through our relationship with them, and the other spectacular species in our galaxy. I could go on about what we have shared and been given in that time, but I think it's best to let you find out about the recent past in your own way. Our colony has at last established quantum communications with Earth. Aedin has grown in population to almost fifty-million humans, in three separate community farms. We have peaceful relationships with several alien species, and our understanding of the universe has grown immensely.

Since your birth, three days ago, you have had many questions. Your mother and I have tried to answer them as best we could. Her letters and dialog with you will also fill in more memory gaps. These letters and the time we share together as a family will bring the most important parts of your heritage into focus. All three of your development-accelerated brothers and sisters were no more, or less, confused and curious as you are now. It takes time for all of this to sink into your mind, and for the implanted images of my life and your mother's to make sense. All of those tangled emotions and feelings of a fractured life will pass soon. We share a bond of family, of father and mother to son that is unbreakable, built by love.

I know I left out many details of my life's journey in my letters, but I am here for you. Never think that you can't ask me a question, I will always answer you in a frank and truthful way. I love you, you're my flesh and blood and I am proud to call you my son. The decision to bring you into this world was not taken lightly; you are a wanted and precious addition to our family.

You are a human being. We are a species with limitless potential. We are also a growing and expanding people and you were born at a time that is full of rapid change and excitement. There has been no better time to be alive and experience all that life has to offer. Your mother and I want you to see and experience this new phase of society as your brothers and sisters have. Humanity is becoming a part of the greater galactic and universal community.

That's why we chose to have you and not to raise you from early childhood. Too much is happening too rapidly in our society for a small child to fully grasp. Coming into the world as an adult, you are blessed with the maturity of emotion and thought that will allow you to process the sweeping changes and discoveries that await you. We wanted you to have the best possible life and a true head start on the adventure ahead.

Quantum networks are not only interlinking human colonies together, but also interfacing with alien social networks, crossing the universe in a grand scale. Not since my youth, when the internet was being created, has so much information and freedom been afforded an individual. You will witness this rapid evolution of technological change the same way I did. I hope that it is all as new and revolutionary to you as the web was to me a quarter-millennium ago.

Now is the time when you can make your own mark on society through innovation, if you choose. There are likely hundreds of billions of species across the universe that we haven't even met yet, all living in digital domains. The Somnium have explained to us in detail how several of the populations they have contacted live, but there is so much more left to explore and learn. We are just now seeing the surface of it all.

Some species are prolific, with millions of colonies spanning billions of years of colonization. Others are quiet and mysterious, with little contact with the galactic community. There are races of beings so different that it strains our imagination, and some that are so similar to us, we consider them cousins. Some ancient species have even spread beyond our galaxy to the spaces in-between, and to other galaxies altogether. Those races are working to establish universe-wide network relays that span all that is known. You can be a part of it, traveling the cosmos in an instant, if you choose.

There are no empires or territories to war over; we all seem to live in peace. Resources are so plentiful and a colony containing even trillions of minds is so very small that it doesn't need much physical space. Fifty-thousand such colonies could fit in an area the size of Texas back on Earth. Instead of borders and the hostility that comes with them, our galaxy, and the universe at large, is open to all and so vast that we can all share the bounty that nature offers.

The same can be said of society itself. As we begin to travel to alien farms, we have been welcomed with warmth and curiosity. We have returned the sentiment. Aedin Beach is filled with visitors from across the heavens, eager to learn about and experience humanity. So many doors are now open for you to walk through and expand your horizon with unlimited possibilities. You will hold conversations with people who are so ancient that they walked their worlds before the dinosaurs roamed the Earth. You will see customs that predate man's ability to speak or use tools.

Fantastical virtual alien habitats exist that dwarf those of humanity in creativity and scale. You may travel to see the Somniums' vast underground kingdom that catacombs their entire home planet. It is a subterranean wonderland with cavern-states and strange eco-systems that populate much of the cool-solid crust of their world. You may choose to visit the bird-like Teneo's glass city. It bridges their home world and only moon together, creating a brilliant ribbon that fills their sky. Many a scholar has found enlightenment by taking an audience with the ancient being called Unus. She is the sole survivor of her species who escaped death by developing AI and transcending. Her now extinct people rejected her and the technology, casting her away into the cosmos a billion years ago.

The known universe alone is incredible in size and scope. Your immortal mind is a ready and willing vessel to capture the grandeur of it all. You will see things that I never could have dreamed of at your age. The sky is no longer the limit for humanity and we are ready for the adventure that awaits. Perhaps we have a naivety in our willingness to explore and there are dangers that we cannot imagine, but that has never stopped our people from finding out what is out there.

Ray is our humble host and constant companion as we navigate the network of worlds open to us. He is, as he has always been, a friend, confidant and leader. Inside Aeternum, he is omnipresent and always available to speak with and assist you. Outside of the human network of farms, he will be with you as an AI companion, just as Val was to me centuries ago. Wherever you go, he will be at your side to advise and guide you. No matter how alien or strange your surroundings become, you will never walk alone.

Your mother and I will always be with you as well. Our digigenetic code is part of you and will be in your DDNA signature for time eternal. You should always remember your origins and never forget that you can always come home. You are part of a loving family and your humanity is a gift you should always cherish, just as we cherish you.

Your father,

William Samuel Babington

###

*Review Request** - If you enjoyed Aeternum Ray, please consider creating a review of this book on the retailer's website where you purchased it. Reviews are very important for independently produced books like Aeternum Ray. Your time and effort to compose a review is appreciated.

Thank you for reading Aeternum Ray.
Tracy R. Atkins

About the Author

Tracy R. Atkins is an author and technology entrepreneur. He is a passionate writer whose stories intertwine technology with exploration of the human condition. A dedicated family man, Tracy credits his success to his four wonderful children and supportive wife.

www.TracyRAtkins.com

Visit the Aeternum Ray
website today!

Watch the trailer for Aeternum Ray.

See special offers and shop for
Aeternum RayMerchandise.

AeternumRay.com